Filling in the Blanks

A Father's Fight to Get His Children Back

by C.C. Pitts

DORRANCE
PUBLISHING CO
EST. 1920
PITTSBURGH, PENNSYLVANIA 15238

Dorrance Publishing Co
585 Alpha Drive
Suite 103
Pittsburgh, PA 15238
Visit our website at *www.dorrancebookstore.com*

ISBN: 978-1-6461-0507-6
eISBN: 978-1-6461-0620-1

Author's Note

I met Jacob Johnson, not his real name, in October 2011 when I was assigned to represent him in a child custody case he was fighting against the State of Washington. He has given me permission to write this biography of his life as a child in foster care and then as a father entangled in the child welfare system based on his recollection of past events and what the various records say about him. But beyond the permissions he can give, many of the documents created in the course of his life by the State of Washington and others remain confidential. Therefore, names, locations, and identifying details have been changed to protect the anonymity of the children, their parents, and other caregivers. This is unfortunate because as Jacob observes the guilty can hide behind the innocent. Protecting the innocent means others such as social workers, therapists, court personnel, and attorneys who are not so innocent are also shielded. Laws and policies that prohibit the disclosure and dissemination of confidential records that are created in the course of child abuse and neglect investigations can have the effect of preventing the community from holding accountable a whole range of people in each branch of government. The people in agencies of the executive branch such as social workers, their supervisors, and the people hired by them to provide services to families are especially invisible to the public eye. Unless the conduct of these people reaches the level of causing serious abuse or death of a child, the public remains uninformed about the day-to-day decision-making that wrecks families, often forever.

In addition to biographical information, part of this story is my own compilation of events and opinions based on my experiences as an attorney working for and against the state, the experiences of others told to me, over the thirty years of my practice and pure flights of imagination.

Chapter One

The family was living with Grandma Dee in South Fork, Washington when the trouble started. They were crammed into a small house: Jacob Johnson, his girlfriend, Rose Faraday, five-year-old Lexie, and baby Lucille in one bedroom, Grandma Dee and her eleven-year-old son, Richard, in the other. Uncle Jerry lived in the attic and cousin Darlene lived in the unfinished basement.

Rose hated her brother Jerry. They were little when he first tried to have sex with her, but what she really hated was the way her mother favored him, always defended him, and even flirted with him. It made her sick. Jerry and Darlene spent most days smoking pot in the basement and the smoke drifted up to the bedrooms. There were arguments about this and about money. Grandma Dee was getting social security for Richard and herself, Jacob and Rose worked temporary jobs as certified nursing assistants, but Rose had not been able to work since her pregnancy with Lucy. She got help from a nutrition program called WIC (Women, Infants, and Children) for the baby. She also got food stamps now and so did Darlene and Jerry who pretended to be looking for work. Grandma Dee and Darlene complained often about how Jacob was aggressive toward everyone, especially Rose. Rose wanted them to mind their own business. Jacob and Rose were desperate to move out.

Sometimes when the arguing got to be too much and there was a little extra money, Jacob and Rose did move out. Once they stayed at a nearby motel.

One time, for almost a year, they rented a house down the street. When Lucy was born, the family moved back in with Grandma Dee. Lexie liked living with Darlene because she enjoyed hearing Lexie complain about her parents. She wanted all the details, and Lexie loved to tell stories.

One morning Lexie told Darlene about how her daddy tried to break her leg. This wasn't exactly what happened. The night before, Lexie and her parents were all on the bed in their room watching TV. The mattress was lumpy and sagged toward the middle. Lucy was asleep in an open dresser drawer. Jacob was on the inside, and when he got up off the bed he rolled over onto Lexie's leg. Lexie screamed because it really hurt. Jacob was very sorry, and Rose said he didn't mean to do anything, which Lexie found very unsatisfactory.

The next morning, June 8, 2010 Lexie told Darlene: "Guess what he did last night." Darlene was all ears. "He wanted to break my leg." They were the only ones at the kitchen table, Lexie with her oatmeal, Darlene with her cigarette and coffee.

Darlene was outraged. "Lexie, that's awful. Let me see your leg, honey." Lexie pulled up both of her pajama legs and stuck out her legs. They looked fine. Neither of them looked red or black and blue.

Sensing this was working against her, Lexie said, "It still really hurts on the inside!" Then she left the room. Darlene did not know what to do, but she had a vague idea she should do something. She didn't want Jacob to get away with it. She called her mother, Doris, and told her what Lexis said.

Darlene no longer lived with her mother because her mother's boyfriend was a total creep, but mother and daughter talked to each other every day.

"Mom, something terrible has happened to Lexie, and I don't know what to do." Doris knew exactly what to do, and hanging up on her daughter, she called the police and told them they needed to go right over to that house because, according to her daughter, Lexie was assaulted by her father.

When a South Fork police officer arrived at Grandma Dee's house a few hours later, Grandma Dee and Darlene were the only people at home. Darlene said she had issues with the way Jacob used discipline. She said that he tried to break Lexie's leg, but she admitted she saw no injury, and Lexie was not crying when she told Darlene what happened. The officer talked to Grandma Dee who told him Jacob was verbally abusive, but she could not say if he was physically abusive. The officer left the house and marked his report "information only," police speak for "nothing more to be done"

Later that same day, Tuesday, June 8, after dinner, Rose and Darlene got into it. Rose was in the kitchen doing dishes. Darlene came up from the basement. She told Rose she should have her kids taken away from her because she was an unfit parent. "Somebody should call CPS on you," she said.

The Child Protective Services threat really got under Rose's skin. It made her furious this little pot-smoking freeloader thought she could mess with her family. She put down the dish she was holding and faced Darlene: "Bitch! Mess with my kids and I will cut you up."

"That's right, blame me. You are the one staying with Jacob when he hurts Lexie!"

"What are you talking about?"

"Jacob tried to break Lexie's leg last night!"

At this point Lexie ran to the family's bedroom, and Jacob went out the front door. Grandma Dee called 911 to report a fight in her home, and yes, she heard threats of physical violence.

A South Fork Officer arrived at the home twenty minutes later. It was the same man who came by earlier. He talked to Jacob first. Jacob was not too sure what started the argument this time, but all of the sudden he was accused of trying to break his daughter's leg. He told the officer, "I have never hurt her. Nothing like that has ever happened."

The officer then went into the house and talked briefly to Darlene and then to Rose and then to Grandma. Everyone was telling the same story. Grandma admitted she did not like Jacob. Darlene acknowledged Rose never touched her. Rose explained she would never hurt Darlene. This time the officer was able to see both children. Lucy was barely awake. Lexie was shy but cooperative. Neither child showed any sign of any injury. He told Rose to think about finding another place to live, and he told Grandma he could smell marijuana. She should not be allowing it in her house. He told Darlene to mind her own business. He duly noted the actions he took in his report on which he wrote, again, "Information only."

Doris had made another call after she called the police. She called the local office of Child Protective Services, CPS. She told the CPS call director Jacob broke Lexie's leg. Even though this was not true and even though the South Fork police officer saw with his own eyes Lexie and Lucy were fine, CPS exploded into action. In Washington state where Jacob and Rose lived, CPS is a vast governmental agency with hundreds of social workers standing ready to be assigned to investigate parents who might be abusing or neglecting their children.

Roberta Lawrence was the social worker assigned to the file created as a result of the false information Doris provided to CPS. Lawrence came to Grandma Dee's house the very next day, unannounced, to talk with Jacob and Rose. Lexie was off grocery shopping with her Grandma, but Lucy was home, and Lawrence could see she was a happy, healthy baby girl. Roberta Lawrence had been a CPS social worker for two months.

Roberta said CPS received a referral. She couldn't tell them who called CPS. The referent said Jacob broke or maybe tried to break Lexie's leg. Jacob told Roberta what happened when he rolled over on Lexie's leg accidentally and Rose explained there was no damage done and no intention to hurt. Jacob described Lexie as very smart and very good. He admitted for discipline he used his hand to slap her hand or butt. Once he used a wooden spoon. Rose told Roberta the time he used the spoon it caused a red mark, and they agreed he would only use his hand after that. Jacob was a good father. In fact, he was overprotective of the children and worried about them all the time. It drove her a little crazy. The parents talked about the counseling services Jacob had been getting last spring at Kane Mental Health and the help they were both getting from Mr. Ledford, a case manager at the Veteran's hospital in Bay Center.

The parents were clearly frightened. Jacob was talking rapidly. Rose was nervously bouncing Lucy. Jacob wanted Roberta to understand he lived for years in foster care and he wanted her to promise his children would never go to foster care. Roberta assured him foster care was not an option she was considering, but to prevent any such possibility she wanted them to sign some papers. As she pulled the forms from her folder, she explained this would allow her to confirm everything was all right by letting her gather information about them from local medical providers, from mental health providers, and from the welfare office. Of course, they signed.

Roberta Lawrence also asked the parents to sign a voluntary contract with her, one she was busy drafting as she sat on the living room couch. She wanted them to take a parenting class, to agree to let her know if their living situation changed, and to submit to random urinalysis testing (UA) to prove they were not abusing drugs or alcohol even though no one said they were. Jacob and Rose would have signed anything, and so they signed the contract.

Jacob watched the social worker drive away from the home, a copy of the contract dangling from his fingers. "What the hell was that all about—did Darlene really call them?"

Rose, equally stunned, replied "I have no idea. I never thought she'd call."

———•———

Roberta got a call from her supervisor as she drove away.

"How'd it go?"

"Dad is dumb as a post. The mom seems okay."

"Do we need to pull the kids?"

"No, no. The baby looks fine. Let's see what the little girl says when I interview her tomorrow. Should I ask for a welfare check too?"

"Good idea. You know who to call?"

"I have the number here somewhere."

Roberta pulled over to call the South Fork police and requested they drop by the home in the next twenty-four hours just to make sure the girls were okay. When the officer, a different one this time, did his welfare check that evening, he asked to see the children. Lexie and Lucy were dutifully produced. Lexie shook hands with the officer and allowed her hands and arms and legs to be examined. Lucy was less cooperative. She squirmed in her father's arms as the officer examined her. He saw nothing of concern and wished the family good night.

It took a few days for Roberta to find a time to interview Lexie. Grandma Dee brought her to the CPS office but waited in the lobby. Roberta knew there was no evidence Lexie had been abused or neglected. A police officer had seen her the day after her leg was allegedly broken by her dad, and she was clearly all right. Adults interviewed by the police, including Grandma Dee, Darlene, and Doris, admitted they saw no signs of any injury to Lexie or her sister. The social worker was following a procedure based on the "just in case" rationale that dominated a lot of what her agency did.

Once Roberta was satisfied Lexie knew the difference between telling the truth and telling a lie, she asked the child about the people with whom she lived. Lexie complained bitterly Darlene was causing her a lot of trouble. Roberta was not interested in Darlene. She asked Lexie to list five things she liked about her mom. Lexie said "She makes spaghetti, she lets me play with her old Barbie doll, she understands I am a princess, she lets me hold Lucy, and once I got to give her a bottle. It dribbled all down her chin, but Mommy wasn't mad about it. She tells my dad not to worry so much, and she never lets Jerry or Richard take care of me. Grandma Dee is okay."

The social worker's next question was more direct. "How does it make you feel when your daddy hits you?"

"Spanking is bad. They kind of gang up on me when I get caught. Sometimes. My daddy is repeating and repeating what he is telling me all the time. I ignore him, but Mommy gets mad. Once he used a spoon. She got really mad that time."

"What else does he hit you with?"

"His hand."

"Anything else?

"No."

"Do you have your pajamas on or off?"

"I always have my pajamas on. And then he gets us ice-cream."

"Do you feel safe with him?"

"Not every time. Because sometimes, even when I know Daddy has some money, he will not buy me what I want."

"Like what?"

"Pie."

Roberta also interviewed Grandma Dee, who said she never saw Jacob hit Lexie or Rose. She confirmed there were fights at home between Rose and Jacob on one side and Darlene and Jerry on the other. They argued about everything, but she couldn't ask anyone to leave unless she was sure they had a place to go.

Summarizing the results of these interviews, Lawrence told her boss, "Lexie is very bonded to both of her parents. She might already be smarter than her dad, but she definitely loves him. There is no evidence of any injury, current or past. I think the allegation of physical abuse is not true. I don't mean uncorroborated. I mean false. My guess is Lexie made it up or exaggerated something, and Darlene embellished it when she called her mom about it. The kids are safe with their parents. It would be great if they could find another place to live."

Her supervisor, Casey Carlson, who had his legs stretched out on his desk and his hands behind his head, tilted forward to a sitting position. "Okay, but don't close the case yet. Make sure the parents follow through with the contract. I will explain to Virginia (the big boss) the allegation should be unfounded and draft a letter for her."

Meanwhile, Jacob called CPS almost every day, begging for help trying to find a place to live. The call director explained CPS could only offer a temporary placement for the girls in foster care if the parents were homeless. Sometimes Jacob would hang up. Sometimes he would yell, "Have you ever been in foster care? I have, right here in South Fork, I would not send a dog to one of your fucking foster homes." At still other times he tried to be reasonable, "What about a voucher for first month's rent—could we get that?" or "Are there any shelters that would take the whole family?" or "What about other counties? If we moved to another county could we get help?" but the answer was always the same, "You can sign your children into foster care temporarily."

At the end of June, Rose's old friend Candy Olsen offered to have the family move in with her and her family. Jacob and Rose jumped at the chance and moved out of Dee's place. Candy lived with her husband, Bill, and their baby girl, Suzie. Bill was significantly disabled. He had fallen from a crane at the shipyard, and he was pretty much bedridden permanently, and Candy was his official caregiver. This was a positive move for Jacob and Rose because everyone in this house got along, no one was yelling, and no one was using drugs. Jacob could help out Candy with Bill's care, and Rose could take care of the children in a quiet home. Once they were all settled at Candy's house, Lexie was reenrolled in a summer Head Start program, to make sure she was ready for kindergarten in the fall. She was more than ready and liked to line up all her books to play teacher with Suzie. Rose and Jacob dutifully enrolled in a parenting class. They had done their UAs and heard nothing bad about them. They stayed in touch with Roberta, keeping her updated on the move and any problems they were having.

On June 30, 2010 Jacob got a letter from CPS acknowledging, based on their investigation, the allegation he physically abused his daughter Lexie was unfounded. Rose got a letter, too, stating the investigation of her failure to protect Lexie from Jacob's alleged attempt to break Lexie's bones, legally termed "negligent treatment," was unfounded. By the end of July, the case that had been opened by CPS based on the false allegation that Jacob attempted to break Lexie's leg was ready to be closed.

———•———

On a warm summer Friday, August 13, 2010 early in the evening, Lexie and Lucy were home with Jacob. Rose and Candy were out. Jacob was keeping an eye on Candy's husband and little Suzie too. Lucy was in her crib, an antique lent to them by Candy. Unfortunately, Lucy dropped her beloved rattle, and it fell between the crib and the wall. She was able to reach down and pick it up, but could not figure out how to get her fingers holding the rattle, back into the crib. She pulled and pulled, but the rattle would not come through. She would not let go of the rattle, and her wrist and fingers were rubbing hard against the wooden slats. She started to cry and then to scream. Jacob came running in. He pulled the rattle out of her hand, pulled her arm back out of the slats, and gave the rattle back to her. He picked her up. She was happy again. He checked her wrist and could see it was red, and one of her fingers looked a little raw and puffy. He thought it might be a good idea to take her to urgent care.

This was Jacob's first reaction to any hurt Lexie or Lucy suffered—take them to the hospital. At this stage in his life, he did not know much about his tendency to go from 0 to 100 percent anxiety in a fraction of a second, but as he looked at Lucy's little wrist and hand, he was ready to fly out the door to the emergency room. But he could not leave the house. He had to take care of Lexie and Bill and Suzie, so he called Rose, explained to her what happened and told her to come home and take Lucy to Stevenson hospital ER. Rose and Candy came back to the house, looked at Lucy's wrist, and agreed it would be best to go to the ER. Jacob stayed at the house while Rose and Candy took Lucy to the hospital.

After waiting an hour, an ER doctor saw Lucy around 8:00 P.M. The doctor noted her hand got stuck in a crib and her finger may have been injured when her dad pulled her arm out. Jacob was not there to give any of the specific details about how the injury occurred.

The ER doctor made a chart note:

> *Child fussy on mother's lap. Given Tylenol 2 mg. No bruises any-where else than wrist and finger on infant. Wrist red, finger tender, applied wrap. Referred mother to family's pediatrician at Uniform Family Clinic. Prescribed more Tylenol. Think crib should be checked. Consistent with story? Safe? Recognize mom, may have seen the father here before; if it's the man I am thinking of, he has a temper.*

Over the weekend, Jacob called the twenty-four-hour nursing hotline twice to clarify the treatment plan, which consisted only of the pain pills and keeping the wrist and sore finger wrapped up, if possible. Lucy did not like the wrap and kept pulling it off. Jacob worried Rose was not remembering everything the ER doctor said.

Monday morning Rose and Candy went to Walmart to look at cribs. They took Lexie and Suzie with them. Two social workers arrived at the house around 11:00 A.M. Jacob answered the knock on the door. He had never seen these women before. They said they were from the hospital and came to examine the crib. Jacob let them in and explained to them what happened as he led them to the room where the crib was located. Lucy was asleep in the crib. He picked her up and she stayed asleep in his arms. He watched in surprise as these women proceeded to dismantle the antique, explaining to him as they did so it was not a crib that should be used. Before he could stop them, the antique was in a heap of wood at his feet, Lucy was wide awake and crying and the women left the house. *What the hell?* Jacob called Rose and told her what just happened. She told him they were getting a new crib. Give Lucy another Tylenol and they would be home soon.

The ER chart note from the Friday visit was faxed to the South Fork CPS office on Monday, August 16, 2010. It is not known why this was done. The fax cover page just said it was from "Stevenson ER records." The fax was routed to the desk of Roberta Lawrence because she had not yet closed her file on the family. At almost the same time, a call from a nurse at Uniform Family Clinic was directed to Roberta for the same reason, she showed up as the assigned social worker in the system. Roberta answered the phone. The nurse was concerned about the father's behavior. She said her record showed he had called the consulting nurse hotline three times over the weekend with questions about Lucy's medication. The nurse thought he should not even have these questions. She wondered if he was high. She did not realize Jacob was not at the hospital on Friday night when the medication was prescribed, and she did not know Jacob was always overprotective of his children and super vigilant about their care. In any case, she went on to complain to Ms. Lawrence the parents had made an appointment with their pediatrician when they should have set up an appointment with an orthopedic doctor.

Lawrence was alarmed by these communications. She didn't have a new allegation of abuse or neglect, just gossip, really: a doctor who saw the dad at an unknown time being angry, a nurse who thought dad called too much, and a mom who had made an appointment with a pediatrician instead of an orthopedist. This was not enough to open a new case, but because the computer showed she still had an active case with this mother (even when parents are married, the CPS files are opened under the mother's name only) the new information landed on her desk, but why did it land like a grenade?

Chapter Two

In the preceding month, Roberta Lawrence had made a terrible mistake in another case. She had failed to follow up, failed to make sure services were provided to a mother who was struggling to raise her children all on her own. The result was tragic.

Just a few days after she interviewed Lexie, on June 14, Lawrence was assigned to another case—a mother with four children all under the age of eight. The oldest had been found wandering in the neighborhood after dark. A teacher coming home from dinner with friends saw him and stopped. He was far too young to be out, she didn't recognize him, and he was filthy. She called the police. The boy was able to lead the police officer back to his own house where his mother greeted the child with tears of joy. All the children gathered round to welcome him back.

"When I got all this oil on me I was afraid you would be mad," he explained. The officer looked at each of the other children, three other boys. Their pajamas were clean, their faces washed. It looked like they were ready for bed. Everyone was smiling, impressed their brother Jimmy knew a real police officer.

"Can I come in?" the officer asked. The mother made no objection, and the family crowded into the small living room. The place looked tidy enough under the mess of toys and scattered clothing. There was a laundry basket full of folded clothing by the TV. In the kitchen, the officer looked into the cupboard and found it was full of cereals and top ramen. In the fridge he found milk and juice. It was adequate. He returned to the living room.

"Ma'am when do you think Jimmy took off?"

"It was just after the news," Jimmy offered. "I told her I was going to see if I could find our cat."

"That's right," his mother agreed. "He loves that mangy old tom. He's not really our cat, just comes around sometimes to see if Jimmy will give him some of our milk. We don't really have much to spare, but Jimmy told me the cat could have his glass from dinner and before I could say no he was out the door. At eight I started calling for him, but I guess he went too far."

The officer asked to speak to Jimmy alone. They went into a bedroom with a double set of bunkbeds. The beds were unmade, but the bed clothes looked clean, and there was no smell.

"You are the oldest, right son?"

"Yes, sir!"

"Where is your dad?"

"I don't know."

"Have you ever seen him?"

"No, not really. I have a picture of him and me. I look at that sometimes." Jimmy went to the dresser and started digging through a drawer. "I think I put it in here."

"Never mind. Any other men around here? Does your mom have a boyfriend?"

"No, sir."

"How long have you lived here?"

"About two months, I think."

"And before that?"

"We lived on a farm with my grandpa. He died."

"Okay. Are you in school?"

"Yes, sir! I start next fall."

"That's good. But from now on I want you to stay close to home, okay son?"

'You mean not go to school?"

"No, no. I mean like tonight. It's one thing to play outside around here, but don't go too far, only as far as you can hear your mom call. You understand?"

Back in the living room, the officer had a few more questions for the mother. "Have you lived here long?"

"Only a few months. We moved from Helena."

"Do you know your neighbors?"

"The woman across the street is nice. She works all the time. She waves."

"What about your family?"

"There isn't anyone left."

When the officer filed his report, he identified the family as in need of some help and made a non-emergency CPS referral, asking that a social worker visit the home just to see what services could be offered to help the mother. At the bottom of his report he wrote, *She's doing okay, just overwhelmed with so many boys. She is all on her own.*

A few days later, Roberta was assigned to the case. When she visited the home, she found things a little more chaotic than the police report indicated. The mother was very friendly, though, and welcomed any help Roberta could provide. A homebased aid could be set up for her to help keep the house clean and manage what little money there was. The aid could also drive the mother to the grocery store and make sure she was getting welfare money for the children. Since they had moved recently, they needed to sign up again for some things like food stamps. Roberta also drafted a voluntary contract, which included the mother's agreement to work with the homebased provider and stay in touch with Roberta. The mother seemed definitely overwhelmed. Roberta added a homebased therapist to the contract to help work with the whole family and give the mother support and maybe some parenting instruction. The mother thought this was a great idea. She signed all the paperwork Roberta asked her to and agreed she would see if she could find the immunization records for each child. They were misplaced in the move and were somewhere in one of the boxes that still cluttered her own bedroom. That was on Monday, June 21.

Roberta put a copy of all the paperwork in her supervisor's box. She thought he needed to approve the homebased aid and the homebased therapist to authorize the expense. She tried to locate information about the mother in the state and county she had previously lived in and found the food stamp information. She found the birth certificates for each child, but there was no father listed on any of them. She also found what she thought might be the grandfather's obituary. The name was right, but it was from more than a year ago. She got a call on an emergency investigation, and she set aside her file and headed out the door.

On August 3, the receptionist at the CPS office told Roberta as soon as she walked through the door that her supervisor needed to see her immediately. She went to his office.

"Close the door."

Roberta closed the door and sat down in front of the big desk.

"When was your last contact with Jane Perkins?" That was the mother of all the little boys.

"I'd have to check the file."

"I have your file right here, and the last entry is June 22, a reference to a grandfather's obituary."

"Okay, that sounds right. I have been waiting to find out when the aid and therapist will start."

"What do you mean?"

"She signed a voluntary contract for those services."

"I can see that, but I don't find anything else in here."

"I put all the paper work in your box. Did you approve the services?"

"Me? I would have assumed those were just copies for my information."

"But I thought you approved services first, and then I could set them up. It's a budget thing, right?"

"I don't know what you are talking about, but you should have set up those services yourself, and because that never got done, nobody saw the family again."

Roberta nodded. "I am sorry. I screwed up on the procedure. I can go out there today to touch base with her, explain the delay."

"Jane Perkins is in the hospital in an alcohol-induced coma, and one of her boys is dead. Looks like a head injury of some sort. The others were taken into care late last night, hungry and dirty. There were twenty-six empty beer cans and two empty vodka bottles in the mother's bed. Quite a binge."

Roberta had trouble breathing. "Who found them?"

"Some neighbor called the police. Not sure why. The boy had been dead at least a day. He was in his bunkbed. The police don't think the mother hurt him. Seems more likely he came home injured, and she was too drunk to do anything for him."

Several emotions were sweeping over Roberta Lawrence. Shame. Fear. Sorrow. She was in a state of shocked disbelief when she heard her supervisor say, "We need to play this carefully. There was nothing in your notes or the police report to indicate the mother was a drinker, much less a drunk. The cop saw the children and so did you—nothing to indicate malnourishment, just thin, scrawny kids. Of course, there will have to be an autopsy. The news people will make a big deal out of this, and there will have to be a death investigation. The area administrator is on her way with our lawyer. They should be here by ten, maybe ten-thirty.

"The fact you didn't get those services in place is a big deal now. You might want to save the tears, though. I'll call when they want to talk to you, but don't talk to anyone else here or anywhere else. This will hit the front pages hard, so no talking. We can stand behind the confidentiality of our records for now, but after the death investigation is finished, you may be looking at a personnel action. We have to find placements for the three boys too. Can you do that?"

There was plenty of fallout from this incident in the media, in the agency, and in the courts. The mother was sent to prison and lost her parental rights. The surviving siblings were eventually adopted and much later awarded a million-dollar settlement, each, from the State. Roberta was reprimanded and the story of her failure to get timely services in place for this family was recited in her personnel file. After a year, though, anything negative associated with her handling of this case would be expunged. Roberta would work hard on forgiving herself in the therapy the agency provided, but for Jacob, Rose, and their children, the tragic outcome in the Perkins case would become a tragic outcome for them too. After August 3, 2010, Roberta Lawrence and her supervisor made their social work decisions on the basis of potential liability, and they saw every child as needing to be immediately rescued.

———•———

Roberta Lawrence called the South Fork police office late Monday morning, August 16, 2010 and requested an officer meet her at Candy Olson's address as soon as possible. She thought a child might be in danger. Forty minutes later, Roberta and the police officer knocked on Candy's front door.

"Can we come in Rose? We need to talk."

Rose opened the door widely, said "Sure," and felt a little flutter in her stomach at the sight of the police.

Jacob was on the couch with Lucy on his lap. He could see Rose was frightened. Then he saw the officer with Roberta. He started right in, talking about the problem with the crib and the social workers who showed up to tear it down. Candy was in the background, and the officer moved toward her. They chatted softly in the background.

Roberta wanted to know how Lucy was injured. Jacob gave a rapid-fire explanation. "She dropped her rattle. I came in when she was screaming but not hurt. She just could not figure out how to her rattle back in bed with her. She kept trying to force it through the slats, so I grabbed it and turned her wrist and pulled it through. She was okay, but that's when I noticed the redness, kind of puffiness round her index finger, and the wrist looked a little raw too. I called Rose because I couldn't leave."

"Is that what you told the doctor?" Roberta was examining Lucy's wrist.

"I didn't go to the doctor. Rose went with Candy."

"How come you called the visiting nurse service so much?"

"What?"

Rose spoke up. "He wasn't with us and thought I was not telling him everything. It was no big deal. He was checking on the medication."

Roberta turned her attention to Rose. "Do you think you might be minimizing this injury? Shouldn't you see an orthopedist today?"

"I don't think so. The ER doctor told me to see my pediatrician first and get a referral from her if she thinks it's necessary. Lucy is fine. What's the big deal?"

Roberta ignored that question and wanted to know why Lucy was not wearing a wrap around her wrist and fingers. Jacob explained Lucy had been pulling off the wrap. Her fingers were too tiny for it, so they left it off. Jacob started nervously trying to wrap an ACE bandage around Lucy's whole hand and wrist, but she would not sit still. Roberta told him not to be so rough with her. Tensions were rising.

Roberta called the same nurse with whom she spoke earlier. The nurse told her the parents could bring Lucy over in an hour, and they would be seen by an orthopedist. Roberta told the parents they needed to follow her over to the clinic with Lucy. The parents agreed and started packing up Lucy. Candy agreed to keep an eye on Lexie if she got home before the parents got back.

While this was being arranged, Roberta stepped aside and privately asked the officer, Patrick O'Connell, if he would put Lucy in protective custody. He said he would not. Police are sometimes in situations where they see a child is at imminent risk of harm, and they must act to protect the child. The law allows for an officer to remove a child from a parent in such an emergency situation. Social workers, on the other hand, may not act in this way. If the situation is urgent, the social worker is expected to contact law enforcement. When a social worker believes a child is at risk and needs to be removed, but it is not an emergency situation or, when contacted, law enforcement does not agree, then the social worker must go to court to get permission from the court to take a child from a parent. In South Fork, Washington, social workers had developed a friendly relationship with some local law enforcement officers and often asked them to place children in protective custody based solely on the social worker's opinion and his or her convenience.

But not this time, not this officer. He told her he understood he had the authority to place a child in protective custody, but he saw no imminent risk to Lucy. Not only that, he thought the parents' explanation of the injury was likely the way it happened. He saw no red flags. Candy seemed like a competent, caring friend. The officer left Candy's home and told Ms. Lawrence to call him if there was any new information.

Ms. Lawrence told the parents to meet her at the Uniform Family Clinic. About an hour later when the family brought Lucy into the clinic, Rose showed Roberta the paperwork she was given in the emergency room the previous Friday. It showed an appointment had been made with the pediatrician for Tuesday at 11:00 A.M., the next day. The parents explained to the orthopedist Lucy would not tolerate a wrap. The doctor took X-rays and determined there was nothing broken but offered to put a tighter bandage around the wrist and fingers for a few weeks to make it easier for the parents to keep Lucy's finger stable. Roberta spoke to the doctor privately hoping he could give her something she could use against the parents, but the doctor told her he had no concerns about the injury or the parents.

The shell-shocked parents went home with Lucy. They had no idea what had changed the social worker's attitude toward them. Why was she so intense, so mad at them? Their living situation had improved 100 percent. They had provided UAs that were positive for drugs, which would have been illegal to possess, but each parent had a legitimate prescription for these pain medications. The last time Jacob was called to provide a UA, he was told the contract with CPS had lapsed and he would not be tested. The parents had missed a parenting class when Rose was ill. They couldn't figure out what was going on with Roberta Lawrence.

Roberta returned to her office on a mission to remove Lucy. She did some research about Candy and her husband, Bill. She discovered Bill had a drug-related felony conviction ten years ago. She believed this disqualified him from living with any children not related to him who were under CPS supervision. Bill's conviction meant Candy's home could not be approved for placement.

Lawrence again contacted Patrick Connelly and asked him to place Lucy in protective custody. Again, the officer declined to do so. He stated Candy was a good backup for the parents if they needed help with Lucy. Roberta told the officer about the drug conviction she found.

"That's for the guy in the bed?"

She had to admit it was.

"No deal, ma'am. Sorry, but I just don't see an imminent risk."

Roberta reported her lack of success to her supervisor. He was undaunted. "Go ahead and start drafting a petition to bring this family to court. I think there is enough evidence to take those kids, and if the court disagrees then it's on the Commissioner. She's the one with immunity."

Roberta returned to her desk and started preparing a dependency petition that would start the formal legal process of bringing the Johnson girls to the court's attention because of her concern or belief the girls were being abused or neglected by their parents or were living with their parents in circumstances that endangered their physical or psychological wellbeing. Petitions like this one were typically based on a preliminary investigation that has found some evidence the concerns of abuse or neglect or endangerment may be true.

In search for such evidence, Roberta called the ER physician who had seen Lucy. The doctor mentioned Jacob kept changing his story in the ER. This was very helpful. Roberta thought Jacob did not go to the ER, but the physician's recollection would trump a parent's statement any day.

Next, she called Candy who assured her, "I can help out with Lucy, manage any medication if that's what you want. No problem."

Roberta asked Candy if she knew about the drug conviction. "Sure, I know about it! But that was, what, eight, nine years ago. He didn't do any time, and he completed treatment. You know he is bedridden or in his wheelchair, don't you? Are you thinking he's using? No way!"

Casey Carlson came by Roberta's cubicle.

"How's it coming along?"

"The doctor gave me something good. Jacob changed his story about the accident when he was at the ER."

"Excellent."

"But I can't get the police on board."

"Come back to my office. Let's call them again."

Ms. Lawrence again called Officer Connelly. She let him know what the doctor had said. The officer replied, "I didn't think the dad went to the hospital, did he? Anyway, he was a nervous wreck. That doesn't make imminent risk in my book."

Ms. Lawrence handed the phone to her supervisor.

"Look, we have information coming in from all kinds of sources, and it's nearly four o'clock. Do you want this child to die on your watch? Because I think that's what might happen if we don't get going. Let us protect this child by keeping her while we work on our investigation. We think there is more to discover. We just need to keep the little girl safe for now."

Officer Connelly gave in. He agreed to meet Roberta at Candy's house and take Lucy into protective custody.

When Roberta arrived, the officer was already in the living room explaining to Jacob and Rose he was there to authorize CPS to take Lucy away.

"There are just too many questions about the injury."

Lucy held on to her mother's finger as she chortled on the couch, propped up between her parents. They were stunned. Tears ran down Rose's cheeks and Jacob's face was turning a dull red, but amazingly, they held it together hoping to make it easier for Lucy. The officer apologized to Rose as he picked up Lucy and handed her to Roberta along with the necessary paperwork and left the house.

Lucy recognized Roberta. She continued chortling and admiring her fingers sticking out of the bandage on her right hand. Roberta wanted to know if there were any relatives or friends who might take Lucy for a day or two. The trauma to Lucy would be eased if she went to stay with someone she already knew.

Rose asked, "Why can't she stay here with Candy? We could move out."

Lawrence shook her head and set Lucy back down on the couch. "That won't work. Bill has a felony conviction for drug possession."

Rose stared at Jacob. "What about your Uncle Ray?"

Jacob stood up, "Yeah, Ray and Carole would do it. I'll call them right now."

After some preliminary checks, Lawrence was able to confirm these relatives, Ray and Carole Samson, were able and willing to take Lucy. She got the address and then asked Rose to gather together some things for Lucy. She told the parents there would be a meeting at the CPS office the next day at 3:00 P.M. They should both be there. Jacob was having trouble thinking clearly. He sat on the couch, squeezing his eyes shut and muttering something Roberta could not hear. As she got ready to leave, Jacob asked if he could go with her to his Uncle's home.

"No," she said, "its best if I go alone, but can you help me load the car."

"You'll need a car seat," Jacob said getting up to find it.

"No, no, I have one in the car."

"The right size?" Jacob demanded.

"Yes."

All three of them walked to Roberta's car, and Jacob got Lucy settled into the back.

"You're going to see Ray-Ray. He will give you a nice dinner."

Lucy was starting to look around, maybe anticipating her parents would be getting in the car as they always did—at least one of them. Roberta got in and started the engine. As she pulled away, Lucy struggled in her car seat to turn and see her parents, but she couldn't, and she started to wail.

Jacob could not understand what was happening. He went over and over the events of the last few days but could not make sense out of what was happening. Rose tried to remain positive. As soon as the officer had appeared, Candy left the house with Lexie and her daughter, Suzie. They had gone to the Dairy Queen and then the park. When they got back, Candy was very positive and upbeat.

"We had a great time!"

"Why is Lucy going to Ray-Ray's house?" Lexie wanted to know.

Rose explained, "Carole was feeling lonely, and we let her take Lucy for a day or two to cheer her up."

Jacob admired the ease with which Rose told this lie. *Nice one*, he thought.

Rose added, "Daddy and I are going to a meeting tomorrow, so we won't be here when you get home, but Candy will be waiting for you. Just like today."

"That's good," Lexie said and went off with Suzie to watch a princess movie.

———•———

The parents showed up for the meeting at the CPS office about an hour early. Jacob was always early. In the lobby of the office the chairs were lined up in two rows, back-to-back. Their upholstered seats were stained, probably by ink, juice, soda, oily lotions, make up, and coffee. The thin blue carpet was also stained.

A receptionist sat behind a glass panel. The parents checked in to let the receptionist know they were there for a meeting with Roberta Lawrence. She told them to wait. They were early. On the far side of the lobby there was a heavy, locked door that could only be opened with a keycard or by the receptionist.

The lobby was full nearly to bursting with parents, children, grandparents, aunts and uncles, family friends, foster parents, visitation supervisors, special advocates for children, and lawyers. The din of humming conversations was punctuated by children's cries and the raised voices of some of the family members, especially parents. Jacob did not see anyone who even looked like a social worker.

The Samsons arrived early too, and they brought Lucy with them. Jacob and Rose were elated, and so was Lucy. At the appointed time, a social worker unknown to them came through that heavy, locked door, asked if they were the parents of the Johnson girls, and introduced herself as Sharon Peabody. She escorted all of them down a long hall to a big meeting room at the end. Jacob noticed the men's bathroom on the left was out of order and all visitors were notified to use the women's room.

There were several people in the room, but the parents did not know anyone in the meeting except the Samsons. Lucy sat happily on her mommy's lap and played peek-a-boo with her daddy. Roberta Lawrence was not present.

The parents were each handed a copy of the petition Roberta Lawrence had drafted. It had been filed that morning and the first court hearing was scheduled for the very next day, August 18, 2010 at 1:30.

"This is when we can get Lucy back?" Jacob asked.

"Maybe," a woman answered. He thought she might be the head honcho. "But let's go over some other things first. Do you or Rose have any questions to start?"

Each parent looked dumbly at her and shook their heads no.

"Good," the woman exclaimed as if they had given a prize-winning answer. "We have discovered some things we want to share with you so you will be able to understand where the agency is coming from. First off, Roberta Lawrence is not able to be here. Jacob, the ER doctor says you kept changing your story about how the injury to little Lucy happened."

"He wasn't at the ER," Rose piped up and Jacob agreed.

"I wasn't there!"

"Okay. You were supposed to do something as part of a contract you signed with Ms. Lawrence when she was investigating the accident to Lexie."

"There was no accident! We got letters from you saying so."

"One of the things you were to do was complete a parenting class, but you didn't do that, did you?"

Jacob looked to Rose. "We missed one I guess."

Before Rose could answer, the woman went on.

"Okay. Now the UA results are really a concerning part."

As Jacob started to speak, she raised her hand to him. "I know in the beginning you each had these prescriptions for different painkillers, but the last few times you were called you never showed up."

Jacob was starting to lose his temper. "I went in, but they told me at the front desk you guys didn't renew our contract for UAs."

"Roberta or Sharon can sort that out, but are you going to sit there and deny you and Rose have a problem with painkillers? It's all in the records you released to us."

Rose and Jacob exchanged a look.

Rose began. "We know there could be a problem. Jacob hurt his back, and something happened to me when Lucy was born. I haven't been able to rest on my left side. But Jacob and I will stop using any painkillers if that's what it takes to get my baby back. It's been a hard year. We could do treatment too."

There was an uncomfortable silence round the large table broken only by the sucking noise Lucy was making as she bore down on the leg of a plastic horse.

Finally, Sharon Peabody broke the silence. "Completing a drug treatment program would be great, and it will be recommended along with a parenting class. You'll have to find a safe place to live, of course. We can't approve the Olsen home because of the felony conviction. These are just the basics. Oh, and Ray and Carole have agreed to take Lexie, too, if the court wants her removed."

"Take Lexie?" Jacob jumped up. "What are you talking about? Nothing ever happened to her, not even close."

Rose tried to pull Jacob back down into his chair, but it was hard to do with Lucy in her lap.

The woman who seemed in charge explained, "You know we have that previous case with you about Lexie. Anyway, you will each get a lawyer tomorrow, and they can dispute anything the agency is recommending, including the removal of Lexie. Where will she be, by the way, tomorrow afternoon?"

Jacob, sat back in his seat, still fuming. He wiped away tears. Rose told the woman where Lexie would be and then asked if they could have a few more minutes with Lucy outside. No one objected, and the meeting was adjourned.

When Jacob reached the door, one of the women at the table called out, "Do you have any Native American heritage?"

Jacob said yes but did not stop moving. Rose was ahead of him carrying Lucy followed closely by Jacob and his uncle and aunt. Once outside by the Samson car, Ray put his arm around Jacob's shoulders.

"You can beat this, JJ. You're not your mother."

Rose put Lucy in the car seat, but the child was squirming and crying. She did not want to go. Rose got her strapped in somehow and stood back with Jacob as they watched the Samsons drive away.

"I want to make sure that bitch understands this is not my first rodeo," Jacob announced, but Rose held him back from reentering the CPS building.

"Don't even think about going back in there. Let's go find Candy and Lexie and have a nice dinner."

"How can you think about dinner? More like last supper for fuck's sake.

———•———

The CPS dependency petition alleged as follows:

Jacob Johnson tried to break Lexie's leg.

Jacob Johnson and Rose Faraday were receiving mental health services due to domestic violence.

Jacob Johnson appeared to have anger issues, and records show he also has PTSD and anxiety.

Substance abuse accounted for the injury to Lexie's leg.

Urine samples provided by the parents contained oxycodone; medical records show a pattern of prescription drug abuse.

Jacob Johnson's explanations of Lucy's injury in ER were inconsistent.

Jacob Johnson has at least one DUI.

Parents failed to participate in the parenting classes they had agreed to do.

Much in the petition was not true, but it sure looked official. The hearing the next day was at the county juvenile court. The parents arrived at the single-story pre-fab office building an hour before they were due. The narrow, noisy hallway at the court gradually filled up with people, some of them very sad, some of them very angry. Little kids were running up and down, squealing and crying. It was a warm day, and there was no air conditioning. The petition said they were supposed to go to court at 1:30. At 1:15 one of the social workers from yesterday's meeting came into the hallway and greeted them.

"Hi. I'm Sharon Peabody. We met yesterday. We are third on the list, so we should get in soon."

"Where's Roberta Lawrence?" Jacob asked

"Oh, she was the investigating social worker. I'm your court social worker, and when we have our next big meeting you will be introduced to the ongoing worker."

"Did you bring Lucy?" Rose asked

"No, as you can see, this place is a bit of a mad house."

"But aren't we getting her back today?"

"Well. Probably not. This hearing is just to make sure you each get a lawyer and a trial date gets scheduled. There will be another hearing next week to discuss the girls' placement."

"Trial?" Jacob was incredulous.

"Placement?" Rose was too. Then she added, "Jacob and I have been calling around to places for drug treatment, but is there a special place the agency wants us to go to?"

"That's great. There are a couple places we can approve—ones that we can pay for. I can get a list for you. Here is a form about Indian Heritage. You each need to fill it out."

Jacob thought his head would explode. He stuffed the form in his back pocket. Cases started being called over a PA system that was loud but scratchy and hard to understand over the din of all the conversations in the hallway. There were many more people than chairs. At 2:10 the Johnson case was called.

Jacob and Rose followed Sharon Peabody into a tiny courtroom. Other people were also crowding into it, and some people were coming out, but Jacob recognized no one. A court commissioner—a silver haired woman in a black robe—sat at a big, raised desk in front, facing the door. She waved them in, impatient to get started. On either side of the commissioner and lower down sat two more women in front of much smaller desks. One had a computer on it. A single row of straight-backed, armless chairs lined the back wall. In front of these were two small, narrow tables. Jacob and Rose were told to sit at the one to the right and Sharon Peabody sat next to her lawyer on the left. The commissioner hit her gavel, and the room fell silent.

"All right Mr. and Mrs. Johnson."

Sharon's lawyer immediately corrected the Commissioner, "These parents are not married, Your Honor."

"Oh, all right then, I'll start with the mother. Have you got a copy of the petition that has been filed against you?"

Rose nodded her head.

"Ma'am we are recording this hearing, so I will let the record reflect the mother just nodded in the affirmative, but I want you to speak up from now on. Good. As you can see, this is a very serious matter, and the legal consequences of these proceedings can be very grave. You have important rights that need to be protected. You understand me?"

Rose said, "Yes."

"Good. You are entitled to have an attorney represent you in this matter. Do you have an attorney?"

Rose looked at Jacob.

"Let me ask you this: Are you in a financial position to hire your own lawyer?"

Rose said, "No."

"No? Well, because this is such a serious matter you can be appointed an attorney to represent you at no cost to you. You will have to complete some forms to show you do not have a sufficient income to hire your own attorney, but if you tell me that's the case, I am able to appoint you an attorney today. Would you like me to do that?"

Rose said, "Yes."

"Fine. Who is next up? Okay, Dianne Turpin-Smith will be assigned to you. I think she is somewhere in the courthouse today, so hopefully you can meet her before you leave. Same questions for you, Mr. Johnson. Would you like me to appoint an attorney to represent you, or do you want to hire your own lawyer?"

Jacob was having trouble with the process. "I thought I was here to get my baby back?"

"All in good time, sir. But first, what do you want to do about a lawyer?"

"I guess I need one."

"All right, who's next? Okay, Mr. Johnson, your attorney will be Sandra Omak. We'll see that you get her card so you can call her and discuss your case with her. Now, I have reviewed the petition, and I think it justifies holding the child until we have the shelter care hearing—looks like next Monday has a slot still open. It will be right back here at 1:30, and that's when you'll both have a chance to dispute what the agency is saying. That's when you ask for your baby back, Mr. Johnson."

"Anything else...Oh, the trial date. Looks like October 18 is still open. Let's set it for that date, and if the attorneys who are not here have any conflicts we can fix it for a different date. Anything else?"

Sharon's attorney explained there was one more thing. "Your order covers only one of the girls, the baby who has been placed with relatives. It's the agency's position Lexie, the other child, should also be placed with these relatives until we have our hearing on Monday."

"What's the basis for your request?"

"The allegations in the petition warrant removal of Lexie at this time. There was an historical allegation she, too, might have been abused."

"How old is that history?"

"The referral came in just four months ago."

"But, Judge, they said that didn't happen," Jacob spoke up, and Rose agreed, nodding her head vigorously. "We have letters."

"Hang on, Mr. Johnson. I suggest if you have letters that you show them to your attorney. Where is the older child now?"

"With her parents where they live with Candy and Bill Olson."

Sharon Peabody added "That's part of the problem, Your Honor. Bill Olsen has a felony-level, drug-related conviction. This makes the home unsuitable for a child under our policies."

"That is years old, and the guy is disabled," Jacob spoke up again.

"That's enough, Mr. Johnson. You'll have a chance to present your evidence and your position on Monday. I am going to sign the pickup order for the older child. You indicated there are relatives who can take her?"

"Yes, Your Honor."

"All right, I will see you all back here Monday afternoon."

Everyone but Jacob and Rose stood up and headed to the door. Jacob looked at Rose. "What's happening?"

"Mr. and Mrs. Johnson, I need to have you clear the room so I can get on with the next hearing, thank you."

As they entered the hallway, Peabody told Rose the woman standing next to her was her new attorney, Dianne Turpin-Smith. She turned to Jacob and said "Your attorney is not here, but she has a box here, and I will put a copy of the petition in it with the information about the next hearing and how to contact you. Okay? Here's her number."

Jacob nodded his head.

Dianne said, "I'd like to talk to you now if you have a minute. We can use one of these rooms."

Dianne led Rose to a small room with two chairs and a small table. Jacob followed them, but Dianne stopped him.

"Sorry, I can only meet with mom." She gently closed the door.

Jacob looked down at the card in his hand. He marched outside saying, "This is all bullshit."

He was able to get a weak signal on his cell phone and called his new attorney. He could not reach her but left a message on her voice mail. "This is Jacob Johnson. CPS has just ripped off my girls, and I need to talk to you as soon as possible." He left his number.

The hearing was, as the law required, a hearing within seventy-two hours of the removal of Lucy from the care of her parents, but the court did not consider—within seventy-two hours, also as the law required—if the actions taken by CPS were reasonable. It was more of a "meet and greet affair" at which the parents were told their rights, assigned attorneys because they could not afford to hire attorneys, told to talk to their attorneys, and told to come back on Monday for a real hearing. It was Wednesday afternoon around 4:00 P.M.

On the strength of the allegations in the petition, the commissioner signed an order that allowed CPS to take Lexie away from her parents and place her with Lucy in the Samson home. The petition did not mention the allegation Lexie was hurt by her dad was unfounded and could not be substantiated, not by physical evidence, nor by the police officer who saw Lexie the next day. Of course, Lexie knew all that and so did her parents, but her parents had no say in the matter on this day.

Rose joined Jacob, and they headed home. Jacob was reeling from all that was happening, but after talking with her attorney, Rose felt able to reassure him all the mistakes would get cleared up and Lexie and Lucy would come home on Monday.

"Where is Lexie?" Jacob asked

Rose explained Candy was taking her over to the Samson's.

"When can we see them?"

"Sharon said she would try and arrange something on Friday."

"This is bullshit."

—•—

While Jacob and Rose were in court, Roberta Lawrence was at the sheriff's office to pick up a new report on the case. At this stage of the investigation there was no report from the county sheriff because Lucy was put into protective custody by a South Fork police officer. Roberta's supervisor thought it would strengthen the case, though, if she could get a Kane County Sheriff report too.

Detective Sargent Scarborough spoke with Roberta. "I sure can have a Deputy create an incident report about Lucy's trip to the ER based on this South Fork police report and your own statement. Just wait a minute, let me see who is available."

Within an hour, Roberta walked out of the sherriff's office with a copy of an incident report. It used the date of the report filed by the police officer who finally gave in and took Lucy into custody. This incident report summarized the information gathered from earlier reports and from Lawrence. Most of the information was false. The most damning bit of false information was that Jacob Johnson's explanation at the ER of how the injury occurred was not consistent with the injury. Lawrence returned to her office to prepare this incident report as an exhibit for the hearing on Monday. Her colleague had already texted to her the time and date of the next hearing.

On Thursday Sharon Peabody met Rose and Jacob at Candy's house. She confronted them with the medical records that were now pouring into CPS. They had each made frequent trips to the hospital complaining of pain. They did not dispute the frequency. Jacob explained he had injured his back when he worked as a Certified Nurse Assistant. He also explained he suffered from PTSD related to his army service and anxiety from his nine years in foster care. Rose explained again she sought medication for pain issues associated with Lucy's birth, and again both parents expressed their willingness to give up these medications if that meant the girls were coming home. They would do anything

Then Peabody delivered the bad news. "Carol Samson fell last night. She can't take care of the girls anymore."

"But Ray's retired," Jacob said. "They're not much trouble."

"Actually, the girls are having a hard time right now, especially Lucy."

"What about my mom?" Rose asked, "She can take care of them."

"I'm afraid not. The dynamic in that house is not good for your children. Your mom has too much going on at the house. Darlene does not deny she smokes weed and neither does Jerry. As long as they live there, your mom is not an option. I found a place for them, though—a foster home over in Parksville. I'll take them over there after you have your visit tomorrow."

Jacob started crying and pacing the room. "Not foster care, not foster care, please," he said, "they can't go to foster care. It's not safe." Jacob explained he had been in foster care for years. He was abused in foster homes. Bad, bad stuff went on there. He couldn't let it happen to his children. Rose was a good parent, and he was too. Foster care was worse than detention.

Peabody tried to calm him down. "It's not that bad anymore, Jacob. You'll be able to get them back before you know it. Once you are both fully engaged in services and making progress and you have a safe place to live, we can look at return."

"You don't understand. I still have nightmares about foster care. When the damage is done, there is no going back. Lexie can be mouthy at times. Foster parents hate that. They will come out swinging. You can't do this to my girls." He wiped his eyes and blew his nose with a tissue Rose handed to him. "But what about other relatives? What about the Bakers?"

"Yeah," Rose chimed in, "Jacob has family in Clarkson. Why can't the girls go there? Then we would know they are safe."

"Who are these people?" Peabody demanded. She was miffed that Roberta did not tell her about these other relatives.

When Jacob went into foster care for the last time, his baby brothers were with him. Rus and Cathy Baker ended up adopting Jacob's baby brothers back in 1990. They wanted to adopt all three boys, Jacob included, but the adoption social worker told them it wouldn't work. Jacob was too protective of his brothers; he was practically their dad. The Bakers accepted this wisdom reluctantly, but they maintained contact with Jacob. They let him know how his brothers were doing, and they brought the boys to the South Fork area a few times for a sibling visit. When Jacob turned eighteen he started spending Thanksgiving or Christmas with them. It felt good.

Jacob knew Rus and Cathy would take the girls. They lived over in Clarkson on the other side of the mountains, but that was okay. Jacob and Rose could drive over every weekend for visits.

Peabody quickly snuffed out this option.

"I can make a note in the file the Bakers should be considered for placement even though they live so far away, and I am not sure they are really relatives—adoptive parents of the girl's paternal uncles? Do they even know the girls? The thing is, no one will start the process of checking them out until the Bakers contact us. Have them call my office, but right now all we have is this foster care placement."

Jacob sat down on the couch and put his head in his hands.

Rose confirmed, "But before you take them to foster care, we get to see them, right?"

"That's right, Ray said he could manage one more night. I will bring the girls over here tomorrow afternoon."

The next day, Sharon Peabody brought Lexie and Lucy over to Candy's house to see their mommy and daddy. Lexie threw herself into her dad's arms. Peabody put the car seat Lucy was in on the floor. Lucy reached and strained to be picked up. Rose undid the snaps and picked her up and Lucy fastened her hands to her mother's blouse and refused to let go. Peabody retreated to the alcove by the kitchen within hearing distance. The family had a snack in the living room while Lexie told her parents all about what happened to Aunt Carole.

"She really broke her arm. I heard her fall. I think it was on the basement stairs. I was awake, but Ray thought I was asleep. I could hear her moaning. Then the ambulance came but with just lights, no siren. Ray gave us breakfast. Then Aunt Carole came home. She sat in the big chair by the window. Uncle Ray wrapped her up in a blanket. She had her arm outside the blanket but not really her arm. It was in a big, white cast like cement or something. She could kind of smile, but she said it was sore, and poor Lucy has been so bad, Mommy. She won't cooperate with anyone, not even me. She threw her cereal down and made a mess this morning." Then Lexi asked, "Where's Candy and Suzie?"

Before either parent could answer, Peabody emerged from the alcove.

"Why is she still here?" Lexie wanted to know.

Sharon Peabody addressed Lexie directly. "Remember what I told you about in the car? I want you to pick out some clothes for the weekend and your mommy will do the same for Lucy. Okay?"

Jacob and Rose had agreed before the children arrived they would not show any negative emotions around the girls. Jacob took some convincing, but finally he understood if he acted like they were just spending the weekend with friends it would be easier for Lexie to go.

The parents gathered together some things for Lucy's diaper bag, and Jacob asked Lexie to select a few of her animals for the weekend. She selected ten creatures, but her Dad told her she needed to leave most of them at home, just take three, and a bouncy ball. She complied and was soon packed up.

The parents helped get the girls into the car. Lexie cooperated, but Lucy screamed when Rose pulled her out of her arms to secure her to the car seat. The parents watched the car pull away and could hear Lucy's wails. Lexie looked out the window at them, unsmiling. She waved her hand. Seeing Lexie and Lucy being driven off to foster care was the worst thing that ever happened to Jacob, and that's saying something.

Chapter Three

Jacob Johnson, "JJ," was born on September 30, 1980. He lived with his mother, Jeannie. She was a drug user and a prostitute. Jeannie was into lots of different drugs: marijuana, alcohol, and cocaine mainly. Whatever was cheapest. She used to give Jacob drugs to keep him quiet, to keep him out of the way. She would also tie him up to keep him from running around. In her own mind, this might have been the best way to keep him safe when she couldn't watch him, but for a toddler it was torture.

Jacob remembers lots of men hanging around Jeannie. He was intimidated by them and did not understand what they were doing to his mother. Given the noises she made, he thought these men were hurting her. He didn't know what to do to help her. Some of the men Jeannie slept with lived with them for a while. All he ever knew about his own dad was his name was Frank and he lived in California.

JJ had nightmares about things he saw when he was living with Jeannie. One of his mother's "friends" slit his wrists in the bathroom. There was blood everywhere. When that didn't kill him, the guy took off all his clothes and jumped out of the second-floor window. An ambulance came and took him away.

Another time, Jeannie tried to drive the car into the water because she believed she saw demons in JJ's eyes.

From time to time, South Fork CPS would get a referral claiming JJ was abused or neglected by his mom. These allegations were certainly true, but for the first several years of his life there was never any serious investigation because if Jeannie felt CPS was getting too nosy she would move with JJ to another state. They moved from Washington to Oregon to Colorado to California and back around again. Jeannie could be smart about avoiding the trouble CPS would bring into her life. Because they moved so often, no one really got to know them or see what was happening to JJ behind closed doors.

When they would move, they usually left everything behind. Jeannie would take JJ to an all-you-can-eat buffet restaurant, and while they ate all they could eat, she filled her bag with knives and spoons and forks, with salt and pepper shakers, and with plates and cups to stock up their new kitchen. Sometimes they lived in motels, sometimes in apartments, and sometimes they moved in with people Jeannie had known for a few weeks.

Jeannie believed in the importance of education—or maybe just in getting JJ out of the house—so when he turned five she enrolled him in school. He was never able to finish a school year in the same place because they moved so often. This meant each time he started school he was far behind his grade level. Even though he liked school, it felt like he could never get it right. He knew the other kids did not like him much, and he did not know how to make them like him. He was dirty most of the time and hungry all the time.

Jeannie's drugs and prostitution exposed JJ to a life of emotional and physical abuse. Routinely she called him "idiot," "bastard," and "butthole." Years later he would tell a psychologist what he really wanted when he was little was a mom who knew more than he did, but all he ever had was Jeannie.

JJ and Jeannie were living in California when CPS, armed with referrals from the school district, finally caught up to them and took him away. JJ was seven. This was his first experience with foster care. He doesn't remember anything about his foster parents. Jeannie voluntarily signed him into foster care. She did a drug/alcohol evaluation and even completed the inpatient phase of the recommended treatment. She continued to do well and established a home she appeared to live in without boyfriends. CPS returned JJ to his mother. Almost immediately she took off to Colorado, JJ in tow. CPS in Colorado was on the lookout for them this time, having been alerted by California CPS Jeannie might be in the Denver area. When she went into a welfare office there to apply for food stamps and money for JJ, she was taken into an interview room and interrogated about her recent time in California. Luckily, she had left JJ with a new friend and was able to leave the office with just a promise to return with him the next day. The next day she moved again, this time back to Washington state. Somewhere along the way, maybe in California, maybe in Colorado, Jeannie got pregnant. When the family was back in Washington, she gave birth to twin boys.

JJ had turned nine just four days before the twins were born on September 26, 1989. Jeannie brought the babies home with a man who might have been their father. This man put JJ in charge of the newborns. JJ thought this was a good idea because Jeannie was not always around, and even when she was, she was usually not in any condition to watch the babies. The guy he thought might be the father had another family he stayed with most of the time.

JJ had learned to take care of himself and his mother, and now he took care of his baby brothers too. He used Jeannie's food stamps to feed the boys. He cleaned them up, changed their diapers, and made sure they went to sleep early. He became their only reliable parent. He knew he could not trust his mother with the boys; he had to be vigilant, always standing ready to protect them. JJ wanted to go to school now that they were back in South Fork, but he was afraid to leave the babies alone with his mother. The only other relative he had was Uncle Ray, but he lived in Germany, and JJ didn't know how to reach him.

South Fork CPS started to get some referrals about the family. It is not clear how long it took for CPS to investigate the situation, but just before the babies turned one year old, on September 14, 1990, a CPS social worker from the South Fork office came to the home prepared with a court order to take the twins away from Jeannie. Jeannie was not home. The social worker's file had not mentioned there was an older sibling in the home. When JJ answered the door, the social worker quickly discovered he was the primary caregiver for the younger children and was apparently not in school. She took JJ into custody too.

All three boys were placed together in the same foster home. At first JJ liked the home. He was finally getting enough to eat. His clothes were clean, and he was enrolled in school. Evelyn, the foster mom, helped him take care of the twins, but he couldn't quite let go of his job as their parent.

One day when JJ came home from school he checked around for his brothers. He found them together in the bathtub, face down. He immediately pulled them out. He could not find the foster mother, so he called 911. The twins were sputtering and crying but okay. They may have been playing a game. The foster mother, however, got into a lot of trouble for leaving them unsupervised in the bathtub. JJ and his brothers were immediately taken away by a social worker who placed them in separate foster homes. This felt like punishment to JJ for calling the police.

JJ had to be enrolled in a new school. He asked the new foster mother when he could see his brothers, but she didn't know. Then a few weeks later the social worker who took him out of that first home came to the school at lunchtime and said she had something to tell him. They walked out to her car.

"Look JJ, there is no easy way to say this. Evelyn died. In fact, her funeral is this afternoon. I thought you might want to go."

JJ said, "Sure," as much to get out of school where he was having the usual trouble fitting in, as to show respect to the foster mom, but he did like her.

When the simple service was over, and people were leaving the small church, Evelyn's daughter came up to JJ.

Before the social worker beside him could intervene, the daughter berated him. "You killed my mother, you little bastard! Calling the police forced CPS to take away her license. It killed her!"

The social worker pulled JJ away as another family member did the same, pulling the daughter away. JJ couldn't care less what the woman thought. Taking care of his brothers was job number one for him.

A few months later, when JJ was ten, he became a ward of the state of Washington. So did his brothers. Jeannie was again provided with some services, most notably, evaluation and treatment at Kane Mental Health. Not much is known about Jeannie's own childhood, but JJ knew she was a breach baby and her umbilical cord had been wrapped around her neck. In any case, she was by all accounts consistently argumentative and abusive. Her IQ was determined to be fairly low, and as JJ would agree, she was easily overwhelmed and defensive. She was considered to be a native woman, at least 50% Seminole, but when the Tribe was contacted they found no reason to believe she was ever enrolled in the Tribe or could now be eligible to do so.

JJ struggled with everything. In school he felt picked on. Sometimes he would get up from his desk and wander around the classroom. He alternated between being belligerent toward his peers and teachers and expressing profound helplessness. Sometimes he would cry for no apparent reason. The CPS social worker assigned to him discovered his Grandma Schneider who was found living in California. Could she help? She could not take all three boys, but she wanted JJ to come and live with her. This was good news.

A psychologist gave JJ his first psychological evaluation when JJ was 11. What stood out in the report was the clear acknowledgement of what he had endured as a child.

> *JJ is the product of a chaotic, unpredictable, and dysfunctional home. He has been raised in an environment which was repressive, exploitive, and which punished him emotionally and physically for engaging in normal behaviors. His disruptive behavior at school comes from intense, overwhelming feelings of despair and it is clear that this child is very depressed. At a deeper level, he experiences rage resulting from the extreme level of deprivation he has suffered.*

The psychologist recommended weekly individual counseling for JJ with a male therapist. It was also suggested he would benefit from active participation in youth organizations like a Boys and Girls Club, which would give him more opportunities to learn how to socialize with his peers. None of these services were provided because JJ would be moving to California soon.

Some time between this evaluation and the fall of 1992, JJ was flown down to California to live with his Grandma Schneider. He struggled with going so far away from his brothers, but he rarely saw them anyway. It was great to move in with someone who really wanted him. He was enrolled in a new school. He had a California social worker who set up counseling for him. Living in California was going to be all right.

But just eight months after his arrival, JJ came home from school to find Grandma Schneider on the living room floor, barely breathing. He called 911. As the EMTs took Grandma away on a stretcher, one of the men assured him she would survive. It would turn out to be a heart attack, but for a couple of days JJ was home alone, watching TV, waiting for news. His social worker came to the door on the afternoon of the third day.

"Hey, JJ. You grandma wanted us to check on you."

"How's she doing?"

"Pretty well, but she is very sick. She won't be able to take care of you."

"That's okay. I'm doing fine."

"Not exactly. You have not been at school."

"Well, no, not recently."

"Okay, buddy. Get your things together. I have to take you with me."

"Why?"

"I'm sorry. I can't leave you here. Who knows when your grandma can come home? For now, I found a place at a boys ranch in Sacramento."

Ranch sounded good. JJ did not have much stuff and was quickly ready.

What happened next is mostly blank for JJ. He recalls a big sprawling place that was hot and dusty. He was in a dorm with many other boys. He hated it when the lights went out. He cannot remember how long he was there. At some point that same California social worker took him to an airport and waited with him until a plane arrived to take him back to Washington state. He was alone on the plane. The stewardess lady was nice to him and gave him lots of Coke to drink and peanuts to eat. When the plane landed and he was walking to the terminal, the last social worker he had seen in Washington greeted him at the gate.

"Hello, JJ. Let's see if we can't get your luck to change, okay?"

JJ was driven to a temporary foster home, the kind that only keeps a child for thirty days or less. At the end of thirty days he was driven to the Boynton foster home about fifty miles from South Fork. He had not seen his brothers since they were in foster care together. He had not seen Jeannie at all.

A petition to terminate the parental rights to JJ was filed against Jeannie Cranston and Frank Johnson. In September 1992, Jeannie voluntarily gave up her parental rights. Frank Johnson was never located, and his rights were terminated by default through a notice published in Kane County. As a result, JJ was placed in the permanent custody of CPS. A little later Jeannie gave up the twins too. After the father of the twins met the Bakers, he gave up his rights voluntarily too.

The Bakers adopted the twins as soon as they could. Cathy Baker continued to worry about JJ. The adoption social worker in South Fork explained to her JJ did not have a lot of his childhood left to live, and it was hoped he could salvage some of it with happier times, without feeling responsible for his brothers. The Bakers were assured JJ was doing well, in counseling, and thriving in his foster home. Cathy didn't buy this because she had read the entire CPS file on this family and because she knew JJ had only recently returned to the state from his grandma's home. All she could do was to make sure he continued to see his brothers from time to time. She wrote to JJ to let him know how the twins were doing. At first she sent the letters in care of CPS and then directly to him at the Boyton home. She and her husband even drove over to let the boys have a visit, usually at a shopping mall. They often bought things for JJ on these visits. When JJ was much older and out of the foster care system, he often spent Thanksgiving or Christmas with them. They wanted him to feel he was a part of his brothers' family. JJ has been forever grateful for their kindnesses to him.

When JJ reached the Boynton home, it was his seventh foster home. He was twelve when he arrived. He had nothing to his name, no toys, no stuffed animals, no books, no pencils, no pens, no paper, no money, and no wallet. He had some clothes, but none of them fit him anymore. He also had a package containing a toothbrush and a comb. This placement was a so-called "pre-adopt" home, meaning the Boynton's were considering adopting him, and that was what JJ wanted too, to be adopted like his brothers.

The Boyntons included JJ as a member of the family. The other children in the home were foster kids too and much younger than JJ. He liked looking after them for his foster mom. JJ liked living with this family because they were nice to him—at first. His "mom," Mary, always made sure his clothes were clean and pressed and he always had enough to eat. He was in weekly counseling with a woman therapist whose office was near his school. These sessions were mostly devoted to his troubles at school. His worst problem was figuring out how to interact with his peers. His anger often spilled over into rage, especially when he felt rejected by them. His therapist thought it would be good for him to write a letter to Jeannie. Here is the letter he wrote:

Dear Mom,

I am really glad that you gave me up. But I am not happy for what you have done to me. If you did not use drugs then I would not be here so it is your fault that I am here. I don't care if you tell grandma because she can't do anything to me no more. I am going to make you feel bad as you made me feel and all the Bad stuff you made me do and stealing perfume and toys. And right now, I like my Home that I have. You would not believe my report card. I got fs on my report card when I was with you. And my mom loves me a lot and they care for me and she taught right and wrong. She taught me manners my mom is very smart because she did not use drugs and my dad is smart too because he did not try to kill himself. And I am going to change my last name.

JJ was enrolled in Sequoia middle school as Jacob J. Boynton, and his parents were listed as Mary and Walter Boynton. This was not legally true, but JJ really wanted a normal family, two parents, and a new name. JJ had an adoption worker back at the South Fork CPS office who was hopeful the changes JJ wanted could become permanent, but Mr. and Mrs. Boynton were starting to have second thoughts about adoption.

—•—

Mr. and Mrs. Boynton appreciated it when JJ completed his long list of daily chores, and his help with the younger children was also appreciated. They did not want JJ to be moved to another home, but they did not want to adopt him either. They were told if they became his adoptive parents he would be their sole financial responsibility. Not only that, if he did anything bad like hurt a child or teacher at school or cause damage anywhere to anyone, they would be liable for his behavior, and the state would be out of the picture. This was more than they were willing to accept. They would be eligible for an adoption support payment, but it would have been much less than the $1,000.00 they were paid each month for fostering a "special needs" child. Reluctantly, the adoption social worker agreed to ask the court to consider letting Walter and Mary Boynton become JJ's foster parent guardians.

The court did not take much convincing. On November 3, 1993, Mr. and Mrs. Boynton were appointed as JJ's guardians and continued to receive $1,000 monthly, plus exceptional costs as needed for his care. As guardians, they were no longer monitored closely, and there were no more court reviews of his case. JJ thought the guardianship was the same as adoption, and he was thrilled to be finally "adopted." He thought he had become Jacob Johnson Boynton.

—·—

JJ was medicated to control his anger and restlessness and medicated to help him sleep at night and medicated to allay his anxiety, but the medication seemed to have a contrary effect. He became defiant and oppositional at home just as he continued to be at school. His therapist wanted JJ to see a male therapist and to get involved in some of the activities at the Boys and Girls Club, but the male therapist was nearly twenty miles away, and the foster parents had no time to take him on such a long trip once a week. They rejected the Boys and Girls Club because they wanted him to come right home after school. They cancelled his therapy appointments, and told him to work with the school counselor to "get better."

It turned out his guardians were often very aggressive with JJ. Mary often slapped his face and once hit him hard enough to split his lip. He was punished for not doing his schoolwork by being forced to kneel on the small rocks near the outside patio. The punishment for swearing was being forced to wash his clothes outside, even in winter. Walter was more violent, hitting him and punching him for any small infraction. He once threw a log at JJ; it struck him on the head and blood poured down his face. He ran into the bathroom to run cold water on the wound but ended up passing out. He cannot remember what happened next.

When the therapist realized she had been, in effect, fired, she contacted CPS. She was not complaining about any mistreatment. She just thought JJ needed to stay in therapy. Maybe CPS could help the family find someone. JJ had started running away on the weekends. He finally had a friend from school who let him stay overnight. He liked doing this even though it meant Walter would blow a gasket.

JJ's CPS case was reactivated, but nothing changed. A social worker came to the house and talked to JJ and then to Mary and Walter. He made a note in his file, saying JJ alleged physical abuse, but at the time there were no marks, and the foster parent denied ever touching him. The social worker was not sure what to do next. He thought it would be almost impossible to find another home for a kid like JJ.

Then in August 1997, Walter and JJ had a fight. JJ does not remember the details of what started the fight. He thinks it might have been when he lost a tooth and Walter said he would have to shift a lot of stones if he thought he would be taken to a dentist. JJ might have said, "Fuck you," and then Walter slapped him across his face. He was sick of Walter, and he slapped back, knocking a surprised Walter nearly off his feet. Swearing a blue streak, Walter launched at JJ, punching his face. JJ fell down, and before Walter could jump on him, Mary got between them. She sent JJ to his room while she held back her husband and tried to calm him down. In addition to the $1000.00 a month they received for JJ, she had applied on his behalf for social security for minors and had been granted a monthly stipend of $650.00. She did not want to lose JJ.

But JJ was already gone. He went into his room and out his bedroom window without stopping. He went to the house of his one friend. From there he called CPS—not his assigned social worker but the CPS hotline—and made an urgent referral on himself, explaining he was not safe in the Boynton home because they were physically beating him and he now had the marks to prove it. The next day he was taken by a social worker he had never met before to a new foster home in South Fork. He was seventeen years old.

———•———

Mrs. Gustafson and her husband welcomed JJ with open arms. She and her family took him on vacation to a remote island where they had a cabin. They helped him work on his GED. They talked to him about learning a trade. They supported his desire to investigate his Indian heritage. JJ appreciated the Gustafsons.

Mrs. Gustafson tried to set up some contact between Jacob and the Boyntons, but plans always fell through. Even when they agreed to a scheduled phone call with Jacob they would cancel at the last minute, or there would be no answer when he called at the appointed time. Mrs. Gustafson was more hopeful about a visit she helped arrange for Mother's Day. Jacob really wanted to see Mary. The Gustafsons were willing to drive him to the foster home, but the day before, Mary called Mrs. Gustafson to say they would not be at home on Mother's Day. When Mrs. Gustafson asked her to hang on so she could get Jacob on the line to say hello, Mary hung up.

He was better off at the Gustafson's. They never raised a hand to him, but he was not happy. He shared the home with three other teenaged foster children. They liked to target Jacob because it was so easy to get a rise out of him.

One day one of these foster brothers brought the Gustafsons goat into the house and left it in the room Jacob shared with another boy. Mrs. Gustafson caught Jacob dragging the goat by its ears out of his bedroom. Jacob was wearing only his underpants. The goat had just eaten all of his Ken Griffey baseball cards. These cards were one of Jacob's few possessions, and they were precious to him. He had been in the process of changing his clothes when he discovered the goat and what the goat had done. He was very angry with the goat and yanked and pulled his ears to get him out of his room, all the while yelling at the animal. When this incident was reported to his CPS social worker, it was interpreted as an extremely concerning incident of aggressiveness against a vulnerable animal with overtones of sexual aggression.

There were any number of incidents of sexual exploration among the boys, including masturbation competitions and examination of the bare breasts of tribal women found in the family's old National Geographic magazines stored in Mrs. Gustafson's sewing room. Most of these incidents were undiscovered by the foster parents. Jacob's deep longing to belong among these boys led him to engage in behavior and submit to behavior that left him uneasy and anxious. He became more and more vigilant, trying to anticipate any pranks and checking his bed every night and his clothes the next day

His one sexual encounter with a girl, a teenager in the neighborhood, had been derailed when she began to makes noises exactly like the ones his mother used to make. He thought he must be hurting the girl, and no number of requests to continue made it possible for him to go on. Without being able to tell her why, Jacob admitted to Mrs. Gustafson he was having trouble sleeping. Medications were increased, but Jacob was careful not to take them for fear he would sleep too heavily. He mouthed the pills and later flushed them down the toilet. By the spring of 1998, Jacob was ready to leave foster care behind. He thought about trying to get where the Bakers lived, but he knew that they lived a long way away, and he was afraid of getting picked up before he got there. He did not want to be returned to a disappointed Mrs. Gustafson who had tried to do so much for him.

———•———

Jacob's big chance came when he saw a flier at the drive-in next to his school advertising a powwow that was to be held at the fairgrounds in the next town over from South Fork. It was designated a Pan-Indian event which meant Indians and non-Indians were welcomed. The event was scheduled to last from the upcoming Friday afternoon to Sunday evening. The Gustafson foster home was designated a native home based on all the special training they had done and the fact Mr. Gustafson was one-eighth Cherokee.

When Jacob asked permission to go to the powwow, Mrs. Gustafson was pleased at the interest he was taking in the event and readily gave permission. She even bought him a sleeping bag and gave him a ride to the event. One of the other boys in the home was allowed to go with Jacob.

The boys slept out in the open field and were fed all they could eat of fried bread and beans. Jacob like the drumming he heard. It seemed to go right through him. The dancing was too out there for him, but the music kept him keen to watch. An older white guy started hanging out with them on Saturday. He called himself Dizzy Lizard and wore a band of what he told them was real lizard skin around the base of his Stetson. As they were settling down to sleep on Saturday night, Dizzy Lizard told the boys about an even bigger native gathering in North Cape starting on Sunday. This was Jacob's chance. He agreed to go with Dizzy the next day.

On Sunday, May 31, 1998, Jacob would not let the younger boy he was with stay with him. He found him a ride that would get him back to the foster home or close to it. Then he hopped into the old VW Rabbit Dizzy drove and shared a joint with the old guy, but there was no gathering in North Cape. Dizzy got the dates wrong. This was good, he said because he knew for sure, for sure, there was a Rainbow Gathering down in Oregon. It was going on for weeks, maybe even months. Dizzy was a vet, and he said that was why he knew all about it. Jacob was happy to tag along. Eight hours later they were in Prineville, Oregon.

The Rainbow Gathering was an annual event that had been held at different places, mostly national parks in the west, since 1972. The first gathering was held in Colorado, and about twenty thousand people showed up. They came together to celebrate peace and spend time in the wilderness, to test their survival skills. There was music and dancing. People were expected to bring their skills in the service of others far from the urban world.

Jacob found himself among the homeless youth at the Rainbow Gathering. He enjoyed the free meals in exchange for work around the camp. He lost track of Dizzy, but that was okay. Everyone was really nice and friendly too. For a few days he enjoyed the smiles and food and music, but he had no money, and he knew he needed to find a paying job. There was no real work in Pineville, and the Gathering, with its free food, was closing down for another year. One of the women he met there, Ginger was her name, offered to drive him to a job she heard about in California picking marijuana plants. He accepted the ride and they headed south. At a rest stop near Shasta he discovered she was a junkie when he saw her shooting up. It turned out she expected him to pay his way. He explained he had no money. Maybe he could pay her back when he got a job, but she said he needed to help with gas now, and if he had no money he needed to get some. She told him to panhandle. He told her he would not do that, and so she kicked him out of the car when they were passing through Redding, California.

All Jacob had with him was his sleeping bag and the clothes on his back. He slept under a tree near a church. He learned from a church lady there was a local food bank that passed out food cards once a week, no questions asked, and the vouchers were good for a meal each day at McDonalds or Wendy's. He found a plum tree with ripe fruit and got permission from the owner to take some fruit. After two weeks of living rough in Redding, using the McDonalds restroom to wash up, and listening to his rumbling stomach, Jacob had no idea what to do next. He decided to start hitchhiking back north.

Chapter Four

The truck driver who picked up Jacob on a ramp on to interstate 5 was a kind and generous man. He asked JJ to tell him his story, and JJ told him all that had happened to him in the last few years. The truck driver let Jacob know he was a religious man and talked to JJ about his faith. JJ didn't mind. The cab of the truck was nice and warm. Then the fellow told JJ he was going to take him home with him to his family. Apprehensive, JJ told him he didn't have to do that.

"Have you heard about the Good Samaritan?" the man asked. "This is what God wants me to do."

He introduced JJ to his wife and four children. Then he explained to his family they were all traveling the next day on a special excursion to take JJ home. The man wanted to know who he should call to let them know JJ was coming back. It was odd, the first person he thought of was Mary Boynton and to his surprise, when Mary answered the phone she agreed he could come home. She said Walter was away for a while. JJ had a bath, and the fellow gave him some clean clothing too. They had dinner, and JJ slept on the couch. Early the next morning, JJ and the family crowded into a passenger van and drove for hours.

The wife and oldest boy shared in the driving and that evening about 7:00 P.M. JJ found himself on the front steps of the Boynton house. He was having second and third thoughts about this idea. It was a comfort Walter was not home, but still. When Mary opened the door, she greeted him affectionately. After the surprise of her big hug, JJ noticed the silence. There were no little kids scrambling round his legs hollering hello. He thanked the Good Samaritan family for their kindnesses. They drove off with a wave and JJ went inside with Mary.

"Where are all the kids?" JJ asked, feeling uncertain of his welcome now that no one else was around.

"I thought you must have heard. Isn't that why you called?"

JJ drained the last of an energy drink he still held in his hand from the road trip. "Heard what?"

"About Walter."

"No, I've been down in California. What happened?"

"I had to give up my license. I had to sell his pickup truck. It's been really hard.

JJ thought she might start to cry, something he had never seen her do before. Mary went on. "You remember Shawna?"

"Sure."

"She told her school counselor Walter raped her—more than once. Of course, it can't be true, and that's not exactly what she said. That was what the school people told her to say, I'm sure of it, but these days kids are believed even when they are lying through their teeth."

"What did Walter say?"

"He tried to explain to the officers that she was an over-sexed little bitch, in so many words. That if he helped her dress or combed her hair it was because she was only eleven years old and he was helping me out getting the kids ready for school. We still had Tricia and little Tommy; you know what the mornings were like here."

JJ nodded. He had really liked Shawna. He used to let her ride him like a pony. And then he felt a surge of happiness, that bastard Walter got caught. JJ did not doubt whatever Shawna said about him.

"That very first day they took him to jail for questioning and he never came home again. We couldn't make his bail because they set it so high, $500,000. Then CPS was here the very next day, interviewing me and packing up Tricia and Tommy. They said the kids could not stay. I told them Walter was innocent and in jail, they should wait. They gave me some papers—they're around here somewhere. They accused me of knowing what Walter was doing to Shawna. He wasn't doing anything. I told them to look at her records. When they brought Shawna to me they warned me she was a liar. How could they just take everything away from me!"

Mary was sniffling.

JJ sat frozen in his place. Mary knew what Walter did to him. She was in charge of everything. He thought about how Walter liked to walk through the living room after a shower. He would be wearing just a towel. He would pull it off and whip it at Shawna. Then he would be naked and she would run away.

Once after he did this he looked over at JJ and said "Women, JJ. Hard to live with, but harder to live without, right?"

JJ nodded and went back to the Game Boy with which he was playing. He had no idea what Walter was talking about.

"They said it would be best for me to hand in my license, then there would be no hearing against me, no record. I thought about it. I visited Walter, and we prayed about it. I needed the money from the kids, especially because Walter was not working. Walter said I should not fight it. Maybe fighting it would be bad for him."

"What's happening with his case now?" JJ asked.

"It's over. Walter's attorney told him to take the deal the prosecutor was offering. They charged him with rape but said they would accept it if he agreed he was guilty of child molestation. Stupid man. He still told me he was innocent. He said it would mean less time for him, and it was too risky to go to trial. I don't understand. He always talks like such a big shot. I went to the hearing. Even though the prosecutor only asked for two years, the Judge didn't buy it. She said so. I'll never forget it. 'Mr. Boynton, I will accept the conviction you are pleading to so Shawna doesn't have to testify, but I won't accept the sentence the prosecutor is recommending. You need to be in prison a longer time. The maximum sentence I can impose is ninety-six months, and I so order.' Not such a big shot! 'I so order!' Walter looked back at me as they took him away. He was really pissed."

JJ thought Mary was almost was enjoying this part of the story. He certainly was enjoying it.

"They sent him way out to Oceanside. His sister drove us out there once but it's too much gas and time. The bank let me refinance, but all I got was a line of credit for $15,000. That's what I live on, that and what I can sell. I didn't get much for the pickup. Walter calls every Saturday evening around six. I try to put money on his books, but I have to make the line of credit last until I can find work. I thought I could get a job at the daycare center next to the school. I filled out the application, and they seemed happy to get me. I knew most of the girls working there, but a few days later Flora, the director, called me. She said when they ran my background check I was on a list. They couldn't hire me. I asked her if this was just their daycare, and she let me know it was supposedly all vulnerable people. I shouldn't bother with the nursing home or the hospital either. I should have fought for my license! More bad advice from big-shot Walter. I am thinking about getting a divorce, but that costs money. You'll stay, okay? There are things that you could help me with."

"Sure," JJ said. "Should I tell CPS am here?"

"No! Aren't you almost 18?"

"Yeah—in two months."

"Then we can start the social security application process right away. I have enough paperwork on you for disability. Okay? Do you have your medications with you? We can get that started again too. You can have your old room!"

JJ celebrated his eighteenth birthday on September 30 at the Boynton house. Mary bought him new clothes and a pair of sneakers. He wanted to learn to drive, but she made excuses. Her car was not reliable. She could not afford the insurance. Maybe when he was nineteen she'd teach him. Mary was true to her word about the SSI money. He started to receive $720.00 a month. Mary was the payee. Every week he cleaned the house, swept the patio, went with her grocery shopping, washed her car, did the laundry, and learned to make breakfast for both of them. He went with her whenever she had an appointment, to get her hair permed or see the doctor. He went to the doctor too, and the medications helped him this time to sleep and stay calm. Mary gave him an allowance of thirty dollars a week.

Jacob went to church with Mary. She had lots of friends there, and he was welcomed. After the main service, he attended a Bible study class while Mary met with the church ladies. He enjoyed the class. It was run by a woman named Mercedes. Over the months she started to give him odd jobs to do from time to time, at the church and then at her house. He liked having the extra money. A few days after his nineteenth birthday, she asked him if he knew how to drive. When he said he couldn't she offered to teach him. This was terrific! He loved to drive. Mercedes helped him get a driver's license. JJ was in seventh heaven! He could officially drive. He proudly showed his new license to Mary, thinking she would be delighted. He was wrong.

"Why are you disobeying me like this?" she demanded one day. "I do everything for you and this is the thanks I get?"

JJ was mystified. He thought she liked Mercedes.

"Don't think I am going to put up with this!"

"With what?"

"Don't smart guy me! You know what I am talking about"

"No, no I don't."

"Go get in the car and wait for me," she yelled

JJ did as he was told. About twenty minutes later, Mary came out of the house lugging a big black plastic bag that was nearly full. She put the bag in the trunk and then got into the driver's seat.

"You think you are all grown up, don't you? You and Mercedes!" And then she didn't say any more.

They drove for an hour in silence and finally pulled into a strip mall. It was nearly dark.

"You know where we are, Jacob? This is the Salvation Army of Chester County. Looks like they are closed now, but there are good people in there, and they will help you now."

Mary got out of the car. JJ followed her. Yanking the garbage bag out of the trunk, she marched over to the locked front door of the Salvation Army and dropped the bag.

"This is all your stuff, JJ," she said and then, walking to the car, she called back to him, "Good luck, JJ!" and off she drove.

The next morning JJ was still there inside his old sleeping bag, using his bag of stuff for a pillow.

"What's happening, young man?" a voice woke him. A man towered over him. "Let's go inside and put the coffee on. You must be cold."

This was the beginning of JJ's life as an adult.

Chapter Five

Jacob was terrified about what might be happening to Lexie and Lucy in foster care. He could not help imagining the worst. He was having trouble sleeping. He was anxious all the time. Although Rose talked to her appointed attorney several times, Jacob was having trouble connecting with his. He grilled Rose about what she was being told, and she explained to him they might have to do some services, but when they went to court on Monday, August 23, 2010, they would try to convince the judge to let Lexie and Lucy come home.

They would tell the judge they had a safe place to stay with Candy and the girls loved her and Suzie—that was home, but they already knew CPS would not agree with this plan. Candy was going to come with them to court and bring Bill too, in hopes the sight of him would be enough to convince the court he could not be a danger to any child, but that might not work in the short run, so her attorney had suggested a plan-B.

Rose said plan-B was to move back to Grandma Dee's house. Darlene was gone and Dee was willing to try it again. Maybe Jerry could leave too, but what her lawyer told her was the chances of getting the girls back were much greater if Rose made the move on her own.

"If we separated for a while," Rose explained.

"You mean a pretend separation?" Jacob asked.

Rose assured him it would be make-believe. Then once the girls were back with her and they jumped all the CPS hoops they could get back together again.

Jacob could see the merits of this plan. He knew without a doubt he and Rose were way better parents than Jeannie had ever been, but he could also see the writing on the wall. The social workers thought Rose, the mother, was better. He didn't really disagree. He knew he had never hurt his children, but he also saw Rose was more nurturing. She did not sweat the small stuff the way he did; she could sort things through with Lexie. Rose looked better on paper. She had never been in the system before, never arrested. Rose looked better to CPS, and they needed to accept that for now. Jacob's only goal was to get his children out of foster care.

Rose had her issues, though. The question of prescription drug abuse hung over them equally. Based on those wide-open releases the parents had given to CPS back in June, information about them was still rolling in—an avalanche of medical and treatment records. Jacob and Rose had too many visits to clinics and ERs in the last twelve months. The parents did not dispute the numbers. Not every visit resulted in a prescription for a pain pill, but in almost every visit the complaint was about pain of some sort from a sprained ankle to a headache. Jacob's visits often included complaints about night terrors and severe anxiety.

The random urinalysis records were also working against them both. Jacob's first UA was perfectly clear, no drugs at all. Subsequent UAs sometimes showed oxycodone, but he was able to produce a legitimate prescription for this drug. Then, about two months into the process, the parents were told Kane Recovery Center's contract for these UAs had ended. Still later, when CPS renewed the contract, Jacob did more UAs. These results were mixed. The oxycodone was still consistent with his reported prescribed use, but one UA showed benzodiazepine too, which was not consistent with any prescriptions he was able to provide.

He had taken a xanny Rose gave him.

Another knock against Jacob was his checkered driving record. He had a DUI in 2009, the result of his careless use of Ativan. He had a legitimate prescription for this drug, but he immediately took the pill as he left the hospital in Ashland County with the new prescription, not knowing or appreciating what its effect could be. He was pulled over on his way home for weaving all over the lane lines. After this incident, his license was suspended. He was also ordered into a drug treatment program. He had tried the program, but he was not able to attended all the meetings they had. His counselor, aware of Jacob's anxiety and possible PTSD symptoms, suggested Kane Mental Health (KMH) might be a better fit for him and referred him there for evaluation. Jacob started working with a psychiatrist at KMH who prescribed a variety of medications for him. Jacob did not, however, follow through with the mental health counseling the shrink recommended, and he never went back to the drug treatment program.

One day, about three months before CPS came to the door, Lexie woke Jacob up and said she could not get mommy up. She was going to be late for her preschool that started at 10:00 A.M. It was too late to walk. Lexie insisted if they tried to walk she would be late for sure. He had to drive her.

Jacob hurried Lexie out to the car. The preschool was only about ten blocks away from Grandma Dee's house. Jacob let Lexie hop in the front seat. Three blocks into this trip, Jacob drove right by a police car parked along the street. The officer could see Lexie's little head in the front passenger seat and recognized she was too small for that seat. The officer hit his lights and immediately pulled Jacob over. Jacob asked the officer for a warning so he could get Lexie to school on time. The officer was not interested in negotiating, but simply asked for identification. Jacob gave him his ID card.

The officer said "No, I need to see your driver's license."

Jacob had to admit he did not have a license; all he was trying to do was get Lexie to preschool because her mom had overslept. The officer checked his computer and saw Jacob's license was suspended and he had failed to appear for a hearing in connection with that old Ativan DUI. As a result, there was an outstanding warrant for his arrest.

The officer explained he had to arrest him, but he agreed to call Rose so she would come and get Lexie. After about fifteen rings, a very pregnant Rose answered the call and then came hurrying down the street a few minutes later.

The officer wanted to see Rose's identification before he let her drive away with Lexie. When he looked her up, he saw her driver's license was suspended too for unpaid fines. This was a surprise to Rose. The officer told her there was no warrant for her, but he could not let her drive the car. She should get those fines cleared up. Rose and Jacob frantically called as many people as they could think of to come and get the car for them, but they couldn't find anyone, so the car was towed away. Jacob was taken to jail, and Rose walked Lexie the rest of the way to school.

Although he got back home by breakfast the next day, Jacob had a new court date in Ashland county with no way to get there, and he was ticketed for improper child restraints. With all this history, no wonder the parents thought they needed to be ready to temporarily split up, so Rose could get the kids back immediately.

—·—

Finally, Monday arrived and the parents went to court again for the hearing—the real hearing—at which CPS needed to prove the health, safety, and welfare of the Johnson girls would be seriously endangered if they were allowed to go back and live with either or both of their parents. According to CPS, the risk of harm was imminent. At this stage of the lawsuit, there was little proof Lexie and Lucy faced any imminent risk, but CPS did not have to offer what was true at this hearing. A social worker—or anyone else for that matter—could state under oath things other people told them that might turn out to be false, and the standard of proof at the hearing on August 23, 2010 was as low as it goes, just reasonable cause to believe the social worker was justified in thinking Jacob might be dangerous based on the lies in the file. Under this standard, false impressions and false reports created by people who did not like him or who thought he was too stupid to be an adequate parent were good enough. The petitions CPS filed and documents such as that sheriff incident report full of inaccuracies were handed to the court commissioner a few hours before the hearing began as state exhibits. Copies were provided to the parents' attorneys.

The parents again arrived early to court. The narrow, noisy hallway at juvenile court again gradually filled up with mothers and fathers, grandmothers and uncles, aunts and children. Again, there was no air conditioning. Candy was there too, with Bill slumped in his wheelchair. Rose had a chance to meet with her attorney while they waited. Jacob wanted to meet with her too, but again this was not allowed. He was told his attorney was in court and would see him when she was free. Sharon Peabody came by and explained again Bill's felony could not be ignored. It was disqualifying. Jacob and Rose told her about plan-B. She accepted their decision to separate, but could not immediately agree to using Grandma Dee as a placement. The parents told her they had already signed up for a drug alcohol treatment interview. She applauded their efforts, but said she needed more of a track record before she could support the idea of the girls being returned. The parents wanted to know how the girls were doing and if Lexie was in a preschool. Sharon said she would try and find out.

People were coming in and out of the courtroom. The announcements over the PA system were still garbled and scratchy. Jacob was pacing the hallway. How was his attorney going to know what to say if they never had a chance to talk? It was 2:30 and still their names had not been called. At three, their case was announced.

Again, they all filed into a tiny courtroom. It was the same court commissioner. It took a few minutes to get Bill situated at the back of the room because some of the chairs had to be moved out of the way. Jacob and Rose and their attorneys sat to the right, and Peabody sat next to her lawyer on the left.

Jacob's lawyer whispered in his ear, "It doesn't look good for return today."

Jacob replied loudly, "But I didn't do anything!"

He was shushed by several people. Each person introduced themselves giving their name and role, including Candy and Bill.

Then the court asked the lawyers if the previously scheduled trial was okay for them. She told them to block out three days for the trial. Jacob did not understand why people were focusing on the date for trial, but he held his tongue. Then Rose's lawyer said it was her understanding the parents were separating and Rose wanted the children given back to her immediately, so a full hearing right now would be necessary. Jacob's attorney said the father supported the mother's request.

The court asked if everyone had a copy of the petition and the exhibits CPS prepared for the hearing. Everyone did. Ms. Peabody was sworn in. She testified about Jacob's prior mistakes, the DUI, and driving without proper restraints for Lexie and about his negative and positive UAs. She described what she thought were the questionable injuries to Lexie and to Lucy. During her testimony, Jacob was getting more and more upset. Couldn't his attorney do something? He knew it was all bullshit, but everyone seemed to be listening to Ms. Peabody as if she were telling a true story.

She testified Rose was likely an addict and had no safe place for the children. Rose might deny there was domestic violence with Jacob, but she was now separating from him and that spoke volumes about their relationship. Right now, the chances the girls would be neglected or abused if returned to their mom only or to both parents were unacceptably high. Then she explained why CPS policy prohibited her from even considering Candy's home as a safe place for the girls because of Bill.

At this point, Jacob stood up and said, "This is all bullshit," and stormed out of the courtroom. He went out to the parking lot where he paced up and down.

Rose was sworn in, and her attorney led her through a long set of questions. She described how much she loved her children, how she and the girls could live with her mother, and how she was willing to do anything the court asked of her. Her attorney also handed around the exhibits she made of the two unfounded letters the parents received. Then the attorney for the state questioned her about her drug use, her angry fights with Jerry, and her failure to protect Lucy from that wrist injury. Rose sputtered and cried. "Lucy is fine," she said, "Jacob never did anything to our girls. That thing with Lucy was just a stupid accident."

The attorney for Rose then called Candy to testify. She led her through questions about her home and the circumstances of her husband's disability.

"The state made me his caregiver because he can't manage anymore. Look at him! He is no danger to anybody. Rose and Jacob are good parents. I see that. They love those kids. They need a place to live. This is a no-brainer."

Then Sharon Peabody testified again saying almost verbatim what she had already said. She added, "Even if the parents have really separated—which I am not sure I can believe—Rose, on her own, has many issues including prescription drug abuse that has never been addressed. The children, especially Lucy, are at a very vulnerable age. As for Grandma's house, I am happy to visit the home. I'll take the court advocate with me if there is one yet, and we can look at a placement there, but we cannot do it today or even next week without more information from Grandma and seeing who else is living there now."

The attorney for Rose explained to the court it was better for the children to live with their mother than to remain in foster care with strangers. Rose had done nothing to injure the children. She was willing to accept any restrictions the court wanted to put on her. If she could not live with Candy, then the children should be immediately returned to her at her mother's home.

"The most important thing is the children are well-bonded to their parents and further placement with strangers can only traumatize them."

The attorney for Sharon Peabody highlighted the real and imagined risks. "Your honor, this family is in crisis whether they realize it or not. Both parents have drug issues, which standing alone would be enough to prove the legal basis for keeping the children in care. With any luck, these parents will now recognize their issues and get the help they need to be safe, as well as loving parents, but any return of the children now would be premature—dangerously premature."

"Has an advocate been appointed for these children?" the commissioner asked.

"Yes," the clerk sitting beside the Commissioner answered. "Raoul Caster has been appointed, Your Honor, but he could not make it to today's hearing."

"All right. Ms. Faraday, I hope you will agree with me the father's performance today here in court suggests you might be minimizing what he has done or not done. In any case, I think your plan to separate from him is a good plan, and I wish you luck with it. I can't let the children go today to homes to which the agency reasonably objects. You need to find a safe place to live, one that is safe for your children, I mean, and when you find such a place that would constitute a change of circumstances, then I could again consider the possibility of returning the girls to you. I would note that clean and sober housing would be an ideal choice."

Rose started to sob.

Everyone filed out of the courtroom. Candy went in search of Jacob. He walked back into the court house with a sense of foreboding. He did not think the hearing could have gone well. Rose, wiping her eyes, gave him the news the girls were not coming home no matter where she lived. His eyes filled with tears. Before he could say anything, his attorney came up to him.

"You are not helping your case," she said.

Now Jacob let her have it. "Really? And how are you helping it? Tell me that. My children are staying in foster care. Do you know what could happen to them? Do you even know their names?"

His attorney replied she was ready to meet with him right then and there, but Jacob refused.

"Why bother now?"

Jacob helped Candy wheel Bill out to the car. Then he and Rose went to find Sharon Peabody.

"Tell us what to do!" Rose lamented.

Jacob stood beside her. "When can we see them?" he asked.

Peabody explained to them it wasn't part of her job to arrange visitation, but she took mercy on these stricken parents and told them to wait while she made a few calls. About fifteen minutes later, she found the parents slumped in chairs by the exit. Rose's attorney sat with them.

"Good news! There will be a visit this week. It's scheduled for Friday at the CPS office at 1:00 P.M. It will be a two-hour supervised visit."

Jacob could not believe his ears. "Friday? Are you fucking kidding me? I have to wait a week to see my own children? Two hours?" Jacob felt like he might pass out.

Rose had calmed down by this time. "It's okay, we will be there, no problem." She pulled Jacob out the door.

———•———

As before, the CPS lobby was full to bursting when Jacob and Rose arrived at noon for their 1:00 P.M. visit. At 12:30, Candy came in too to say hello. When the girls arrived at 1:10, Rose gave Lexie a long, tight hug, then started to cry, and quickly excused herself and stepped outside.

This was the instruction she had previously received from Sharon Peabody. "I know it will be hard, but try not to be emotional. It will make it much easier for the girls if you have a visit without tears and getting upset."

When Rose stepped outside, Lexie ran to Candy and hugged her. Then she saw her dad and hugged him long and tight. Then the woman who had come in with them carrying a sleeping Lucy in a car seat, handed the seat to Jacob and led the family back to a visitation room. Rose almost immediately caught up with them.

The visitation room was small, a ten-by-ten foot square, with a single window. The window blinds were down. There was a single overhead light and a small circular table with one or two straight-backed chairs. There was an overstuffed couch and an overstuffed chair. They did not match. The chairs and couch and floor were stained with easily identified substances: juice and soda and lotions; all kinds of food stains from milk to bananas to French fries to dipping sauces. In addition, there were crayons crushed into the carpet, vomit stains on the arms of the couch, and a stain on the carpet that was hard to identify. Jacob sat on the couch, disgusted by the room. The woman who walked them in now introduced herself as the visitation supervisor, Jennifer Reisenberg. She wedged herself into a corner and opened a computer on her knees. She would write down what she observed, or thought she observed.

"Just ignore me if you can." She said.

Jacob noticed Lexie's knuckles were red and raw. He asked Ms. Reisenberg to discuss with the foster parents changing detergents. He also thought Lexie might have an allergy to some plastics. She nodded her head and then typed in her notes, *Father obsessed by idea of allergies—no evidence.*

Lexie showed to Rose all the drawings she had done that week in her new kindergarten. Jacob told Ms. Reisenberg about some of his experiences in foster care and how he was concerned about protecting the girls from similar abuse. He wondered if Lexie should be checked by a doctor to make sure her hymen was intact. Ms. Reisenberg quickly tried to redirected Jacob, telling him to talk to his social worker about that.

Then Jacob said, "My foster dad is probably still in prison for molesting a girl."

The supervisor shook her head vehemently. Rose pulled out a special gift she and Jacob had for Lexie—a chocolate bunny. Lexie was delighted with this gift and she generously offered each parent a chance to take a piece as she nibbled a paw. Jacob held the still-sleeping Lucy.

Rose and Jacob were relieved to hear the foster home was a Christian home and the foster parents would continue to take the girls to church and encourage them to say their prayers just like at home. Jacob asked Lexie a lot of questions about the foster home: where she slept, what her room was like, what she got to eat, how much television she could watch. He asked Lexie to look at him directly when she answered, and she willingly complied. Rose told Jacob it sounded like he was interrogating Lexie. He explained he just had a lot of questions. He explained he was trying to make sure she was okay.

There was a toy kitchen set up in the room. Lexie played there while the adults talked to each other about her and Lucy. They were sad to see Lexie's beautiful hair had been cut off. Ms. Reisenberg said there had been lice at the school. They told her how Lexie was a finicky eater. They described how much solid food Lucy ate. They had brought Lexie's favorite blanket so she could have it with her. They asked Lexie about the bouncy ball toy she had taken to the foster home. Lexie complained it was something her foster parents wouldn't let her use. Ms. Reisenberg intervened to say she would talk to the foster parents about this.

Jacob again expressed his concern his girls might be hurt in foster care. He was especially worried about sexual abuse, and again Ms. Reisenberg corrected him for using inappropriate language in the visit. He asked if they could have visits at other places like Chuck E. Cheese, and he was told that would likely not be allowed any time soon, but he should talk to his social worker about it, and then Jacob asked Ms. Reisenberg if they could go to counseling as a family. She said she would make a note of his request, but he should, Jacob interrupted her.

"I know, I know, talk to Peabody."

Ms. Reisenberg replied, "No, no, I think it's someone else."

"Who?"

"Sorry, I don't know."

Lucy finally woke up. She opened her eyes and smiled up at Jacob. When she saw Rose, her smile got even bigger. Once Lucy was awake, the parents took pictures, first of Lexie and Lucy with Rose and then with Jacob. Lucy needed to be changed, and the parents did it together, Jacob distracting her because she was such a wiggle worm. Then Lexie needed to go to the bathroom, and Ms. Reisenberg insisted on going with Rose and Lexie to use the restroom. This made Rose mad, but she tried to hide it.

Near the end of the two hours, Jacob asked Lexie if she wanted anything else from home. She got excited at this suggestion and began listing all the toys she could think of and finally said she wanted all her toys.

Jacob laughed. "No, this is just a temporary situation. Your toys will be waiting for you when you came back home.

"But when?" Lexie started to cry.

Jacob tried to reassure her. "Just a little while."

Tears were rolling down Rose's cheeks. She could not talk. Jacob told Lexie it might help to pray now. Lexie prayed God would send her home as soon as he could.

"Amen."

Chapter Six

When the man woke him up at the door of the Salvation Army, Jacob was very tired. The invitation to come inside and have some coffee was a welcomed chance to get warm. There were biscuits too. The man started to talk to him about what he could do next but stopped when he saw Jacob's head bobbing.

"Young man, there's a rolled-up mat on the floor in the back room. You can rest on it. There's a bathroom on the right. You get cleaned up and stretch out for a while, I won't let anyone disturb you."

Jacob did as he was told and slept for hours.

"There's sleeping beauty!" It was the same fellow who let him in. "I know you must be hungry, and we'll take care of that, but I got a few questions for you first, okay son?" Jacob nodded.

"How old are you?"

"Nineteen."

"Where is your family?"

"I don't know. I have been in foster care since I was nine. I think my mother must be around somewhere, but she's bad news."

"Okay. How have you been living?"

"I was with an old foster mom. She was giving me an allowance, and I was helping her out, but she got mad at me for learning to drive. She brought me down here. She's a payee too."

"You mean you are getting social security?"

"Yeah. She took care of all that."

"Let's go get a burger."

The next thirteen months marked a crossroad for Jacob. Larry, the man he met at the door of the Salvation Army was connected to all kinds of people and agencies that helped Jacob get good and truly on his feet. He lived in a shelter, studied his Bible, and completed his GED. He continued with his medications again. Larry helped him get a bank account. Then a woman in Larry's office helped him get his social security transferred under his own name. He moved in with a lady who was having surgery on her knees, and for nearly ten weeks he was able to help her out. He did chores, a painting job, and he drove her to her appointments. She let him sleep in her spare room. He thought about buying a car, and then Jacob Johnson became the proud owner of a 1980 Datsun pickup.

He can't remember all the details, but somehow he got a job working for a carnival down in Oregon. He recalls traveling with the carnival for about four months. He was one of the guys who put up the tents and rides and pulled it all down again when it was time to move. He bought a cab for his pickup and slept in it. When he wasn't working, he liked to wander around the carnival talking to people. He was developing the gift of gab, not trying anymore to make friends exactly, just chatting up people to pass the time of day or night. Wandering one evening down the midway, he saw a woman he had seen before and wondered who she was.

"Do you work here?" he asked her.

"Why do you want to know?"

"I am sure I have seen you before. I work here."

"I was thinking it might be fun to work in one of these games. Is that what you do?"

"No, I set up and tear down, and in between I keep things running." Jacob knew this was on overstatement, but she seemed impressed. Jacob took her over to the woman in charge of hiring, and she got a job making cotton candy. Her name was Dawn.

Sometimes she would crawl in next to him in the pickup, and they would have sex. He told her about how his mom sounded like she was being hurt when her johns were on top of her, and she understood the problem and helped him out.

The end of the season was approaching. Everyone working for the carnival was given the option of staying with the job and moving down to San Diego for winter. Dawn wanted to go back to her home and encouraged Jacob to follow her. She was his first real girlfriend, and he didn't have to think twice about it. He pulled his truck onto her parents' property. He had to sleep out there, and Dawn joined him often. He got to come in for meals. Dawn's parents were foster parents. Her uncle was a local pastor.

One day Jacob came into the house looking for Dawn. What he discovered was Dawn's brother, who was over twenty-one, fondling the breasts of one of the family's foster daughters. She was about fourteen. He backed out of the house, but of course could not forget what he saw. He told Dawn about it thinking she would be willing to turn in her brother, but she wasn't; she did not want to get involved.

Jacob's concluded, "It didn't matter where you went. It's always the same bullshit."

The next day he drove his pickup down the road to another town. The following Sunday he came back to catch Dawn's uncle after church. He told the uncle what he had seen. The girl he saw was not fighting off Dawn's brother. They seemed like a couple making out, but it wasn't right. Jacob wanted someone to know what was going on, someone he thought would have to turn in the brother. The uncle promised to look into it. Jacob never knew what, if anything, ever happened.

—·—

Jacob found himself wandering down the main street of a port town in a light drizzle. He was looking for a cash machine to see if his social security deposit was ready. He walked past an army recruitment office. He stared at the poster.

"C'mon in out of the rain, son," a man in a beautiful uniform beckoned him in.

The man was handsome and fit and friendly. In fact, he was the most well put together guy Jacob had ever seen in real life. Captain Edward A. Hunt happily explained to Jacob how he could become a man just like Edward A. Hunt. He listened attentively to Jacob's story and gave him a few tests that Jacob managed to complete easily. Jacob was given an appointment that afternoon to see a local doctor for a preliminary physical, and then he was told the most astonishing thing. If he passed that physical and signed up to join the Army that same day, he would get a check for ten thousand dollars. He almost ran to the doctor's office, and when he finished the physical, he hurried back to the recruitment office to sign all the papers. He had enlisted in the Washington State Army National Guard. He was first sent to Franklin Army base near South Fork, and from there he was scheduled to go to boot camp at Fort Knox in Kentucky. If he survived boot camp, a check for ten thousand dollars would be waiting for him.

Before he and his buddies were sent off to boot camp, there was a big battalion dance at the base. It was there, when he was no doubt looking his finest in his dress uniform, that he met Rose Faraday. They danced. They talked. They really seemed to hit it off, to connect, but of course, Jacob was leaving the next day and didn't know if he would ever see her again. He was surprised she wrote to him. When he got back to Franklin, she was waiting for him. He proudly showed her his certificate from the Department of the Army showing he successfully completed sixteen weeks of training.

The ten thousand dollars made it easy to move in together. After about two months, Jacob was ordered to Montana for additional weapons training, this time with tanks—M1A2 Abram tanks.

Jacob was learning to love tanks, but one day when he was ordered to pour a pink hydraulic fluid into his tank, a wind came up, and blew the fluid on to his right hand. His skin immediately started to burn. Skin began to fall off, and there was a putrid odor. Jacob went to sickbay where he washed his hands, but could not get the liquid off. He was given a cream and a glove to cover the hand. Small boils appeared, and the cream did little to ease the pain and the condition persisted.

On another day, the soldiers were using live ammunition including hand grenades. Jacob pulled the pin on a grenade, but then held on to it too long. Luckily, his instructor grabbed it, threw it, and covered Jacob as the grenade exploded in midair. Jacob says this guy saved his life.

The men in his unit talked about the many accidents that were rumored to have happened at this Montana facility including an incident in which an officer was killed. It had been a hot day, and the soldiers on the ridge had taken off their helmets. Another team was below them, maneuvering a group of tanks. An officer commanding the tank group had gone down on foot to explain something to a soldier in the turret. For some reason he, too, had taken off his helmet. The helmet held the headphones and microphones that allowed soldiers to communicate with one another. Suddenly one of the other tanks was bearing down on him. He could not communicate with tank's crew. All the soldiers on the ridge were yelling and waving their arms. Finally, the tank driver made a sharp turn, overcorrecting to avoid an accident. The turn was so sharp it flipped the tank over right on to the officer, crushing the man as everyone watched helplessly. Supposedly all those who witnessed this accident were cautioned not to talk about it with anyone, not even with each other, and yet all the soldiers in Jacob's unit had heard the story.

In the third week of training, Jacob's unit was on a sleep deprivation exercise. They had been up for three days straight. They were heading back to their barracks but were called up for extra duty. Jacob was ordered into the gunner's position in the turret of his tank. When the turret began to turn, his field jacket snagged in the gears of the turret. His whole body was being pulled into the turret. He could not tear off the jacket. He was choking and screaming. He thought he was going to die. He kept struggling to free himself but could not. Luckily, his buddies finally heard his screams and the tank stopped. They cut Jacob out of his jacket. He was totally freaked out.

Jacob was traumatized. He knew he needed help. Medication or something. He couldn't sleep. He was jumpy all the time. He thought he saw the officer who was killed when he was in the mess or out on maneuvers. He spoke to a senior man about getting some help, medications, maybe some counseling.

The officer was blunt. "You have two options soldier: Suck it up or run away."

Jacob ran away. He hitched a ride back to Rose. He was reduced in rank and later, effective December 28, 2002, he was discharged from the army under other than honorable conditions.

When he got back to South Fork, Rose helped him calm down. He found a doctor who prescribed the same anti-anxiety medications he used to take before he met Dawn. He moved on with life. He was able to complete nursing assistant training and got his CNA certificate and license. After a few years, Rose suggested they move to Arizona for a fresh start. There was still a little money left in savings from that bonus.

Jacob was able to get his CNA license transferred to Arizona and got a good job almost immediately at a convalescent center. He and Rose bought a better car and were able to get their own apartment. Rose planned to get her CNA license too, but before she could start the program she became pregnant with Lexie.

In spite of all that had happened to him, this was a good time in Jacob's life. He felt like he was finally getting it all together—the job, the money, the relationship, and now he looked forward to being a good dad, a protector, a real man.

Lexie was born on January 10, 2005. Jacob proceeded to drive Rose crazy, worrying that Lexie was not okay, feeling she was too small to hold, and in general launching into his overprotective, hypervigilant dad role. For him, fatherhood was an overwhelming responsibility.

Jacob continued to work. He liked his job, enjoyed the people. He was good at this, helpful too. He saved his angry outbursts for coworkers he thought were lazy or incompetent. Feeling competent himself for a change, he relished having answers. One day he was helping a new patient get into her bed. He had reviewed the chart notes for this sixty-nine-year-old woman, and nothing there alerted him to the fact she suffered from childhood polio. The condition had made her immobile legs very heavy. Reaching down to lift her legs, Jacob heard something pop in his back. He succeeded in getting her into bed, but when he stood up, he felt an extreme burning in his lower back. He had popped a disc.

He was put on a shorter work schedule of lighter duty, no lifting. He saw doctors and had X-rays and an MRI, which showed the problem with his disc. He went to physical therapy, but nothing eased the pain in his back. He was prescribed painkillers, and these seemed to work but left him feeling wonky and irritable.

He had a claim against his employer because this was a worksite injury, and he tried to follow through with it as he watched the amount of his monthly paycheck go down and down. He had to make some payments for his medical care out of his own pocket. There was the promise he would be reimbursed when the claim was settled, but he had no financial cushion to see him through until then. While the lighter duty helped with the pain, the lighter paycheck was turning into nightmare. It was hard to find the money for rent, and the young parents fell behind on their bills. As spring approached, things were getting desperate. When Rose's mother, Dee, invited them to come back to South Fork and live with her for a while, Jacob and Rose packed up and returned to Washington. Lexie would have her first birthday in South Fork.

Jacob found work as an on-call CNA. He was still taking pain medication for his back. Rose was staying home with Lexie. Money was tight, and life was chaotic. As the months and then years went by, Jacob became well and truly addicted to those pain pills. He was unable to find a steady job and didn't really want one. He and Rose scraped by on his occasional CNA jobs, the charity of others, welfare, and food stamps. When living at Dee's became too unbearable, they moved to shelters or motels. In the midst of all this uncertainty, Jacob's untreated PTSD symptoms grew worse. He tried separating from Rose, hoping that would get him some peace, but he missed Lexie too much. Rose wanted him back, and he returned after only a few weeks.

Lexie had just turned four when Jacob got that DUI for Ativan. He was ordered into drug treatment, and he admitted he was in rough shape. He was still taking pain medication for his back and his other symptoms of anxiety, nightmares and sleeplessness, hyper awareness, and flashbacks continued to plague him. The drug/alcohol treatment counselor thought he was helping Jacob when he determined drug treatment was premature based on his array of PTSD-like symptoms, and referred Jacob to Kane Mental Health.

When a person is abusing alcohol or drugs and is also suffering from a mental health disorder, whether it be depression or anxiety or PTSD more generally, it is hard to tell which came first, the drugs and their effects or the mental health issues. There is a fair amount of dispute about which should be treated first or whether they can be treated simultaneously. Some experts say unless a person is clean and sober, they cannot successfully engage in mental health therapy. Others say the insight a person can gain in therapy will help them stop using drugs, and if there are relapses along the way it is a matter of two steps forward one step back. Isn't that progress?

This conflict was compounded in Jacob's case because the Ashland county court ordered him to do drug treatment, not to do mental health therapy, and Jacob continued to ignore the court. It was even more complicated because the drugs he was using were legitimately prescribed for him. He was not taking the drugs to get high. He was taking them to ease the real pain and real anxiety he felt all the time.

Jacob had been very forthcoming at his intake interview for mental health counseling on February 17, 2010. He said, "I was referred by my drug/alcohol counselor. I can't keep a job. I have communication issues. I have nightmares and flashbacks." Jacob agreed his treatment goals were to reduce his fear, nightmares, and panic attacks. He explained his problems related to what happened to him in his childhood.

A few weeks later, Jacob met with the psychiatrist at Kane Mental Health (KMH). He described to this doctor his avoidance of confrontations, his lack of friends, his anxiety over Rose's pregnancy, his frequent flashbacks, and sense of being constantly stressed out. He acknowledged he was hypervigilant with his daughter Lexie and fearful about how the family would manage with another child due to be born in two months. He described his own temperament as nice one minute and angry the next. He discussed drugs he had been prescribed in the past: Serzone, Valium, and Lorazepam (Ativan). He said he got some relief from Cymbalta, but his state welfare insurance would not cover it. He acknowledged using alcohol to fall asleep in the past but was afraid to use it now that he had a child. He acknowledged he sometimes used benzodiazepine for pain relief.

He received a diagnosis of Post-traumatic Stress Disorder, mood disorder not otherwise specified, alcohol abuse of uncertain status, and possible Benzodiazepine abuse. The psychiatrist prescribed another antidepressant, Celexa, and to help Jacob sleep, Prazosin. For anxiety, he was given a prescription for Trazadone. Jacob was scheduled to come in again at the end of April.

Jacob did not make it back to KMH until the end of May 2010. He told the psychiatrist he was scared to change Lucy's diaper because she was so small. He said he knew he was driving Rose crazy with his concerns for Lucy when she obviously was just fine, and he acknowledged his overprotectiveness was a problem. His medication seemed to be doing some good. The psychiatrist noted Jacob was also taking some other medications he got from two other doctors, Neurontin, Prilosec and Alprazolam and Lorazepam. Jacob was encouraged to begin mental health counseling. At this point, Jacob drifted away from any formal treatment for either drug/alcohol abuse or for mental health issues.

Jacob had also been working on another front, starting in 2008, to try and get the resources his family needed to be free of Grandma Dee's charity. This was his quest to obtain help from the Veterans Administration. While he was working at a temporary CNA job at the Vernon Veterans home in South Fork, he met John Ledford who was managing the Veterans Service Center there. Mr. Ledford helped Jacob with his claim and provided counseling and encouragement. Jacob's claim was based on PTSD as a result of the tank accident during which he was nearly choked to death. He also claimed lasting skin damage as a result of the hydraulic fluid that spilled over his hands during this same period of tank training. He also claimed some hearing loss and ringing in his ears from working so closely to the M-1 Abrams tanks as they fired live ammunition.

Making a VA disability claim was and no doubt remains a complicated process. Just getting the release of his army service records required multiple requests. In addition, Jacob had to get corroborating evidence for the facts he claimed as the basis for his disabilities.

He was able to get some verification of the incidents through affidavits from men who had been in his unit, and he also provided the VA with his recent KMH record in hopes it would further support his claim. Throughout the long process, Jacob continued to meet with Mr. Ledford and often the whole family met with him. Mr. Ledford formed a very favorable impression of Jacob, Rose, and Lexie. He never saw the parents under the influence of anything. Jacob was always very respectful toward him and toward his family. Both parents had a very caring relationship with their little girl. Jacob submitted his claim. Then he waited and waited and waited.

Chapter Seven

Visitation between Jacob and his children was limited to once a week for two hours, supervised at the CPS office. Jacob and Rose visited together with the girls at 3:00 P.M. each Friday. At the second visit there were lots of smiles and hugs and kisses. Jacob asked Lexie lots of embarrassing questions: Are you taking a shower every day? Are you changing your underwear every day? Rose told him to stop with the interrogations. They took photos. Jacob held Lucy while he and Rose talked with Lexie about her friends in kindergarten. It was painful to have missed her first day in school, but Rose convinced Jacob they should not let Lexie know how much it hurt.

They had snacks, and Lexie helped feed Lucy. Lexie found a book she wanted to read and she sat on the couch between her parents and read to them. Lucy was restless but eventually fell asleep in her mother's arms. Lexie told her parents about going to a fair. Before long, the two hours were up.

In less than three weeks, the children had been taken from their parents and from Candy and Suzie, too. They had lived in two different places already with two different couples. Lexie no longer saw friends from her old preschool or the neighborhood. The girls had moved to a new town. Lexie had been introduced to three new social workers and to a man named Raoul who came to see her at her new foster home.

He told her his job was to tell the court what was best for her and for Lucy. She wasn't certain what a court was, but what would be best was clear to her. It would be best to go back home to Mommy and Daddy.

Some scholars have suggested the very notion of a child's "best interest" is a false or impossible standard when applied to children removed from their parents. None of the options facing most children suddenly placed in foster care are best. It might be helpful if professionals in the child welfare system took an oath like the one physicians take, a promise to first do no harm. In any case, what might be "best" is rarely accomplished. Just barely good enough is the true standard in the child welfare system.

The third visit was delayed a week because the girls had been sick. Nothing serious, just a flu. Jacob had repeatedly called Sharon Peabody for more details about the illnesses and if the visit would be made up. All he got was the same re-assurance, just the flu. As for a make-up, she would check the schedule. The visit followed the established pattern. It started off with smiles and hugs and kisses again. Pictures were taken again, cupcakes enjoyed. Lexie talked about school. Jacob again asked about bathing every day and changing clothes every day and Lexie assured him she did and Lucy did, too. Rose got on the floor with Lucy because Jacob's back was hurting. Lexie sang her ABCs, and her parents were very impressed and praised her. When the visit was over, Lexie told them she loved them. There were more hugs and kisses as the parents settled each girl into her car seat.

On September 18, Jacob brought a game for Lexie. It was a board game called Don't Wake Daddy. The object of the game was to get around the board first. The squares on the board represented things around the house—a TV, pots and pans, a piano, a chair. Each square had a number. Each player chose a mounted picture card of a boy or a girl to use as a game piece. Each player was also dealt six cards with pictures that corresponded to pictures on some, but not all, of the squares on the board.

There was a dial to spin with numbers on it, which told the player how many squares she could advance on each turn. In the middle of the board was a big, red, plastic bed, and on the bed was a blue, plastic Daddy doll, sleeping. He had a yellow, cloth nightcap on his head. Next to the bed was an alarm clock with a button sticking out of the top.

If a player landed on a square for which she did not have a corresponding picture, the player had to push the alarm button the number of times indicated on the square—it might be two or five or eight times. No one knew when the alarm would actually go off. Whenever the alarm clock went off, the Daddy doll would spring up, his eyes flying open, wide awake, like an explosive jack-in-the box. Sometimes he would wake up so hard his night cap flew right off his head. If a player woke up Daddy, she had to go back to the very beginning and start all over again.

Playing Don't Wake Up Daddy led to much laughter and happy screams. Lexie loved playing this game, and Lucy giggled joyfully every time Daddy woke up and with complete abandon when his nightcap flew into the air.

———•———

While the parents waited anxiously for their trial date, they did everything they could think of to make their case as strong as possible for getting the kids back. They stuck to the plan of separating, and Rose moved back into her mother's house while Jacob stayed at Candy's. Rose's attorney advised her she should get a drug/alcohol evaluation as soon as possible. She also told her to re-enroll in a parenting class. Once she was settled at her mother's house, she should ask Sharon Peabody to come by to do a walkthrough and hopefully approve the home for placement.

Jacob consulted with his attorney too, always by phone. She advised him to first and foremost clean up his outstanding warrant. She explained no court would consider placement with a parent who could be pulled off to jail at any moment, however short that jail stay might turn out to be. It made him look unstable. Jacob dutifully got a court date in Ashland County and Candy agreed to give him a ride down there, Rose could watch Suzie and Bill.

A new social worker was assigned to their case, although Sharon Peabody still seemed to be in charge. Betsy Wilson and Raoul Caster came by at the scheduled time to see Rose at her mother's place and check it out. As Ms. Wilson walked around the house, she found one problem after another. The basement stairs were in poor repair, there was no railing either. Stacks of boxes in the basement were a fire hazard. The light was poor. Rose explained they would not let Lexie or Lucy go down there, they never did anyway. Ms. Wilson showed them the lock on the basement door appeared to be broken.

As the social worker and advocate moved on toward the bedrooms, Jerry came home and went immediately into the basement.

Ms. Wilson asked Rose, "Didn't you tell me your brother had moved out?"

Rose blushed and turned to her mother, "You told me he was moving out!"

"He will, he will! But he has to find a place first, doesn't he? That trial is not for weeks yet."

"You always let him have his way! This is important to me. Don't you get that? Lexie and Lucy can't live here if Jerry is still here."

"That's just not fair! Your brother never did anything wrong! He loves those kids."

Rose turned back to the visitors. "I'm sorry, I'll get him out of here as soon as I can."

Nothing in the bedrooms posed any threats. A few minutes later Rose, Ms. Wilson, and Raoul gathered on the porch. Ms. Wilson explained she thought most of the safety concerns with the house could be fixed, but Jerry's continued presence in the home was a showstopper.

"I know you and your brother do not get along. The girls should not be exposed to your fights, and I think you need to be engaged—actually engaged—in treatment before the girls can come home. Your last UA showed painkillers you had no prescription for—did you get something from Jacob?"

Rose refused to say. Instead, she described the pain she was still suffering associated with Lucy's birth. Ms. Wilson was sympathetic. "I am not saying you should be in pain, Rose. You need to find another way to deal with it. For now, I cannot agree to returning the girls to you here."

"Where do you want me to go then?"

"There are shelters that take mothers and kids."

"You think a shelter is better for the girls than a real home? That's crazy!"

Jacob felt optimistic on the drive down to the Ashland county courthouse for his hearing on September 21. He knew he had not completed drug treatment or the recommended treatment the KMH people, but even so, he hoped his involvement with CPS and his plan to get into a drug/alcohol treatment program for prescription drug abuse now would satisfy the court. CPS would pay for services. He also figured he could make a payment plan to pay off any fines that might be stacking up.

"What have you got to say for yourself, Mr. Johnson?" the judge asked him as soon as his case was called. Jacob explained now he would be able to do treatment with help from CPS. In fact, his social worker told him she could set up parenting classes for him too. He knew he would follow through this time because they had his children in foster care, and he couldn't let that go on. He told the judge what his visitation schedule was—once a week for two hours every Friday. He never missed a visit.

The judge was unimpressed.

"You ignored your obligations here, Mr. Johnson. In fact, I don't think you would even be here now if CPS had not intervened in your life. You owe fines and restitution and it keeps on piling up because you can't be bothered with us here in Ashland County, can you? I sent you to drug treatment over a year ago."

"I have a trial in few weeks!"

"That's your CPS case, right? Let that attorney know you are down here. You had an obligation to let this court know what was happening. Court dates were set and you ignored those dates. You do not respect this court, Mr. Johnson. That much is clear. You do not appreciate the seriousness of your drug abuse that led to this DUI in the first place. You are going to jail, Mr. Johnson, I revoke the treatment option we gave you and sentence you immediately to forty-five days.

"I can't miss visits," Jacob cried out.

"Good day, Mr. Johnson."

The judge waved a deputy sheriff forward and Jacob was handcuffed and led out of the courtroom and into the adjoining jailhouse. There he was given one phone call. He called Rose and broke down.

"They're booking me," he cried, "Candy saw everything."

The next visit was just Rose and Lexie. Lucy was sick again, this time a cold. She had been taken to see a doctor. Reisenberg said someone tried to contact the parents so they, too, could attend the appointment, but this was the first Rose heard about it. Rose told Lexie that Daddy had to go away, but he would be back soon.

"For his back?" she asked.

"No, it's more for business."

Lexie accepted this. Rose read to her while she had her snack. Then Lexie read to Rose. It was a quiet visit. Later Rose got permission from Sharon Peabody to have her mother come to the visits Jacob would miss. Sharon okayed this arrangement even though Grandma Faraday often fell asleep during the visit. For the next five visits, the girls did not see their daddy.

Chapter Eight

The trial was not held at the juvenile court but in the big courthouse down-town, the Superior Court for Kane County. The attorney for Jacob obtained an order requiring he be transported to the Kane County jail so he could par-ticipate in the trial. He now sat across from her in a meeting room at the back of the court room. A sheriff deputy was also present, and Jacob remained hand-cuffed during this meeting with his lawyer.

"What's Rose going to do?"

"What do you mean?"

"She is fighting this, isn't she?"

"I don't think so, but I want to talk about what you are going to do."

"Can we get a delay? Till I get out?"

In another room, Rose was meeting with her attorney.

"Have you looked over the paperwork I gave you?"

"Yeah, you're sure we will lose?"

"Ninety percent sure. I am 100 percent sure the state will accept what I have drafted. Let me go over this again with you—I know this is stressful. The state will not insist that you agree you abused or neglected the girls. I used simple language for the finding. You just agree you need services in order to reunite with your children. That's the easy bit. You also have to agree, at least temporarily, to this formal statutory language: Lexie and Lucy have no parent, guardian, or custodian capable of adequately caring for them right now, and so that means they are in circumstances that constitute a danger of substantial damage to their psychological or physical development."

Tears rolled down Rose's cheeks. She had trouble swallowing. Softly she said, "I don't think that's true."

"I know, but living with this language is the way we get out of here with an agreed order of dependency. It will give you the time you need to clear up any allegations of drug use and to locate housing that would be acceptable to CPS. I don't think it will take you long to do these things. As soon as you complete the first phase of treatment and have a place of your own, we can set a hearing and ask for the kids to be sent home to you."

"When?"

"That's impossible to say, but sooner than later. Maybe within ninety days."

"The evaluation says I have to do thirty days of inpatient treatment. When can I start all that?"

"As soon as there is a bed available, I hope, but that's one of the problems with going to trial. The state has the evaluation with that inpatient recommendation. It will be used as an exhibit to prove you are not really ready to parent because you have to go away for thirty days. I am surprised the evaluator wanted that based on what you told me about your drug use, but that's what the agency gets to rely on now. We could get a second opinion, but I am not sure if what we would get would be any better, and for sure it would cause delays. Oh, and we might have to pay for it. I can get funding, but again, it might not be better. Another problem is that your UAs have been all over the place. In the last thirty days you have been mostly clean, but then the last one from last week was positive for meth."

"I'm so sorry! I knew it was a mistake."

"What the court would want before considering any return is at least sixty days clean, that's all I'm saying. Another problem is how hard on you this trial will be. Remember that first hearing? This will be much worse. You will have to listen to people testify against you. I showed you Jerry and Darlene are both on the state's witness list. I am afraid you will end up being the state's star witness. The state attorney will ask you all kinds of uncomfortable questions about your relationship with Jacob, with Jerry, with Darlene, questions about your recent drug use, and you have to answer. This is not a criminal trial where you can plead the fifth, so to speak. If you are asked about that recent meth UA and you say, 'I won't answer that,' the judge gets to assume you used meth.

"Look, Rose, I want you to get your kids back as soon as you can, and I will fight for that, but you have to look better to the court than you do today, on paper, before that can happen. If we say we want to go to trial, it will not happen today. There are six cases set for trial today and only one judge. It could take days before we could start. Then allow another week for the trial. Then if we lose, as I am certain we will, the order will have findings that will be harsh—that you used meth recently, that you have a serious addiction. They may even bring in the evaluator to testify about how likely it is you will be able to maintain a clean and sober lifestyle even assuming you will complete treatment. It will be bad."

Rose nodded her head. "Okay, okay. Where do I sign?"

—·—

Jacob's attorney did not think it was very likely they could get a delay.

"Look, you are in jail right now, okay? That's all the state has to prove today, okay? "That you are unavailable to parent. The reason we won't get a continuance is I can't seriously argue the minute you get out of jail the girls could be placed with you, can I?"

"Rose is a better choice."

"Agreed, and since that is true, there is no reason to delay your case. You're not even asking for the girls. Right?"

"But what about all the lies they told?"

"What do you mean?"

"The letters I sent you—CPS says I didn't hurt my girls."

"I don't think that's what they say. Those letters say there was not enough information to prove it."

"What are you talking about? I never hurt them!"

"Agreed, but it does not matter anymore. Water under the bridge, okay?

"Can I talk to Rose?"

"I'll see what her attorney thinks about that. It's fine with me. Okay, officer?"

The deputy had no objections either. He felt sorry for this guy.

A few minutes later, Rose came in the room and sat down across from him.

"Jacob, I'm signing the papers."

"Why?" Jacob gave an anguished yelp.

"It's complicated. I trust my lawyer. She thinks this will be the fastest way to get the girls back to me."

"Do you think they might approve your mom so we could get them out of foster care? Or the Bakers?"

"I'm working on it, but they want me to do thirty days inpatient treatment, and then almost a year more."

"Wow."

"Yeah, but I will wait until you get back, so the girls don't miss any visits with at least one of us."

"How are they doing?"

"Good, but I have to get back out there. Can you call me again on Sunday? I think they're doing great, considering."

When Rose traded places with Jacob's attorney, he was ready to sign. She gave him the paperwork and left him to look at it while she went back into the courtroom to handle a few of her other cases. Jacob thumbed through the ten-page document. He was not a great reader, and most of the words were bullshit. He signed off.

Rose and Jacob stood before the judge. They each agreed they wanted the orders that had been handed up. They agreed they had plenty of time to talk to their attorneys and they agreed they had no questions. They agreed they understood they were entitled to a trial and by these orders they were waiving that right. The judge signed the orders.

"I appreciate this was not easy. I will set a hearing for when we can talk about the best services for each of you. For now, good luck!"

Rose and her attorney went off to have coffee and discuss what would happen next. Jacob was led away by the deputy.

The order Jacob signed was not the same as the order Rose signed. His attorney had not drafted any new order as Rose's attorney had done. She accepted from the state attorney the order he had drafted for the case. Jacob's order read: "The following allegations of dependency are not disputed: All the allegations in the dependency petition." This was dangerously wrong. Among the allegations Jacob was now accepting as true were these falsehoods:

Jacob tried to break Lexie's leg

There was domestic violence between the parents that accounted for the "injury" to Lexie's

Jacob's explanation of Lucy's injury was inconsistent.

These falsehoods would haunt his case. Jacob fired his attorney as soon as he could, but the change in legal representatives did not change the language in the order the judge had signed. On October 18, 2010, Lexie and Lucy Johnson became temporary wards of the state of Washington. Another thing neither parent really understood was a clock was now ticking. They only had about eighteen months to fix the problems CPS said they had. If they failed, their children could be put up for adoption.

Chapter Nine

A few weeks after orders were entered, there was another hearing called a "dispositional hearing," at which the court would consider what services the parents should be ordered to do. Jacob was not present for the next hearing. His new attorney asked for a short delay. The commissioner (they were back in Juvenile court) asked the lawyer if she had a chance to talk with Jacob about the report filed by the social worker in support of the services the agency wanted. She acknowledged they had briefly discussed it.

"I think that's good enough counsel. If there is something Mr. Johnson really wants to address and we don't cover it today, you may bring it back in without having to show a change of circumstance. Although I am willing to concede right now his release from jail would be an adequate change."

The Commissioner had before her a lengthy report submitted by newly assigned social worker, Betsy Wilson.

Ms. Wilson included in her report the assertion that all allegations from the original petition were now deemed true.

Jacob had received a copy of the report in jail. He slowly read through the whole thing. He felt—in no particular order—overwhelmed, unworthy and fighting mad. Although the law required there be a connection between the services the parents would be ordered to do and their deficiencies, social workers like to throw the kitchen sink at a parent at this initial hearing to see what might stick.

It was no surprise Ms. Wilson wanted each parent to do a drug/alcohol evaluation, and a requirement to complete a parenting class also came as no surprise. Even being told to continue doing UAs was anticipated by each parent, but requiring Jacob to complete a domestic violence assessment and follow its recommendations, if any, was a shocker. His attorney objected. She had seen nothing in the record to indicate Jacob had ever been involved in an incident of domestic violence. Everyone—including Jacob—agreed he had a temper, even anger issues, but those could be addressed with mental health counseling. Most DV assessments found a need for treatment; most DV treatment lasted at least a year.

Ms. Wilson responded to the objection by reciting a litany of the conflicts between Jacob and Grandma Dee, Jerry, and Darlene. She also noted the assertion he was heard to speak angrily to Rose. And besides, Jacob signed an agreed order that said he and Rose had DV issues. It should be pointed out these hearings at juvenile court were informal affairs compared to the hearings held downtown. The rules of evidence did not apply and hearsay, within limits, was acceptable.

When asked about the Indian heritage of the girls, the social worker assured the court she had done all she could and was now waiting for the Seminole enrollment office to get back to her.

The needs of the children were supposed to be addressed in this report too. A brief paragraph for each child simply commented Lucy had some respiratory problems, and Lexie liked her school.

Commentary on Rose was equally benign. Ms. Wilson believed she was ready and willing to engage in services. Visitation was positive. Jacob was judged more harshly. Ms. Wilson complained she had driven all the way down to Ashland county jail only to be treated rudely. He interrupted her frequently, most notably when she was telling him things she thought he did not want to hear. He seemed agitated. Ms. Wilson recognized Jacob had been partly raised in foster care and she supposed his claims of abuse in foster care might account for his overreactions now. Mental health counseling would be provided to him as soon as his drug treatment therapist thought he was ready. Ms. Wilson concluded it would be a long haul for him.

The commissioner accepted all the services as proposed by CPS without exception or modification, and the proposal became the order of the court. Visitation remained the same. When the commissioner signed the order, the girls had been in foster care for three months.

———•———

Less than a week after the hearing for services, Rose walked Lexie back to the visitation room at the CPS office. She told her she had a special surprise for her. Lexie went into the room and saw her daddy! She ran into his arms. Throughout this visit, Lexie returned again and again to her dad, swinging on his arm, leaning into him. She chatted away happily, and the two hours seemed like twenty minutes. Lucy was at her foster home, sick again. Lexie explained how Lucy had a tent to help her breathe, and they all discussed what Lucy might be allergic to, something in the home or at her new daycare.

Jacob was strapping Lexie into her car seat when he thought she started to tell him about something that happened in the foster home. Jacob immediately unbuckled Lexie, picked her up, and confronting Jennifer Reisenberg, demanded to know what was happening. Lexie started to cry. Rose was unable to calm down Jacob, and when she took Lexie aside could not get any more information out of her.

Ms. Reisenberg spoke sternly to Jacob. "This is neither the time nor the place. If something is wrong, I will check it out."

And with that she put Lexie back into the car and they sped off. Jacob went ballistic. He called the police. He did not know the name of the foster parents or the location of the foster home. Nonetheless, a police officer contacted Ms. Wilson and then called a county sheriff to do a welfare check on the foster home. An officer arrived that evening and found nothing to be concerned about. Over the next few days, Rose and the social worker tried to reassure Jacob there were no safety issues in the foster home. He did not believe them.

There was some fallout from this incident. Raoul, the advocate, chided Jacob for his extreme overreaction and told him he could be arrested for making a false police report. At their very next visit, Lexie hugged her dad but was shy with him, didn't want to play any games, just wanted to read to herself. Jacob played with Lucy, and Rose sat with her arm around Lexie. Eventually, Lexie agreed to read a story to Lucy. Her parents praised her reading. Still later in the visit Lexie sat on his lap and things seemed to be smoothed over between them.

A few days later, Rose got a bed date and started her thirty-day inpatient treatment on November 17. She would miss four to five visits. This meant Jacob was now on his own with his daughters. In the past, Rose would give Jacob some direction during the visits. She sometimes handed Lucy to him to hold or asked him to change her diaper. She might tell him when to read a book for Lexie or when to let Lexie do the reading. She would also warn him off certain subjects, encouraged him to relax, and otherwise guided him. When he was the only parent in the room, he felt a little lost.

The first time all on his own went fairly smoothly. Lucy was in a good mood and didn't mind playing on her own. Lexie talked with her dad about how to handle some girls at school who were bullies. Jacob was on solid ground here since he had known many bullies during his school days. As it turned out, Lexie observed the bullying but was not a part of it and not the victim of it. What should she do?

"If you ever think a child is being hurt, you should tell a grown up." Jacob also suggested that she could pray for all the girls.

Later Lexie hopped on her dad's lap for tickles and kisses. She laughed. There were hugs goodbye.

At the next visit, Lexie's right arm was in a sling. She explained she had cracked her elbow when it got caught in the heavy front door at school. One of the teachers took her to an emergency room and X-rays showed a faint white line at her elbow. Jacob asked Jennifer Reisenberg why he was not notified about this—he could have gone to the hospital.

She had no idea and gave her usual refrain, "You'll have to talk to the social worker."

This seemed a little odd because Jacob knew Jennifer worked for the agency hired by CPS to license and monitor the foster home. They should know more, not less, than the social worker. He turned his attention back to

Lexie. He was very sympathetic and was careful to keep Lucy from careening into her sister's injured arm. Lexie sat quietly, enjoying the snack her dad brought for them, Go-Gurts, crackers, and lemonade. After the visit, he told the receptionist to ask Ms. Wilson to come to the lobby. She could not be found, so he had to leave a note. He wanted her to call him and explain why he was not contacted about Lexie's injury. He could not believe the school could be so careless with his child. The note was lost in the blizzard of paper in the CPS mail room.

At the third visit, Jacob began to flounder. Lexie was getting bored. He had forgotten to bring any games. It was easier for him to cope with Lucy than with Lexie. He didn't have to have a conversation with Lucy, and he knew what to do with her—change her diaper, feed her, hold her, vibrate his lips on her tummy, and keep an eye on her as she crawled around. He tried to include Lexie in looking after Lucy during the visit, but she objected.

"Just let me read," she would say, "you play with her."

This was his only time to be with Lexie and he wasn't going to waste it watching her read all the time. "No let's talk. Let me tell you about the new computer I am thinking of getting."

Jacob had never come first with anyone, and this fact made it difficult for him to appreciate the biggest gift he could give Lexie was the certainty she was the Number One person in his life. Jacob understood his duty to his children to provide the basics of food and shelter and to protect them from all harm. He thought Rose was in charge of the emotional stuff. He was not equipped to put his daughter first, in any emotional sense, by making her the center of his attention, one-on-one. He thought Lexie should give him the attention he deserved as her father as a sign of respect, but she was just a little girl and giving her daddy all her attention all the time was just not possible .

At the fourth visit without Rose, he invited Lexie to put an empty fruit carton on his head. Jacob made faces and when it fell off both girls laughed. Lexie repeatedly put the carton back on his head and watched it fall off. She laughed and laughed, but when Lexie wanted to go read, Jacob again insisted they talk instead. He asked her how her arm, still in the sling was doing. She dutifully answered it was fine. Then Jacob started talking about his back injury and described, not for the first time, how it happened, where it hurt. Lexie looked longing toward the pile of books on the floor.

At the next visit, Rose was finally back. Jacob was relieved, maybe Lexie was too. He told Lexie now it was his turn to go to the thirty-day inpatient treatment. He explained he would be back after four visits. She was more interested in the Barbie doll he brought her.

Chapter Ten

On January 3, 2011, at 10:10 P.M. a CPS after-hours call director took a call from the Stevenson ER. The caller wanted CPS know that the foster mom for the Johnson girls was at the hospital. She was injured in a car accident. The police might be involved.

"Who is this?"

"I am her mother."

"Where are the children?"

"Oh, they weren't in the car. The girls are at home with their dad."

"Foster dad?"

"Yes, yes, foster father."

The information was sent urgently to the assigned social worker.

When Betsy Wilson saw the message the next morning, she immediately called the foster father. He explained he had remained home with the girls when he got word of the accident. His mother-in-law was with his wife. He said Lexie did not know anything about what happened because she and Lucy were asleep the whole time. He told the social worker the children had to go to a new home that day. He hoped the girls could stay together. He was sorry.

"It was a single car accident. No one else was hurt, thank God. They say she was drinking. She's been depressed lately. You understand. Sorry."

Ms. Wilson went into high gear, contacting the placement desk for a new home for the Johnson girls and contacting the Department of Licensing regarding violations of the terms of the foster parents licensing agreement. An investigation would be started. It is certainly possible the foster mother drove the children when she was drinking. This was not a new foster home; the screening was probably done years ago. The agency needed to know if the foster mother was treating her depression with alcohol and why on earth Jennifer Reisenberg never reported any issues.

But Ms. Wilson did not contact the people most concerned about the wellbeing of Lexie and Lucy Johnson. She did not contact the parents. Rose only learned of the move from Lexie herself at the next visit, and Jacob—who was not present—would learn about it from a report filed with the court many weeks later. Months later, in records finally released to their attorneys, the parents would get a glimpse into some of the details of the abrupt move of their children from one foster home to another.

Jacob was still in inpatient treatment when there was a court review of the case. In her recitation to the commissioner for this hearing, the social worker downplayed the change in foster homes and focused instead on her review of the visitation notes. Rose did well during visitation but Jacob, especially when Rose was not there, seemed oblivious to the cues of each child, and as a result, the quality of his visits was only fair. He had no grasp of child development. More generally, the social worker complained Jacob overreacted to things in such a way as to cause upsets for everyone. His inability to manage his behavior was a recurring issue.

Jacob's attorney was disgusted. "Your Honor, this is outrageous. Instead of explaining to the court what services she has provided to address the parenting deficiencies she has identified in my client, she seems to think he should already know things about childhood development, for example, or how to understand cues. The way the social worker is presenting her report makes it clear the agency is not interested in helping fathers and prefers to castigate them in their absence."

The commissioner responded, "I have to agree. Ms. Wilson, you are making it hard for me to find the agency has made reasonable efforts to reunify this family. Are you planning on focusing just on the mother and casting the father aside like a lost cause? You do not get to do that. Aren't we ready for some expansion in visitation?"

Ms. Wilson did not want visits to expand because the agency did not have the staffing to do it, but instead of offering this reason, she tied the limitations on visits to the parents' lack of progress.

"Services have been offered, Your Honor, but Mr. Johnson has been unavailable. Ms. Faraday has also just started phase I of her treatment program, and it would be premature to expand visit at this time."

Raoul pipped up to agree. "It would be awful for the children if we expanded and then had to cut back."

"All right, all right, but I want language in the order that allows for expansion of visitation without another hearing. As long as Ms. Wilson and Mr. Caster agree. Now, Ms. Faraday. I thinking you are making real progress, and I congratulate you. Keep up the good work, and counsel, please let Mr. Johnson know the court appreciates he is moving in the right direction with treatment."

—·—

The first sign that all was not well with Lexie was when she was eating. At the foster home, she pushed her food around as if she was not hungry. Then when she did eat, she complained of stomach aches. She did not mention this to her mommy or daddy and was able to eat the snacks they provided easily, but she let her foster parents know her tummy hurt, especially in the evening. Her foster mom started to keep a log and realized Lexie complained every night. She was a completely obedient child. She wasn't trying to get out of anything, but she hurt. She had trouble with defecating too and spent lots of time in the bathroom, straining to go. Her foster parents told her not to worry, not to try so hard, take it easy. The laxatives they tried made little difference.

One day when the girls had been in their new foster home for about three weeks, Christine, the foster mother was home alone doing laundry. When she took clean things into the room Lucy and Lexie shared, she opened the top drawer of the dresser to put away some of Lexie's underwear. As she did so, she felt a lump in the pair already in there. She took it out and discovered a single small, hard lump of poo and some brown staining around it.

Christine did not know what to make of this discovery. Why would Lexie hide her dirty underwear? Why would she save her poo? She called her husband, and he didn't know what to make of it either. She called Betsy Wilson. She explained what she had found. Ms. Wilson was aware of the stomach issues. She told her to take Lexie to the doctor as soon as she could.

"But don't tell Lexie what you found."

The foster mother told the child they were going to visit the doctor to see if she could give them a better medicine for her tummy. Lexie made no protest.

The doctor was very helpful. "Have you ever heard of encopresis?"

"No, is it serious?"

"It can be. First, I want to make sure it is not something else that's causing the problems—something blocking the bowel, for example, but I suspect it's encopresis. You said she was your foster child, didn't you?"

Over the next few days, Lexie was given a barium enema and did some X-rays too. Meanwhile, her foster mother read all she could about encopresis and talked with Jennifer Reisenberg and Betsy Wilson too. At the next visit Jacob was not there, and Jennifer and Betsy talked to Rose, but only about the tummy complaints. Rose was mystified.

"Lexie can be finicky, but you just have to find out what she likes. She even liked her vegetables. It's the stress of not being home, isn't it? Can we start some kind of family counseling with her? It might help her."

"I doubt it," Ms. Wilson replied repressively. "She has already been out of your care almost six months."

The doctor's final diagnosis was Lexie was in a pre-encopretic stage and making some changes to her diet would likely help a lot. More concerning was the gesture of hiding her stool.

"Something else is going on here. I think she is feeling guilty or ashamed about something, but not necessarily just embarrassment about having trouble with her bowel movements. I am going to recommend she see a child therapist."

Betsy Wilson was able to get funding for this therapy based on the doctor's recommendation.

Ms. Elizabeth Grantham started seeing Lexie twice a week after school. Christine spoke with Ms. Grantham at most of Lexie's therapy sessions, sometimes both foster parents and Lexie talked together with the therapist, sometimes Ms. Grantham talked to the foster parents privately, sometimes the foster mother sat in Lexie's "individual" session for the whole time, and sometimes she sat in on half of the session.

"What was dinner like when you lived with your parents?"

"Good."

"What did you like best about it?"

"Mommy's spaghetti and Grandma's brownies."

"Were there other people at the table?"

"Daddy and Mommy. Richard and Grandma. Darlene didn't eat with us. I don't know why. If Jerry was home he would be with Darlene downstairs. I think they made their own stuff."

"Okay, what was the name of your first foster mother?"

"Judy." Lexie had lowered her voice.

"What was dinner like with Judy?"

"Bad. Not good."

"What do you mean?"

"Her food was all gooey."

"You mean she used sauces?"

"Not like my mom. My mommy made the best spaghetti, and it had sauces, and we had garlic bread too."

"Did Judy make spaghetti?"

"No! It was always gooey, and then it was hard—hard beans and hard green things—and if I didn't eat it all she got mad."

"Okay."

"Really mad. She would be pushing the spoon into Lucy's mouth and yelling at me to clean my plate. I tried to eat more, but I couldn't!"

"It's okay, Lexie."

"How are meals with Christine and George?"

"Good."

"Nobody gets mad?"

"Only Lucy gets mad sometimes."

After this session Ms. Grantham immediately contacted Betsy Wilson. She learned the previous foster family was no longer fostering any children. They had turned in their license after the foster mother's car accident.

"Can they do that? I think they should be investigated for emotional abuse at the least."

"We can't investigate them when they are not licensed. Do you think a crime was committed?"

Elizabeth hesitated. "No, probably not a crime."

At the next session, she asked Lexie more about life at Judy's house.

"What happened if you couldn't clean your plate for Judy?"

"She would say I couldn't go back to my mommy and daddy."

"Like a punishment?"

"She said they would not want me back if I was a bad girl."

"Anything else?"

"Once she made me stand in the corner. I think she forgot about me because I had to sit down. My legs hurt."

"Did you sit down in the corner?"

"Yeah, and Lucy crawled over, and we played."

"Anything else?"

"She used to hit our fingers."

"Lucy too? With what?"

"A spoon, just a regular spoon, but it hurt. Lucy would scream."

"How many times did she hit you?"

"Usually only once, one quick swipe."

"Did she punish you or Lucy like that more than once?"

"I think so."

"Did you get into trouble for anything else, separate from not cleaning your plate?"

"If we made noise."

"Where was the foster dad most of the time?"

"He was at work. He came home when I had to go to bed. He was nice."

"Did he eat with you?"

"He said he ate at his office. It made Judy mad."

"What about breakfast?"

"He made his special coffee, and then he put it in a special thermos, and he would leave. He always kissed me on the top of my head, Lucy too, and said goodbye."

"Other than standing in the corner or hitting your fingers, did Judy do anything else to you or Lucy—I mean for a punishment?

"Maybe. I don't know."

Elizabeth faxed her notes from this session over to Betsy. She wrote in big letters on the fax page, *IS THIS A CRIME?????*

———•———

Over the ensuing weeks, Lexie's stomach aches lessened and her appetite improved. Gradually her bowel movements became more regular. Ms. Grantham advised Christine and George how to manage what she identified as Lexie's emotional immaturity. She told them it was okay to treat Lexie as if she were much younger. They should let her crawl onto their laps and even rock her like a baby. They were instructed to do lots of imaginative play with her, again, as if she were a much younger child.

Christine and her husband threw themselves into working with Lexie. She and Lucy were their first foster children, and they wanted to get it right. They became foster parents to find children they could adopt. After dinner every night, they would suggest roles Lexie could play and encouraged her to think about how she might act if she was a teacher or a doctor or a nurse or a mommy or a pilot. Inevitably, Lucy was the pupil, patient, baby, and passenger. The whole family really enjoyed these pretend shows Lexie was learning to put on for them. As for Lucy, she loved Lexie totally and followed her lead all the time and everywhere.

Unfortunately, Jacob and Rose never knew what the foster parents were being told to do with Lexie. It would have been easy enough to have Lexie engage in make-believe scenarios during the family visits, but no one mentioned this kind of play to the parents, and Lexie was starting to make a neat compartment around her visits. The prohibition on talking about her foster parents with her parents, or talking to her foster parents about her parents inevitably led her to create two worlds. Of course, one of the worlds was big and fun, and the other world was cramped and boring.

What Ms. Grantham did with Lexie did not have to exclude Lexie's parents. On the contrary, the therapy was to help Lexie repair the damage done to her sense of self by being abruptly taken away from her primary reliable adults, Rose and Jacob, only to end up with a stranger who turned out to be a mean drunk.

Lexie and Lucy came into care securely attached to their parents. More than one professional observed the strength of the family bond, but for Lexie especially, living with a stranger who was mean to her, seeing her mommy and daddy for only two hours once week and never alone, the bond began to weaken.

Ms. Grantham was under the impression Lexie's parents were addicts who neglected their girls and her father was physically abusive. She refused to have anything to do with them. She thought the girls were obviously better off with Christine and George. She knew these foster parents wanted to adopt the children, and bringing the parents in could only confuse Lexie and slow down the process.

CPS favored the plan of adoption too, though they were legally prohibited from saying so at this stage of the case. The parents needed to be given time to do their ordered services and show they could benefit from those services by staying clean and sober, improving their parenting skills, and establishing a good home. Instead of telling Ms. Grantham, who was under contract to the agency to work with the parents as part of a legally required reunification plan, Ms. Wilson never required Ms. Grantham to even speak with the parents about their daughter.

Lexie began to form a solid attachment to her foster parents. Her foster parents were falling in love with both of the Johnson girls. Jacob and Rose were struggling to comply with what they had been ordered to do. They still believed CPS favored Rose over Jacob. This meant Rose needed to establish an independent residence, get started with her services, and then get Lexie and Lucy returned to her. Once the girls were home and CPS was out of their lives, down the road, then Rose could resume her relationship with Jacob and he could resume his role as full-time father. Anyway, as he sat in inpatient treatment, that's what Jacob thought the plan was.

Chapter Eleven

When Jacob got out of his in-patient treatment on January 25, 2011, he wanted to see Rose right away. He was going back to Candy's house to live, but as far as he knew, Rose was still at Grandma Dee's and CPS wouldn't return the kids to that place, so the plan had not really started yet. Jacob called Rose several times. When she wouldn't agree to see him, Jacob went over to the house and barged in to the bedroom they had shared as if he were still living there. He found another man lounging on the bed wearing some of Jacob's clothes. Jacob walked right back out. He could not believe Rose would do this to him. Later that night, about midnight, he climbed up the drainpipe on the side of Grandma's house to see if the guy was still there. He couldn't see anything. He could hear the shower and thought maybe Rose was in the bathroom. He crawled back down.

The next day Jacob called Rose several times, but she wouldn't answer. He needed to know where he stood with her. What about the girls? He could not make sense of what was happening. He went back to the house again and Rose was at home. She tried, unsuccessfully, to calm him down. He wanted to be with her, and he wanted that other guy to quit wearing his clothes. How could she just substitute him like that, put another guy in their bed? Rose said it was just a fling. She met him at a bar. He needed a place to stay. Their plan would still work. CPS didn't know what was happening, but what about her treatment. Was she drinking? No problem! She hadn't been called for a UA yet and by now her pee was clean.

On the morning of the next day, January 27, 2011, Jacob asked Rose to take him to a pharmacy to help him get his medication restarted, in hopes that if he could take his meds again he would calm down. He still had a refill for some antianxiety pills and an antidepressant. Rose gave Jacob a ride, first to the pharmacy, and then to Candy's house and then they went their separate ways, but these few medications would not have an immediate effect, and meanwhile Jacob misinterpreted the help Rose gave him as proof she was his girlfriend again.

Later that day he called her again, but she wouldn't answer. He tried her cell and Grandma's landline too but no one would pick up. At about 8:00 P.M. he showed up at the house calling out to her from the street, hollering he loved her and needed her. That's when someone called the police.

By the time the police arrived, Jacob had gone. Rose wanted to make a strong case for herself, so she told the police that she thought Jacob was having a mental breakdown, that he needed help, and she feared for her life and her mother's safety. Grandma Dee helped by showing the officer a record she had been keeping of all the times he called Rose or the house. As Rose was explaining how frightened she felt, Jacob called her again. She handed the phone to the police officer, who made an arrangement with Jacob to meet at Candy's house. When the officer arrived, Jacob was waiting for him. The officer immediately arrested him for stalking and read him his rights. Jacob submitted to arrest but said he did not assault Rose. The officer explained stalking was not the same as assaulting. Jacob then admitted he had been calling a lot and he had gone into the house a few days earlier without asking for permission.

Betsy Wilson wanted to know why Jacob missed the visit on January 28. She knew he should be out of his inpatient program. She called Rose and asked if Jacob had a new phone number.

"He's in jail," Rose told her and gave her version of events, omitting any information about the new boyfriend.

Betsy told her to immediately go to the downtown courthouse and get a protective order against Jacob. The court clerk copied the police report for her, and she attached a note to the incident report, to the statement she had written. She wrote, *I'm really afraid of him,* three times in her statement. She got her order, met up with her new boyfriend and enjoyed the meth he gave her.

———•———

Jacob was given twenty-five days in jail, adding more time to his long absence from the girls. Every few days, he talked on the phone to Cathy Baker, the adoptive mother of his bothers. Although she refused to bail him out, she gave him good counsel. She told him to use the time to think about what was best for Lexie and Lucy. Did he really think Rose should be the one taking care of them?

"You are not a bad man, Jacob. You just need help. Take advantage of what CPS can give you – treatment, parenting classes. I'll talk to the social worker again and find out where they are with looking at me and Rus. Maybe they would let you live here too. I know you can learn what you need to. You can make a family, and we can help you. Rose will always be their mother, but I don't think she can handle it right now."

From the moment he was released on February 21, 2011, Jacob understood he needed to make an independent life for himself, and that included becoming an independent parent. He was like a rocket, fired up and exclusively aimed at what he needed to do to get Lexie and Lucy out of foster care. He abided by the no-contact order. This meant he would always see his children on his own. He redoubled his effort to get as much parenting instruction as he could, but Lexie especially found the visits with her dad very boring. She didn't mind playing games with Lucy, but she didn't want to clean up after her. She preferred to read to herself or to her sister. This was okay with her dad some of the time, but he wanted to talk too—about his life, not about her life.

Jacob committed to a two-year drug/alcohol treatment program. He continued to provide clean UAs. He was accepted into clean and sober housing. He started a yearlong domestic violence treatment program. He never missed any sessions or classes. He never missed any more visits. When Betsy Wilson acknowledged he was now on track, Jacob let her know Rose was not. Between her continued drug use and her new boyfriend, who turned out to be a man who had just completed nine years on a conviction for aggravated assault, Rose was in collapse.

When Jacob finally received a letter from the VA regarding his disability claims, he was disappointed but not surprised. He knew enough about governmental agencies to know denial was always the first response. All of his claims were denied. For his hearing loss, tinnitus, bilateral dermatitis, there was insufficient evidence to establish these problems existed. The claim for PTSD was denied because the evidence was insufficient to confirm he was in combat or in a stressful event while he was on active duty. The existence of Jacob's PTSD was not disputed, but

...evidence shows your PTSD is due to childhood abuse and not due to your military service. We also considered treatment for your PTSD. However, evidence shows you were first diagnosed with PTSD nearly eight years after your military service. Therefore, treatment purposes for PTSD is also denied.

This total denial did not stop Jacob. He went back to see Mr. Ledford. They reviewed the denial letter together.

"My attorney asked CPS to give me a psychological evaluation. They said they couldn't afford it. I am not crazy enough to justify a big price tag. Do you think you could help me get an evaluation here?"

Mr. Ledford was happy to do so. "Yes, I have authority to do that, and we have a counselor right on site who does them. I'll make a referral for you to get a general mental health assessment. Let's see if it can help your case."

A therapist named Christy Anderson completed an assessment on May 4, 2011 based entirely on what Jacob told her. Jacob described his mother's addictions and how they used to live like nomads. He told her how he tried to look after his brothers. He also described beatings at the Boynton home and how he felt like their servant. He described the different jobs he had before he joined the army.

Ms. Anderson's explained to Jacob he would not be eligible for services, much less benefits, because he had a less-than-honorable discharge. The chance a soldier could get his discharge status changed to honorable was almost nil. How her evaluation was paid for was a mystery, but she helpfully stated in her assessment she thought he might benefit from completing a comprehensive psychiatric evaluation. He could hardly be expected to recover quickly from PTSD, but eventually he might get clear of it with therapy.

As soon as he received a copy of Ms. Anderson's evaluation, Jacob took it to his attorney's office. With her approval, he took it to Betsy Wilson. This evaluation put CPS on notice Jacob's issues were not insurmountable. He was capable of making positive progress if he was provided with the right services. Ms. Wilson assured Jacob this was all she needed to justify the expense of a psychological evaluation, which would include a parenting component.

Chapter Twelve

There was a review hearing coming up called a "permanency planning hearing." It marked twelve months since Lexie and Lucy were taken from their parents. This twelve-month mark was a very important point in the life of any dependency case. It was at this point predictions started to be made about the likelihood of the children ever going home.

Although the applicable state law required a plan of reunification in the initial stages of most dependency cases, it also recognized children need to be placed in safe, permanent family environments as soon as possible. The hope was this type of placement would be achieved back with the child's biological parents or parent. Over the last many decades, the pull to put children in safe environments as soon as possible steadily increased and was finally memorialized in the Adoption and Safe Families Act passed by Congress in 1997. The federal law emphasized the solution of adoption for children who were spending too much time in temporary foster homes, judged to be fifteen months or more. The law provided a significant financial incentive to the states to increase the number of adoptions completed each year.

The federal law required state courts to frequently review dependency cases to make sure cases were staying on track to be completed within that fifteen-month range. The push to increase the number of adoptions in the 1990s relegated the emphasis on reunification with biological parents to the back burner, policy wise, as many parents could not possibly correct their parental deficiencies in the time allotted. In Washington state, the number of adoptions from foster care dramatically increased from about four hundred in 1996 to about sixteen hundred in 2010.

Nationally, adoptions from foster care increased from about 26,000 in 1992 to about 57,000 in 2009. New financial incentives put in place to encourage people to adopt foster children also fueled these increases. The federal government agreed to pay each state four thousand dollars for each adoption over a baseline number. The baseline number was an average from a three-year period when the number of adoptions were relatively low. The federal government also agreed to pay each state six thousand dollars for each adoption of a so-called special needs child.

This incentive did two obvious things. There was a reduced emphasis on reunification, and most children in foster care were now deemed special needs children. Money talks. The state provided its own incentive too. It would provide adoptive parents with a monthly stipend that would offer financial support to anyone who adopted a foster child until that child turned eighteen. There was also the prospect of additional money as needed. The intent was to ensure no person should have to decline to adopt a foster child for purely financial reasons, but an inevitable result was to further fuel the increase in the number of adoptions happening in Washington state. There was no monetary incentive for reunification. The agency received no cash award for successfully returning children to their parents. This was a national phenomenon, and not surprisingly, reunification rates declined.

Ms. Wilson was required at the upcoming hearing to identify a permanent plan for Lexie and Lucy. She could recommend to the court a single plan of reunification, but after a year—unless that reunification was going to happen in a matter of weeks—she would be required to suggest an alternative plan. She named the Bakers as the alternative placement and started the process of getting a home study done of them.

It was possible to justify exceptions to applying the fifteen-month rule in this case. Jacob was fully engaged in services and making progress. CPS did not yet have the parenting assessment and psychological evaluation it agreed to provide to each parent. These were likely to contain recommendations for further services that would need to be provided.

In addition to her own recommendations, Ms. Wilson was also required to let the court know the opinion of another group, the Local Indian Child Welfare Advisory Council (LICWAC). The council reviewed the case because the children had been identified as having Indian heritage. To preserve the recognition of that heritage, and/or to stand in for a specific tribe to whom the children might be linked, these local Native American community members reviewed the case, met with the parents, and gave the court a recommendation on the permanent plan that would protect the Indian interest. There was general agreement the Johnson girls' only potential tribe was the Seminole, and notice sent to them with an ancestry chart had not yet received a response.

The council preferred the plan of sending the girls to the Bakers as soon as possible. They determined this option was best because it was the fastest way to get them out of foster care. The council also wanted CPS to keep working with each parent in hopes of reunification. The social worker provided the court with the LICWAC position as an attachment to her report.

Ms. Wilson's report stated the primary plan should still be return to the parents. This was welcomed news to the parents, but still a little odd. While she gave Rose some credit for finally reengaging in a drug treatment program, it was too recent a development to put much faith in. She disparaged the mother's judgment by starting a new relationship and being now pregnant.

The court received another report in advance of the hearing—this one from Raoul Caster, the advocate for the children—but before he filed it he made a visit to the foster home. Raoul was a volunteer. He was employed as a manager at a local grocery co-op. He had just completed the advocate training, and this was his first big case.

Lucy paid him little attention as she sat on her foster father's lap, playing with the buttons on his sweater. The foster parents reported Lexie had been making progress in therapy. She beamed to hear this praise. She was not certain what progress meant, but she could tell from the tone of their voices and smiles it was a good thing to be making.

She chatted with Raoul about school and the prospect of a summer camp. She listed what she might need if they went on an overnight: flashlight, sleeping bag, matches etc. Raoul asked to see where she slept, and Lexie led him to her bedroom. It had a definite princess theme. Once in the bedroom, he began his private conversation with her.

"Do you know where Clarkson is?"

"No."

"Pretty far. Have you ever met the Bakers, where your uncles live? For that matter, have you ever met your uncles?"

Lexie was confused. "I did once, before a visit. I think I talked to them on my daddy's phone sometimes."

"Okay. How are you feeling about your mommy and daddy?"

"Good."

"Why do you think your tummy was hurting so much?"

"Elizabeth says it was Judy."

"Not Mommy and Daddy?"

"No!"

"Here's the deal, Lexie. We have a big important court date coming up, and I have to tell the court what I think."

"Okay."

"I have to tell the judge what I think is best for you. What should I think about you? And about Lucy?"

"You mean if you like us?" she asked uncertainly

"No, not exactly. This hearing is about where you should live."

Lexie, who had been standing in front of Raoul as he sat on her bed, slumped into the kiddie chair by the door. She couldn't believe it, but now her tummy was hurting again.

"I live here, with Christine and George."

"Exactly. Do you want to stay here?"

She looked at him in amazement. "Yes!"

"Good, good. Have you ever heard the word adoption?"

"No."

"Like Minions."

"Like Minions?", Lexie repeated again uncertainly.

"Yes. Let me ask you this—would you like to live with Mommy and Daddy, if you could?"

"Yes," more tentatively, "that would be good. Where?"

"I'm not sure where, not yet. Thanks for talking to me, Lexie."

And off he went.

Lexie crawled onto her bed and started to cry.

Christine came in to comfort her. "What's wrong, honey?"

"Are Mommy and Daddy back together?" she asked sitting up.

"I don't know, why do you ask?"

"That man asked me to live with them."

"Oh, Lexie. That's not bad, is it?"

"I want to stay here with you too!" And she threw herself into her foster mother's arms.

It would take Ms. Grantham and the foster parents several weeks to guide Lexie back to a feeling of security in the foster home. Before that could be accomplished, the permanency planning hearing was held at juvenile court. While Raoul's carelessly traumatizing conduct was reported to Betsy Wilson and to his supervisor, it was never mentioned to the parents or to the court.

Lexie's increased whininess with her dad and clinginess with her mom was attributed to things that might be coming up in therapy.

"Like what?" Jacob wanted to know, and was—as usual—referred to his social worker.

His social worker described the issues as "adjustment problems." No one suggested Lexie would benefit from family therapy with her parents where she could discuss their lives and plans and how she felt about the possibility of returning to them, of leaving her foster home. Obviously, if CPS had told Ms. Grantham to see the parents with Lexie, to normalize the whole process of being separated from them for so long, it would have helped everyone. It would also have given Jacob and Rose a chance to hear about the techniques they could use with Lexie to help her feel attached and safe with them as well as with the foster parents. Nothing like family therapy ever happened.

Chapter Thirteen

On Wednesday June 29, 2011, Jacob and Rose with their attorneys, Ms. Wilson with her attorney, Advocate Raoul Caster with his supervisor, and many others trooped into the commissioner's court room at the Kane County juvenile court facility. This hearing was before the same commissioner who heard the last hearing.

Jacob had not read Ms. Wilson's report from the beginning to the end. As often happened, he got through the first three pages and had to stop. From his point of view, these reports were full of lies and false assumptions. He had confidence in his attorney though, Geraldine Stanley-Brown, and knew she had read it thoroughly. She had even submitted her own report on his behalf, but this meant he was hearing some things for the first time when Ms. Wilson summarized her report for the court. Now he heard her criticize him for not following cues or understanding child development, and he wondered whose side was she on? Betsy also said some positive things about him, especially about his treatment, and at least she talked about the Bakers in a favorable way. *Okay, so far so good.* She concluded her summary with information about Rose, her recent return to sobriety, and the fact she was pregnant. Jacob's head was starting to spin.

Raoul Caster was up next, summarizing his report. This was harder to take. Jacob could not stand the sight or sound of Caster. He was the one who threatened Jacob with jail for making a false police report when Jacob called the police in desperation to investigate that first foster home. Before this hearing, Ms. Wilson's supervisor told Jacob and Rose and their attorneys on the courthouse steps, about the abuse in the first foster home.

"I was right to call the cops!" Jacob said triumphantly "What were they doing to my girls?"

The supervisor explained the nature of the abuse disclosed by Lexie.

"What's being done with that home?" Jacob's attorney demanded.

"Nothing, there's nothing we can do They turned in their license, so any investigation was stopped before it even started. I'm sorry."

"But what about making a call to law enforcement?"

"Our lawyer advised us not to pursue that, and we didn't think it was a good idea to start a case that would require Lexie to testify." Rose nodded her head in agreement

Jacob just stared at this woman. Before he could say anything more, their case was being called in to court.

Now Jacob had to listen to this guy Caster, who should have done something to protect his children, tell the court what he thought about the case. Raoul appreciated the mutual love and affection between these parents and their daughters, but he could not see Rose—and certainly not Jacob—becoming adequate parents any time soon. The girls should be adopted by Christine and George. Adoption was an unexpected and hard word for Jacob to hear, especially coming from this guy's mouth. Although Jacob did not know it, adoption had been a hard word for Lexie to hear too.

When Geraldine Stanley-Brown was making her presentation, listing all of his accomplishments, including how he got an evaluation from Ms. Anderson all on his own without any help from the agency, the commissioner interrupted her.

"Counsel, exactly where is your client living?"

"Your Honor, he secured a place in a clean and sober house. He's been there four months."

"Could a child be placed with him in that house?"

"I don't think there are any clean and sober houses for men in this area that allow children to live there too. They can visit there, and we would ask for the expansion of the father's visits so he could."

"I am not thinking about visitation right now. I want to know when the father is likely to get his own place to which the children could be returned."

"Well, Your Honor, that question highlights what we are asking for in terms of placement. The Bakers are family, and they are willing to have the girls immediately placed with them, and we anticipate Jacob would move to their town too and could even live with them."

"Ms. Stanley-Brown, I appreciate the imaginative approach you are taking, but this is a permanency planning hearing. I need to know where these girls will live permanently now. I do not think it is realistic this father can provide them with a home, assuming the agency would approve of it, in less than six months. Do you?"

"I think six months is probably reasonable, Your Honor, so long as the agency provides Mr. Johnson with the services he needs."

"Let me hear from the mother's attorney."

The attorney for Rose summarized with as much fervor as she could muster the mother's recent return to the straight and narrow requirements of her drug/alcohol program.

The commissioner again interrupted, "That is all well and good, but I will ask you as I did your colleague, when can the children be placed with the mother?"

"We are hoping she will be accepted into drug court, and if not, she will apply to a program specifically designed for mothers with children. That way she can work her program, and the children can be reunified with her at the same time."

"You also conjure a rosy picture. How long to the imaginary point of re-unification?"

"It could be as soon as three months"

"Really? She has not been accepted into any such program, has she?"

"No, but—"

"Please. Sometimes I think you lawyers believe I just fell off the turnip truck."

Jacob, who had been trying to follow these exchanges, now dropped the tread, although he thought the Commissioner's statement was funny. He grinned.

"There is nothing funny in this case, Mr. Johnson! The mother of your children has been back in treatment for sixty days. That means she has not yet gone sixty-one days without using illegal substances. I commend you, Mr. Johnson, for stabilizing yourself and engaging fully in services, but you are living in a men-only, clean and sober home to which the children cannot possibly be returned. Time is running out. I reject the agency's recommendation, and while I appreciate the LICWAC work on this case, their recommendation is simply too hopeful. The primary plan for the girls must be adoption. The backup plan should be a third-party custody arrangement with the Bakers. Call my next case!"

Jacob nearly knocked his chair over as he stood up and left the courtroom. He had spent every waking moment doing what he was told (or thought he was told) to get the girls out of foster care. He understood Rose was not moving forward fast enough to suit some people, but he could not understand why the court was in such a hurry to go in the direction of adoption.

Rose caught up with him in the lobby. "Hang on, Jacob, we have another way to slow this down."

"You're pregnant?"

"Just listen."

He was listening

"I'm going to try and get accepted into drug court. We get a new commissioner, maybe even a judge. We get a new social worker. It lasts a full year; I think I can do it."

"Sounds good," he said and went to find his lawyer.

She was by the check-in desk. "I'm waiting to look at the order before she signs it. Sorry that was such a bummer. She acted like she had nails for breakfast."

"Rose was telling me about this drug court. What do you think?"

"Yeah, her attorney told me. It's good for her, but I think you should stick with your own program."

"How will it work, then for me? I stay here, and she is in another court?"

"No, the whole case will get moved there. It may make it harder to get the girls to the Bakers."

"How come?"

"It will focus almost exclusively on Rose. They won't want the children to be living so far away because as she shows stability and sobriety, assuming she does, visitation will be increased for her. The girls need to stay close by for that. If Rose is serious, this might be the fastest way to get Lexie and Lucy out of foster care and back to their mom. Would that be okay with you?

"I want them out of foster care. If she is sober and that creep is not around, I'd be okay with that."

———•———

The drug court option, officially called "family treatment court," was a fairly new alternative court for parents whose primary issue was drug or alcohol abuse. Instead of court hearings every six months or as scheduled by special motion, treatment court hearings were held each week, every Friday afternoon. In phase one, a parent was expected to appear at the weekly hearing ready to discuss their progress with the judge in open court. During the week, they were expected to fully engage in their recovery programs, seek employment, seek adequate housing, and pursue additional services as required by their social worker. The treatment court team for each parent consisted of the drug court judge, the specially assigned CPS drug court social worker, the representative from the parent's treatment/recovery program, the parent's attorney, and the child's advocate. This team provided much more support than a parent routinely received. Children could be returned to a parent at any time so long as the basic requirements were met: well established clean and sober lifestyle, suitable housing, means of support, and commitment to working on any remaining parental deficiencies.

After three months of compliance, a parent could move to phase two, which required hearings only every other week. After this, a parent could move to phase three where the contact was less frequent, and in most cases, a parent in phase three already had his or her kids back.

In order to participate in this special court, however, a parent had to waive several important rights. For example, if it was reported at the hearing a parent had a positive UA, he or she could not challenge the result or the consequences—immediate jail time for at least twenty-four hours. The jail time could be longer at the recommendation of the team.

A participant's life was an open book, and very little information was confidential. The team and the participants were expected to maintain confidentiality outside the program, but within the system of treatment court there was none. A participant's progress was intensely scrutinized by many people, and demands made on a participant were far greater and wider ranging than what the regular juvenile court commissioner was likely to demand. For example, a mother might be prohibited from having contact with people she used to do drugs with, and if such contact were discovered she would be punished with additional requirements like having to attend an AA meeting every day for two weeks. This intrusive "support" made family treatment court a rigorous option many parents were unable to complete successfully, but those who did were better able than most to keep out of the child welfare system forever.

Jacob was already highly self-motivated in his services and had been clean and sober for a year. He got all the attention he needed, but it was a good fit for Rose who needed the frequent and supportive contact with the professionals that the treatment court team gave her.

On occasion, both parents might be accepted into treatment court, but in this case, if Jacob had wanted to join this family treatment court with Rose, he would have to give up his own treatment program and begin again with another agency. Switching agencies would also cost him his housing. Jacob did not join the family treatment court, but when Rose was accepted, the whole case went on to the treatment court docket and was heard by the family treatment court judge. In other words, the entire social and legal focus of the Johnson case was now on Rose and on her recovery.

Rose was accepted into family treatment court in August. Jacob's treatment providers continued to work with him separately but were not on the family treatment court team as were Rose's providers. The drug court judge became very familiar with Rose and to some extent with Lexie and Lucy, but she had only a tangential view of Jacob. The focus of CPS, of the court, and of the team was now firmly fixed on a sole plan of returning Lexie and Lucy to Rose as soon as possible. The plan of adoption, as directed by the commissioner, was ignored.

———•———

Jacob hated the word "adoption." He hoped Rose did well and could get the girls back, but he was not going to give up. He stayed right on track. In fact, at the time of that permanency planning hearing, Jacob had already met with Dr. Chan on three occasions to complete the psychological evaluation with a parenting assessment CPS was now funding. Unfortunately, Dr. Chan's twenty-two-page *positive* report was not completed until a week after that hearing.

Dr. Chan gave Jacob a battery of tests including the MMPI 2, the adolescent adult parenting inventory, a personality assessment inventory, the Wonderlic personnel test, the child abuse inventory, and the Peabody Picture Vocabulary Test. Dr. Chan conducted an extensive interview with Jacob and had him complete a background history questionnaire. The psychologist looked at collateral information too, such as Jacob's evaluation from the VA and the social worker's last report, but he looked at these things only at the very end of the process. He wanted to avoid being swayed by the social worker. A good thing, too, because Ms. Wilson repeated lies in her report about the nature of Lucy's injury and failed to mention the allegations of child abuse were all determined to be unfounded.

Dr. Chan diagnosed Jacob with mixed anxiety disorder with PTSD and obsessive-compulsive symptoms; a cognitive disorder affecting decision-making, concentration, and attention; opioid dependence in early remission; and alcohol abuse in sustained remission.

The parenting part of the evaluation was to determine if the parent had the capacity and motivation to parent. This assessment relied on an observation of the parent with his children and on specialized testing. Dr. Chan observed a visit between Jacob and the girls at the CPS office.

He noted both girls were excited to see their dad. Jacob brought the fixings for peanut butter and jelly sandwiches. After lunch he brought out a family album and Lexie was especially interested in these pictures. In general, Dr.

Chan observed Jacob was affectionate and he was an active participant in the visit. He noted it was not easy for Jacob to keep up with all of Lexie's suggestions for imaginative play, but he was encouraging. Lexie and Lucy both initiated and responded to eye contact with Jacob. Dr. Chan concluded Jacob had an adequate attachment and/or "reciprocal connectedness" with each child. He demonstrated empathy, but could at times be insensitive to cues. He certainly had the ability to set limits. At times he could be inflexible, and at other times he was willing to accept feedback from others and apply it.

Dr. Chan concluded Jacob was capable of parenting and very amenable to treatment. He identified two primary services not yet being provided that would enhance both his parenting skills and his life skills. These services were hands-on parent coaching and individual mental health counseling, specifically cognitive behavioral therapy. The service of a parenting coach was a service that had the potential to significantly enhance the quality of the visits and could lay the groundwork for significantly expanding visitation.

This evaluation was sent first to the agency. Ms. Wilson then dutifully sent a copy to Jacob's attorney, and when she passed a copy on to Jacob, he was able to read it cover-to-cover. It was good! But when Stanley-Brown contacted Ms. Wilson to find out how quickly the recommended services would be provided, she hit a wall. First, she learned the case had been transferred to another social worker, the special family treatment court social worker, Lois Thorpe. Then Lois explained she knew nothing about the evaluation and had not seen it yet. In fact, she had only received part of the file so far. Finally, Lois told the attorney she would not be able to get funding for a service like a parenting coach without a court order. The fact Dr. Chan had recommended it was great, but a court order was what her supervisor would demand.

Still fuming from this call, Stanley-Brown received more bad news. Her contract to represent parents in Kane county would not be renewed. She still had contracts for other counties, but the state wanted to try to use attorneys who actually lived in the county they were hired to serve. She would be replaced in two weeks.

—•—

The Chan evaluation remained a very important milestone in this case. Along with the acceptance of Rose into drug court, it effectively blocked the road to adoption. The assigned social worker might ignore Jacob, but legally, CPS was obligated to continue to work with both parents to achieve the goal of reunification. As long as Jacob was engaged in services and demonstrated he was benefitting from services, it would be impossible to eliminate him as the legal parent of the children, and as long as she fully participated in family treatment court, Rose could not be eliminated as the legal parent either.

Betsy Wilson and Lois Thorpe had a meeting to discuss the transfer of the case. Betsy thought the most pressing issues were completing the Bakers' home study and providing additional, new services for Jacob. The court order also needed to be changed. The next hearing would be in two weeks, and they needed to be sure the new order recited the changes in the permanent plan. The primary plan would now be reunification, and the Bakers, assuming the home study was positive, would be the alternative, back-up plan. It might be a good idea to have Cathy Baker start writing to the girls in anticipation of developing a relationship with them. The social workers agreed reunification with Rose was far more likely than with Jacob, but Wilson cautioned Thorpe not to discount Jacob too much. Dr. Chan thought he could be, with services, a viable option. Thorpe scoffed at the idea.

"I have seen him in the lobby. He could never parent, not on his own. He's a hothead."

Something else was happening at the same time these social workers were meeting that would thwart any reunification of the children with their father no matter what he did. Raoul Caster was quietly taken off the Johnson girls' case because of the upset he caused Lexie. He was offered other cases with older children. He thought this was unfair and refused to take any new cases, but before he quit, he did two things. He gave Elizabeth Grantham a copy of the last court order, the one that said adoption by Christine and George was the primary permanent plan for Lexie and Lucy. He explained to her the reference to the Bakers was some type of alternative plan—with people who were unknown to the girls, were not even related to Jacob, and who lived about five hours away. Then Caster went to the foster home to see Lexie. He told her the commissioner decided she would not be going back to either parent. Lexie said nothing, but hugged her foster mom until Caster left.

When she pulled away, she asked Christine "That's okay?" Christine smiled and assured her it was more than okay.

The court order she was given did not order reunification. Therefore, Ms. Grantham concluded she did not have to consider working with the parents or even speaking with them, much less including either or both of them in Lexie's therapy as she was including the foster parents. George and Christine were going to adopt Lexie and her sister, but she was worried about the Bakers, whoever they were, and she wrote to Betsy Wilson to object to them. Any contact with the Bakers would be harmful to Lexie.

This letter was not meaningful to Ms. Wilson. She was no longer on the case, and it was up to Lois Thorpe to explain to Grantham the turn the case had taken. The fact the child's therapist did not realize reunification was still very much on the table only meant she was out of the loop. Lois Thorpe would set her straight. Ms. Wilson put the letter on top of a stack of documents she then took over to Thorpe's desk. What Ms. Wilson did not appreciate was the fact Lexie herself was now under the false impression she was never going back home.

Chapter Fourteen

This is how I met Jacob Johnson. It was a warm sunny afternoon in September, 2011. I was at the juvenile court, between hearings, and having trouble finding a private place to work. I went outside and sat on the low wall around the facility. I was dressed in my lawyer costume: black slacks, black blazer, pink shell and pearls. I was reading a file. A white man approached the door. He was about thirty, wearing jeans and a beige t-shirt. His very round head was shaved and he had a nose like an eagle.

When he saw me, he veered over to where I was sitting and said, "Are you my new lawyer?"

"I might be."

"Well, there is no way I could be that baby's daddy. I had the snips."

"Snips?"

"You know, the operation, and now I can't make any more babies. Lexie and Lucy are all I have, and that's plenty—CPS won't let me have them. I don't need any more."

"Jacob Johnson?"

"Yeah, how did you know?"

"I recognize your daughters' names."

"So you are a smart lawyer?"

"I am good at what I do. I used to represent social workers, so I know their ways."

"This whole thing started when I went home from inpatient and that baby's daddy was in my bed and wearing my clothes! She doesn't want him to be the father because now she knows he is a violent felon, but that's on her. How could I not react to that?"

"To him being the father?"

"No! Him being in my bed and wearing my clothes!"

And Jacob gave me a big grin. Initial client interviews can feel like a roller coaster ride, and this interview was no different, but perhaps sensing we might get along, Jacob launched into what I later learned was his definitive test for compatibility:

"Does the brown bear shit in the woods?" he asked.

"I am not sure what you mean. Literally, where else would he do it?"

"Exactly. There has been a load of crap from the beginning of this case, and it is not just in the woods!"

I burst out laughing. And passed the compatibility test.

I had represented parents for about three years. Before that, I represented CPS social workers for almost twenty years. As an agency attorney I believed I was, by and large, doing the right thing when I appeared day after day in court, arguing CPS social workers were right when they removed children from parents, when they restricted parents' access to their children, when they sought to terminate the parental rights of parents who were unwilling or unable to properly care for their children. Occasionally, I was able to take the happy position of supporting a reunification, asking the court to authorize expanded visits, trial returns, and even asking for dismissal of a case when a parent had demonstrated their capacity to care for their child.

But the celebration of the increasing numbers of successful termination trials and subsequent adoptions began to wear me down. In some cases, a parent's deficiencies were so glaring, terminating his or her parental rights was a pleasure even after a long trial, but those cases of obvious neglect and abuse and the terrible harm caused to children began to seem few and far between. What we saw on a far more frequent basis were marginal parents, women and men who could take care of their children if only they got clean and sober, if only they could follow a medication regime, if only they could get probation instead of prison, if only they could find a decent place to live, if only they separated from an abuser, if only they had money, if only someone told them about time out, junk food, the value of cuddling and holding and kissing. And more and more often, along with trainings on trial strategy and effective appellate argument, we were given lectures on trauma, disproportionality, the critical period of zero to three in a child's life and the singularly important value of visitation in securing reunification. Eventually, I decided to switch sides, or as my colleagues said, I decided to go to the dark side. Of course, that always got a giggle, but the reverse was true for me. I was escaping from the darkness.

There were many things that changed once I was on the parent's side of the courtroom. The biggest change was how I received information about my cases from the agency. The day or two before most hearings—and these hearings in a typical case would be many months apart—I would get a great pile of paper or a disc or a flash drive with hundreds of pages of documents containing information CPS had gathered as part of its ongoing work on the case. The information was presented in a disorganized way. There was no coherent numbering system, UA results were thrown in with visitation notes, social worker notes were jumbled together, as many as three or four different people making notes on the same case, and usually a supervisor's monthly review of the case thrown in too. Also in the mix were letters, fax cover pages, medical records, and evaluations. There was no order to this either. Documents were often copied double-sided, whether there was any connection between them or not, to save money on the cost of copy paper. There was also extreme duplication of the material and often there would be 2 or 3 copies of the same document.

It is fair to say the typical parent representative, like me, with a case load between fifty-five and ninety active cases, had no time to pore over these records in the day or two before a hearing to discover the nuggets that might be in there, so like other attorneys who represented parents in these court cases, I relied on information from direct conversations with social workers, other attorneys, treatment providers, and my clients. These CPS cases tended to move from crisis to crisis: visits were suspended, UAs were suddenly dirty, a terrible evaluation was received, a motion was filed to prohibit contact or change services or remove a relative supervisor. The parent representative in response tended to move from crisis to crisis too. The records were reviewed for what was needed that day. The Big Picture review was reserved for trial preparation, when time would be taken to examine the whole file carefully, when the nuggets would be sorted.

When the money poured into my old state office from the feds to promote adoption, it really helped the agency attorneys. I had had a paralegal and a legal secretary assigned to me, and they kept me on top of my daily court work, especially my trials. In fact, they were constantly preparing cases for trial, doing both the substantive preparation and the creation of glossy notebooks and ring binders. During the years I was a state attorney representing the agency in termination of parental rights cases, the office I worked in was essentially a legal factory, and the product we produced was legally free children, children ready to be adopted. While I was glad to be on the other side of that factory wall, so to speak, I would discover I missed some important nuggets along the way in Jacob's case.

When I got his case, Jacob was starting to feel written off in spite of his great progress in services. He watched Rose take center stage in the snug, protective environment of the family treatment court. Lois Thorpe was much harder to reach and never returned his calls. He would go to the CPS office and try to catch her. Invariably she was out, but her supervisor would sometimes talk to him. He asked her about getting a parenting coach, but she had her own ideas about how that service should be handled.

"You know Jacob, you're not the only parent who needs services. It's a real juggling act. I have to guard our precious resources. As for mental health counseling, aren't you getting that at the VA? I want you to exhaust any other source of funding before we pay, stands to reason."

This was a misunderstanding. Jacob had the letter denying him benefits and services, but because he was also still talking to people at the VA about services, going to appointments with VA advocates, meeting with veterans' groups and filling out forms, Thorpe and her supervisor assumed the option of services from the VA was real. When Jacob listed all the people he was seeing to *try* and access services from the VA, social workers assumed real options might exist through the VA. He also had a tendency to speak of options as if they really applied to him when it turned out these were options certain vets might qualify for, but he would not. As his pursuit of such phantom services progressed, he would give Thorpe the names and numbers of people he was talking to, which further cemented her supervisor's belief he might be able to access counseling services without CPS having to pay.

Jacob was very patient with me, explaining all the ins and outs of his quest for services from the VA. Eventually I understood he would be unable to access anything given that less-than-honorable discharge. I also learned Jacob loved to talk to people, especially vets, about his situation.

Although his previous attorney had explained it to him, Jacob did not fully appreciate why everyone was suddenly focused exclusively on Rose. It was good news that adoption was off the table and the process for a home study of the Bakers was well underway. Jacob wanted his children placed with the Bakers, still envisioning he would move to their neighborhood, if not their home, and resume a parenting role under the guidance of Cathy Baker. He was glad the home study was moving along because he was not optimistic Rose could stay drug-free. He was doing well in his drug treatment program, leading some groups and managing the house he lived in. He even enjoyed his DV class. He was open to learning new skills and effectively used the techniques his instructor taught him, including recognizing the physical symptoms of anger, learning to remove himself from the situation in which he was angry, and giving himself timeouts. He really wanted to get started with the services identified by Dr. Chan, the therapy and working with a parenting coach. Unfortunately, there were no referrals for these services from Lois Thorpe, and even though in drug court there were court hearings every week, I did not get updated information more often than every three to four months.

I thought the first battle I should fight on behalf of my new client was getting the court to order the services recommended by Dr. Chan. Since it was the drug court judge who would hear the case, and Rose had a hearing every Friday, it took only a few weeks to get a motion set.

I prepared a motion asking the court to order CPS to provide Jacob with the parenting coach and mental health counseling Dr. Chan had recommended. Jacob and I decided to also ask the court to immediately place Lexie and Lucy with Rus and Cathy Baker. It was a long shot, but I wanted the judge to hear about the Bakers. In support of the motion, I attached Dr. Chan's evaluation and this declaration from Cathy Baker.

> *I am a sixth-grade teacher and my husband runs a franchise restaurant in Clarkson, WA. We adopted Jacob's brothers 20 years ago and have known Jacob since that time. He calls me Mom and we often talk by phone. When his girls, Lexie and Lucy, were first removed from his care, my husband Rus and I stood ready and willing to provide a home for them if necessary. The children were thought to have some Indian blood and so our home study was done through an Indian Affairs agency. The only plan anyone ever talked to us about back then was third-party custody.*
>
> *We passed the home study and I was ready to come and see the girls and let them get familiar with me. Then the plan for third party was put on hold because the mother was going to drug court and would be getting the children back. We stayed out of the case at this point because I thought it would be too confusing for the girls to move back and forth from here. Jacob continued to ask us if we would take the girls in case things did not work out for the mother or for him and we said we would, we have always been an option.*
>
> *I have just recently learned that the department wants the girls to be adopted if the parents can't get them back. We want to adopt the girls. I would be happy to do an updated home study and happy to start visiting with the girls. We have not wavered at all in our desire to have [Jacob's] girls placed with us if they cannot go to either parent.*

I was confident we would get some relief from the court. The girls could not be adopted unless there was a termination of Jacob's parental rights, and this could not happen so long as CPS continued to refuse to provide him with the services Dr. Chan recommended. I thought it was unlikely the agency would be ordered to immediately move the girls to the Bakers, but why not ask for it?

The hearing was on Friday September 23, 2011. For the hearing, all the parties stood before the judge at the "bar," the half wall that separated the clerk and court reporter from the parties. Behind them sat the judge, elevated another four feet or so above us. The social worker talked first, then the children's advocate (Raoul's supervisor had taken over the case), then the parents' attorneys. Behind us in the audience, the foster parents sat huddled together. As I recall, it was during the remarks made by the children's advocate, simply saying she thought the girls were doing well in foster care, that Jacob started to lose his temper. He was standing beside me, and I could sense him getting more and more agitated. I put my hand on his arm, hoping to calm him down a little, but the statements being made got harder and harder to take.

"The children do not know the Bakers. They have been in their current foster home for almost a year, and the foster parents have worked diligently with Lexie and her therapist. They are the only realistic adoptive parents for the girls."

Jacob erupted. "Adoption? There won't be any adoption! This is bullshit!"

The court cautioned me to control my client, but by then Jacob had already turned on his heel and stormed out of the courtroom, loudly complaining the whole way about the court's unfairness to him and sharing a few more expletives. The judge and all the other people at the bar then smiled sympathetically at me, and I had to restrain myself from hollering, like Jacob, *THIS IS BULLSHIT!*

When it came my turn to speak, I argued without the recommended services being provided, we had no idea what Jacob was capable of in terms of his parenting skills. For example, the social worker expressed concern Jacob was not picking up on Lexie's cues during visits and the quality of visits was only fair. The correction for this problem was the provision of the parenting coach Dr. Chan recommended who could help guide Jacob with appropriate instruction. Jacob had participated in several parenting classes but really needed this hands-on coaching to put it altogether. Then I focused on getting Jacob into the mental health counseling Dr. Chan recommended. If people thought he was hard to work with, short tempered, and too single-minded, then give him the therapy that would teach him the skills to manage himself. In addition, it was appropriate to focus on the Bakers as an alternative plan to reunification.

Our request to move the children to the Bakers home was denied. Rose was now opposing any consideration of the Bakers. She saw a real chance of having the children returned to her, and traveling to Clarkson to visit the children if they were moved to the Baker home was out of the question. It would interfere with what she needed to be doing in treatment court, the treatment groups, the NA meetings, the search for suitable housing, and what if she found work? Thorpe agreed and said she thought the mother was serious and would get her children back in the not-too-distant future. She also recited Grantham's opinion that introducing the girls to the Bakers now would be confusing. She did not tell us that when she called Grantham to ask about family therapy she got an unexpected earful from the therapist rejecting the very idea.

The judge decided to completely eliminate the option of the Bakers. She ruled the primary plan would be to return the children to the mother and the mother only as soon as she was ready, failing that the girls should be adopted by their foster parents, Christine and George.

The court, in its ruling, considered only a few facts with regard to Jacob. He was largely unknown to her. He had not made a good impression so far. She observed he still lived in a men-only clean and sober house. He could not keep his temper even in the courtroom. Therefore, he was not a viable option for placement. He missed some UAs. The girls had been in foster care continuously for fifteen months. The good news was the mother was doing well.

As for providing Jacob with the additional services he needed, the court's order regarding a parenting coach was deeply unsatisfactory: "In the event visits are expanded, hands-on parenting is to be provided to the father."

It was unlikely the social worker or the child advocate would agree to expand visitation so long as the quality of Jacob's visits was deemed only fair, and how could he improve the quality of his visits? Through the help of a parenting coach—a classic catch-22.

The court ordered the social worker to work with the VA on obtaining mental health services for Jacob. If she discovered (as I knew she would) the service was not available through the VA, then CPS was required to find a provider that could make mental health counseling available to Jacob. This was helpful in that it clarified CPS was ultimately going to have to pay up front for this service.

Jacob was waiting for me outside the court house. I had to admire the guy. He was calm, cool, and collected. I filled him in on what had happened and handed him a copy of the order.

"This was all bullshit."

"I totally agree."

"I need to tell you something. I didn't want to mention it in there, but Rose is using again."

"Are you kidding?"

"My source is pretty solid. Candy told me."

Only a few days after that hearing, Lois Thorpe realized two things. Rose had never stopped using the medication she had been authorized to use a few weeks earlier after she underwent a difficult abortion, and her latest UA was positive for meth.

When she was using, Rose was a woman of great cunning. She was often given the benefit of the doubt by her social worker, by the judge, and even by her treatment provider because invariably when she was "caught," she came around quickly to telling the truth, or something close to the truth, and so she got credit for sincerity and eventual honesty.

At the very next drug court hearing, her treatment provider recommended and the judge ordered a plan of long-term inpatient treatment for Rose. For some reason, her treatment court team remained cautiously optimistic about her prospects for recovery, and instead of throwing her out, merely suspended her participation in drug court while she was in inpatient treatment. The drug court judge continued supervision of the legal case.

Chapter Fifteen

Is there a bias against fathers in the child welfare system? Jacob Johnson confronted a deeply entrenched bias throughout his case.

Although the unique role of fathers was acknowledged as early as 1975, it was not until the mid-1990s the Federal Interagency Forum on Child and Family Statistics developed recommendations for collecting better data on dads, and a federal review of the operation and function of CPS in Washington state found CPS did not focus adequately on fathers. No surprise.

From the start, Jacob himself took it for granted Rose had a connection to his daughters that was superior, even far superior, to his connection. He observed her parenting skills were superior to his and, while he took every parenting class he could, he knew his progress in this area was slow. His own father had taken no role in his life, leaving him to the exclusive, brutally abusive care of his mother. Jacob absorbed the culturally assigned role of father as provider, and most importantly, as protector. He would never allow anyone to hurt his children as he had been hurt. His inability to protect his daughters from real and imagined harm once they were living in foster care not only challenged his fatherhood but his manhood as well, and yet he doggedly pushed on, day after day, week after week, month after month, doing everything that was asked of him and much more in his quest to be a good dad.

Of the nine caseworkers and supervisors who worked with Jacob, eight were women. The allegations against Jacob that he had abused his children were never substantiated. He was, in fact, a garden-variety drug addict who stumbled into his addiction through the abuse of pain medication initially prescribed for legitimate pain issues. Jacob was also a young man with no reference point for a nurturing parent and who fell back on his image of himself as a protector in the vacuum created by his experiences of abuse at home and in foster care. It was another man, Dr. Chan, who saw Jacob's real potential and identified services that were readily available and likely to help him a great deal.

But these services were not provided. No one at CPS ever expected Jacob to become a parent to whom the children could return. No one took the time to modulate the language they used with him, in appreciation of his sometimes-distorted view of fatherhood, and instead wrote him off as damaged goods. He was never taken seriously, and even though this was a response he first learned to expect from his own mother, then from his foster parents, and then from army commanders, Jacob remarkably refused to accept it himself. He would not give up. To his credit, he relentlessly kept his foot in the door of CPS and refused to go away.

The most difficult obstacle for Jacob to overcome was how to preserve and enhance his relationship with his children when he continued to be stuck in a small room seeing his daughters only once a week for only two hours, supervised. It wasn't enough time. The law agreed. Washington state law affirms that visitation:

...is the right of the family, including the child and the parent, in cases in which visitation is in the best interest of the child. Early, consistent, and frequent visitation is crucial for maintaining parent-child relationships and making it possible for parents and children to safely reunify. The supervising agency or department shall encourage the maximum parent and child and sibling contact possible, when it is in the best interest of the child, including regular visitation and participation by the parents in the care of the child while the child is in placement.

(B) Visitation shall not be limited as a sanction for a parent's failure to comply with court orders or services where the health, safety, or welfare of the child is not at risk as a result of the visitation.

(C) Visitation may be limited or denied only if the court determines that such limitation or denial is necessary to protect the child's health, safety, or welfare.

RCW 13.34.138

There is plenty of research to show frequent visitation is the single most important factor leading to successful reunification. There was no reason Lexie and Lucy could not have visited their father more frequently, no reason the visits could not occur at public places like a shopping mall, a child play center, a park, a museum, a bowling alley. That would have been way more fun than sitting cooped up in a small room with a guy who wasn't always sure what to do next. There were many problems Jacob confronted regarding visits with his children.

The law said CPS was supposed to encourage the maximum parent/child contact. In fact, it was assumed maximizing contact would be in a child's best interest, and there was certainly nothing to suggest maximizing contact was *not* in the best interest of Lexie and Lucy. Nonetheless, in this case, as in many others, CPS put up one road block after another to thwart any expansion of his visits.

The first roadblock was the agency's insistence his visits had to be supervised. There was no doubt he could be a hothead, but the allegations he had hurt his children were unfounded. The real knock on him was he might interrogate his children, especially Lexie, about her current foster parents or about how she was being cared for. He was preoccupied with the possibility Lexie and Lucy might be abused in foster care, and no one at the CPS office made any attempt to review his childhood file to understand where Jacob was coming from, and no one made any other attempt to help him cope with his fears about foster care. The potentially positive impact of providing Jacob with a parenting coach to teach him about cues and appropriate child centered talk was not provided. The service of cognitive behavioral therapy that might have helped Jacob manage his obsessive preoccupations was not provided.

But even if one accepted Jacob's visits needed to remain supervised in the absence of these services, why not increase the number of visits and change the location? Jacob was not even allowed to step outside with the girls unless the woman supervising his visits was "comfortable" with that miniscule change in location. Jacob had a couple of serious traffic infractions, and his only criminal activity was the harassment charge made against him when he was arrested following his confrontation with Rose about her new boyfriend.

It is worth noting the harassment charge was dismissed by May 2011 when Rose went to court with Jacob and admitted she had never been fearful of him. She was doing the twelve-step program at the time and working on making amends. She explained to the court she was getting him back for being so needy. In any case, there was no basis for thinking Jacob, if allowed to play with his girls on the grass in front of the CPS building, would try and run off with the children or cause harm to them or the visitation supervisor.

The court order had left the approval for any expansion in the visitation schedule up to Jacob's social worker, Lois Thorpe, in agreement with the child advocate, now a woman named Martha Jones. Thorpe did not trust Jacob. Jones wasn't sure the children wanted more frequent contact with their dad, and even a modest change—adding on additional two-hour supervised visit each week, for example—would be a costly logistical challenge.

The cost of providing supervised visitation was a significant expense in the CPS budget. The children had to be transported to the visitation site, Lexie from school and Lucy from her foster home or daycare. If that took an hour, then a round trip of two hours had to be added to the total visit time. The parents visited separately. That meant the supervisor who was also the transporter was required to spend a minimum of eight hours on the case per week, the better part of a day. It also meant the girls had to spend four hours each week in the same cramped room. If an additional visit was added, the supervisor had to find another time in her schedule, assuming CPS could pay for her additional time. Social workers and their attorneys had become quite adept at convincing judicial officers they should be sensitive to the constraints on the CPS budget. They made this sensitivity seem reasonable by suggesting parents who sought to expand their supervised visits should provide their own supervisors—approved by CPS, of course.

On the face of it, this suggestion seemed reasonable. It would relax the atmosphere of a supervised visit if the supervisor was a relative or family friend, but anyone proposed by a parent as a supervisor had to be vetted by CPS. The vetting process seemed to be conducted with an eye toward eliminating all conceivable liability should anything ever go wrong. There was paperwork to be completed, criminal background checks to be done, driving records to be examined, proof of insurance to be copied. CPS never allowed a supervisor to transport foster children on public transportation.

In Jacob's situation, his only suitable relatives/supervisors were the Samsons, but Aunt Carole had a stroke, and Uncle Ray couldn't leave her. Jacob had his pastor too, but his only time to supervise was on a Saturday, and CPS could not allow that. The visit had to be on a weekday. Social workers were not comfortable with any weekend contact because it meant foster parents would have to coordinate the visit and **What If Something Happened?**

Candy Olsen volunteered to be a visit supervisor, but since she needed to be home to keep an eye on her toddler and disabled husband, visits would have to be at her home. Mind you, this was a familiar place for the Johnson girls, and Lexie loved Candy and would no doubt enjoy seeing Suzie, but her disabled husband's old conviction once again reared its ugly head. She could not be approved to supervise visits at her home, and so on and on it went, each person Jacob could think of was not acceptable to CPS or unavailable.

Jacob was always ready and waiting in the CPS lobby for his visits with Lexie and Lucy. The visits continued to be at the same time, between 3:00 P.M. and 5:00 P.M. every Friday. Jacob always brought a snack or meal. He often brought gifts too, usually clothing. The visits continued to be supervised by Jennifer Reisenberg. Increasingly Jacob needed guidance to manage these visits. He found it hard to take what he learned in his parenting class and apply it to his visitation. For one thing, there was the age difference between the girls. He could see Lexie was sometimes distant with him and even ignored him in her quest to do what she wanted, usually read. Unfortunately, Lucy also started to ignore him, preferring to do whatever Lexie was doing or when Lexie shunned her, amusing herself with toys or playing with food and generally making a mess.

It was not the supervisor's job to provide any guidance to Jacob. She was not there to help him sort out activities that would satisfy each girl. She was there to take notes—what was eaten, how behavior was managed, what games were played and how the father interacted with his children. From time to time, she had to stop Jacob from asking Lexie questions about the foster parents. She never had to intervene for a safety issue. Jacob was good at making sure no one ever got hurt. She also stopped him from making any promises or talking about the future. For example, he once said to Lexie, "I think we should move to California." Ms. Reisenberg immediately interrupted and cautioned Jacob not to say such things. On one occasion Jacob was so frustrated with how the girls ignored him, he turned to Jennifer and said, "They don't listen to me—what is that saying?" She did not respond.

The visits followed a similar pattern. They would often eat first. Then Lexie would turn to a book. She often read to herself, but sometimes she read to her dad and to Lucy, both girls crowding onto his lap. Lucy liked to dash around the room and generally messed things up. Jacob always enlisted Lexie's help in managing Lucy, and she was usually willing to be helpful about half the time. On one occasion, Jacob told Lexie she needed to set a good example for Lucy because Lucy imitated her. There was never any doubt Lucy adored her big sister. Playing Don't Wake Daddy remained a big hit, but Jacob was not always able to bring the game with him. He told the girls stories about the tanks he used to work with when he was in the army. Only Lexie listened politely. At one visit, Lexie and Jacob played tic-tac-toe and then hangman. At another, before she drifted back to her book, Lexie asked her dad for letters and then spelled out I LOVE DAD SO MUCH. One time Lexie opened her own pretend nail salon and discussed with her dad how she would get money doing this. She even made Lucy her business partner, which was awfully generous of her.

On one occasion, Jacob recalls Lexie sat on his lap, acting like she was Lucy. He liked it and enjoyed cuddling with her, but Jennifer Reisenberg intervened saying he should put her down, she was too old for that. At a visit in November, 2011, Lexie thanked her father for his service. Jacob was delighted. Then she went back to the book she was reading. As Christmas approached, both girls took a sustained interest in discussing what gifts Jacob might get them and when he could be expected to deliver them.

At a visit on January 5, 2012, Lexie asked her dad if he had seen the movie Despicable Me. He said it did not sound good. Lexie explained there were funny parts in it. Jacob actually knew about the movie and replied he thought it was a movie about kids being adopted and that was not a funny subject. He wanted to know why she was watching it and suggested it was an adult movie, but Lexie persisted.

"It's a good movie. I liked it."

At this point Jacob changed the subject.

Then to Jacob's surprise, a parenting coach had finally been hired to work with him, Beth Dahlquist. I was not surprised. I knew from past experience this service was finally being provided because the agency was gearing up to terminate the parents' rights and the failure to provide this service was a hole in the state's case. Rose had relapsed while in treatment, and she was thrown out of drug court when it was discovered she was no longer at her treatment facility. It was going to be easy to terminate her rights. The agency was setting Jacob up for termination too, but no judge would grant a termination petition against Jacob so long as CPS continued to refuse to provide him with the services Dr. Chan recommended.

Lois Thorpe described Jacob to Ms. Dahlquist as having emotional or intellectual impairments, lacking parenting skills, lacking motivation to change, and unable to recognize his issues. Her description of Jacob made it clear she had not been keeping up with the monthly reports Jacob's primary treatment providers were sending her.

His drug/alcohol treatment provider was Chad Carlson. His domestic violence/anger management teacher and counselor was Ginny Verlander. These two professionals saw Jacob as a man committed to his recovery and capable of significantly changing his behavior. Mr. Carlson was not only Jacob 's chemical dependency counselor, he also was the instructor for two of the parenting classes Jacob completed. One was a twenty-eight-hour course entitled Parenting as Prevention and one was a forty-six-hour course entitled Teaching Parenting the Positive Discipline Way.

Jacob started his treatment with Carlson at the end of February 2011. Chad Carlson was impressed by Jacob's level of participation as well as commitment and said he had done more than any other client with whom he ever worked, and he took advantage of everything recovery offered. He did additional parenting programs and programs about general health, including learning to use coping skills to manage his emotional reactions. In the month of June 2011, for example, he attended eleven meetings, most lasting two hours. A year later, in March 2012, he was still hard at it, attending nine appointments, all but one lasting two hours. These included group sessions on relapse prevention, parenting classes, a session on educational growth, and an individual session with Mr. Carlson. Mr. Carlson saw how much Jacob benefitted from all he was learning and noted he contributed significantly in groups. Mr. Carlson had no doubt about what motivated Jacob: He had done everything that was available because he really wanted to be a dad to his children. The prognosis for Jacob Johnson was very positive. Chad Carlson concluded Jacob was making real and significant progress. He submitted monthly reports to CPS documenting Jacob's progress.

Ms. Ginny Verlander provided domestic violence and anger management counseling and treatment. Jacob enrolled in her domestic violence program in the fall of 2011. He successfully completed the twelve-month program, which consisted of a class Ms. Verlander taught, and which included not only homework assignments but also keeping a log of feelings. She also met with clients on a weekly basis for the first six months and facilitated weekly support groups. In addition, she provided a parenting class that focused on the impact of domestic violence on children.

Ms. Verlander said Jacob always fully participated in all phases of the work. She noticed his tendency to ruminate but found he was responsive to moving off his preoccupations when she encouraged him to do so. He had a good working knowledge of the twelve-step program, which aided him in his work with her. She did not see him as a typical perpetrator of domestic violence and worked with him primarily on his anger issues. He was open to learning new skills and effectively used the techniques she taught him, including recognizing the physical symptoms of anger, learning to remove himself from the situation in which he was angry, and giving himself timeouts. He demonstrated a capacity for active listening, and she noted he took responsibility for his behaviors. Ms. Verlander observed Jacob benefit from and make real progress in her program. Like Mr. Carlson, Ms. Verlander submitted monthly reports to CPS documenting her work with Jacob.

Maybe Lois was too busy to read the monthly reports about the dad when her focus was on the mother, but happily, Beth Dahlquist kept an open mind. Ordinarily, she would coach a parent who was on the verge of getting his children returned to his care. In fact, reunification was often completed during the course of these sessions, but Jacob was still living in clean and sober housing, and Ms. Dahlquist accommodated these unusual circumstances. The instruction Ms. Dahlquist provided was broken down into three parts: a health section, a parent/child interaction section, and a safety section. For each section, she gave Jacob manuals and homework assignments and then assessed his grasp of the material. They met weekly.

Once the workbook sessions were done, Ms. Dahlquist observed a visit and initially assessed Jacob as an inexperienced father. The children didn't have any idea what their dad wanted of them so they tended to ignore him. Jacob shared with her his concerns that someone—maybe more than one person—was talking to Lexie about adoption. He felt she liked him less and less. At recent visits she didn't want to talk to him, just wanted to keep her nose in a book.

"It's not fair! I only get to see her for this little time. I want her to listen to me. I don't even feel like a father in that room, more like a babysitter."

"We are going to make a plan for each visit. I want you to be the leader, Jacob."

He really liked Ms. Dahlquist and appreciated her no-nonsense style and direct instruction. He made what she described as a "tremendous" effort to do those things she told him to do. If she had a 1-10 scale on effort alone, Ms. Dahlquist said Jacob was above 10. He made an excellent effort.

Even in the unnatural environment of a visitation room at the CPS office, Jacob learned how to take charge and establish structure, boundaries, and routines. He made a written plan for each visit with what activities he would provide and how the visit would flow. The quality of visits immediately improved. In short order, Ms. Dahlquist and Jacob observed gratifying changes in Lexie.

She was engaged in the plans Jacob made and accepted his authority. He established a routine for each visit, from bathroom breaks, to snack time, to puzzles and games and play-acting and face-painting and singing. Lexie got fully involved and embraced the routines and the play with enthusiasm. At the end of the visits, Lexie began to offer spontaneously her assessment.

"This was really fun, Daddy," or "I love you," or "Next time, let's pretend we're going to the zoo!"

Lucy loved being part of the play with Lexie. She continued to ignore her dad for much longer, looking to Lexie for direction, but eventually she, too, came around and squealed with delight when he chased her around the room.

Ms. Dahlquist was aware of Jacob's tendency to go over again and again in his head and in his speech, whatever was weighing on him. She took the time to help him sort out why something had bothered him, why it got stuck in his head. She assured him he could learn to ease his own mind, not from her but from a therapist, and she made a note to tell the social worker her opinion that he could really benefit from therapy.

Follow-through was also an important part of the process. Jacob had some difficulty learning which of the girls' behaviors to actively ignore and which required his attention as he set up interesting things for the girls to do. Perhaps the hardest thing for Jacob to learn was how to simply listen to the girls and take an interest in their conversations without acting as their peer. Both children responded positively to their father's assumption of leadership and style of listening to them without going off on his own tangent.

By their last session in April, 2012, three months after he started working with Ms. Dahlquist, Jacob was independently figuring out what to do during the whole visit and following his plan. The progress he made and the reactions of the children to the changes he introduced made it clear the attachment between this father and his children had been renewed and strengthened.

Ms. Dahlquist recommended the children see their father more frequently and supervision be relaxed. She noted family therapy would greatly benefit Lexie and her father if they were to move successfully beyond the current rigid visitation structure.

Lois Thorpe was not going to seek funding for a service in which the child was already engaged with Elizabeth Grantham. Instead, when Jacob walked out of his last visit session with Ms. Dahlquist, Ms. Thorpe asked him to wait behind so she could talk to him. When she came out into the lobby, she told him she was still waiting for a release of information from him so she could get a copy of his military file. Then she handed Jacob a petition to terminate his parental rights.

Chapter Sixteen

Jacob was surprised to get the termination petition from Ms. Thorpe and called me right away. I was able to assure him if we did end up in trial, it was very unlikely the state would be able to prove its case. Lois Thorpe had still not provided him with any sort of mental health counseling.

Jacob tried repeatedly to get counseling at Kane Mental Health on his own. The problem was, he was not entirely certain what he needed, and KMH was not certain about his eligibility for their services. He asked Thorpe for help, but she was too busy. Did he expect her to go with him? There was no time for that. Jacob kept looking for help. He would go into any agency he could think of and ask for counseling.

A good example of this was when he went to an agency called Sullivan Community Health, which offered mental health counseling among other services. He was unable to clearly identify what exactly he needed, but he mentioned PTSD and suggested, as he did from time to time, the counselor needed to call me and I would explain everything.

He signed a release and a confused therapist called me from Sullivan. Based on her conversation with him she concluded he needed a full psychological evaluation to determine his diagnosis and if medication would help. I almost laughed out loud since we already had two evaluations. It was the job of the social worker to sort this out with Sullivan, but I knew that was not going to happen. I explained Jacob had received evaluations, he was already taking anti-anxiety medication, and the treatment he needed was really quite specific. He needed to engage in behavioral cognitive therapy to address his perseveration, at least to begin with, but it turned out not to matter what he needed because he did not have the right medical coupon for Sullivan. What he needed was a little complicated, what his insurance would cover was more complicated, and CPS needed to get this service started for him and pay for it too.

At the same time Lois Thorpe hired Beth Dahlquist, she started to demand Jacob sign a release to the army so she could have access to his entire military file. On one hand, I had no idea what was in this file, and Jacob was uncertain too. On the other hand, Thorpe would use any refusal to sign the releases against Jacob. When he called me to say Thorpe had served him with a termination petition, I advised him to go down to her office the next day and sign the release for her.

Typically, a parent against whom the state sought termination of parental rights was obviously failing—either not engaging in services or unable to benefit from services. Jacob complied with services, and along the way he started to have realizations and insights that led him to fully participate in services and benefit from them too, demonstrably. Beth Dahlquist, Chad Carlson, and Ginny Verlander all saw positive results. This was a fairly new experience for him to be respected for his accomplishments, to be seen as capable of change. The more he studied, and the more he demonstrated an ability to change his behavior, modify his reactions, and articulate the changes he was making, the more attention and acknowledgement and respect he received.

He was first and foremost driven by his desire to be a good dad and that meant, first and foremost, getting his girls out of foster care, but he was also driven by the sheer comfort of finally having a circle of people around him who believed he had value as a person and as a dad. As a result, in spite of all that he was doing, he wanted to do more. He understood he needed mental health counseling to make even more progress. His attitude and the testimony of his providers would make it hard for any judge to terminate Jacob's parental rights.

To everyone's astonishment, Rose managed to provide a few months of clean UAs and was welcomed back into drug court. Lois Thorpe really liked

Rose. Here, the subtle and not-so-subtle preference for the mother was clearly on display. Rose had managed to find drugs even when she was monitored 24/7 in an inpatient treatment program. She had been in a state of almost constant relapse since Lexie and Lucy were first placed in foster care. She had never been able to successfully engage in treatment, much less establish a clean and sober life style for more than ninety days, but Ms. Thorpe praised her insight and honesty and the drug court team took her back. Six weeks later, Rose was caught using meth. She was finally kicked out of family treatment court and the case returned to juvenile court for review.

The next review was held on May 12, 2012. In her report for this hearing, Thorpe acknowledged Beth Dahlquist had high praise for Jacob but stated it was unlikely his improvements would last. She said he was in only partial compliance with ordered services because he failed to get into mental health counseling at the VA or KMH. After the rest of us presented our updates to the court, refuting Ms. Thorpe's assertions, the commissioner observed she remembered this case from the permanency planning she had heard just before it was transferred to drug court.

"I heard this case a year ago. At the time, I stated the obvious—reunification was not likely to happen within the guidelines we are supposed to follow. No exceptions applied, as far as I recall. In reviewing the court file, I see my last order identified adoption as the primary plan and third-party custody as the alternative. Then the mother entered the family treatment court and an entire year has gone by. What I heard today tells me nothing has changed. Mr. Johnson is still in clean and sober housing unsuitable for the children, and Ms. Faraday is actively using. The only conceivable plan for these children is adoption. I am setting the trial for August 12."

As usual, Jacob stormed out.

———•———

Jacob and I knew he could never get a fair shake from this commissioner, but it didn't matter, our trial would be in front of a judge, downtown. I told Jacob the housing issue could be a problem. What could he do to fix it? He told me he had met yet another veteran who might help. Peter Smith was a family liaison administrator with the National Guard bureau in Bayview, a town near South Fork. In the course of his conversations with Jacob, he confirmed in writing Jacob's discharge status made it impossible for him to get anything like mental health counseling from the VA. I gave Thorpe a copy of this statement in case she tried to hide behind imaginary VA availability to justify her failure to help Jacob.

But there was good news too. Peter Smith told Jacob he should apply to attend school at the local community college. If he got in, the VA might pay for it in spite of his discharge. Jacob immediately sought enrollment and was accepted. The VA provided financial support that covered tuition, books, and a stipend for housing. Are you kidding me?

Jacob found a two-bedroom apartment and managed to secure first and last month's rent plus a security deposit. He started attending his classes at the Bayview Community College in the summer session, and against all odds, he thrived in school. He was taking English and basic computing, but for his elective he signed up for ZUMBA. He was the only man in the class. He was the ZUMBA mascot.

Another thing working in Jacob's favor was a new relationship he started back in May with Melinda Graves. She worked the customer service counter at a local grocery store and sold, among other things, all the lotto games. Jacob was first introduced to her by a buddy of his when they were going to a nearby AA/NA meeting. Jacob slowly courted her, and over ten months convinced her to go out with him. He had clearly mastered patience.

Chapter Seventeen

My initial strategy for trial was to again float the idea of placing the girls with the Baker family on a permanent basis. The state law governing dependent children in foster care was modified to encourage social workers to pursue more relative guardianships as an alternative to having children languish in foster care. It was also an alternative to termination of parental rights and adoption.

The Bakers were considered relatives of the Johnson girls by CPS. The process of getting a new home study done for them was complete at the end of the previous year, but the Bakers had been ignored as an option as the case progressed. Now I suggested to the mother's attorney if we filed a joint petition for guardianship, which named the Bakers as guardians, we might be able to avoid termination.

The mother was open to the idea. Her repeated relapses and failed treatments brought her around to the idea guardianship might save the children from being adopted. I hoped as the trial approached the idea might even gain traction with Thorpe, but then I learned the Bakers' situation had changed. Mr. Baker was ill and increasingly unable to work. He was the mainstay for operating the franchise the family owned while Mrs. Baker taught school. By the summer of 2012, they were no longer available to provide a home for the girls, and the possibility of filing a guardianship petition evaporated.

The task of preparing Jacob for the trial was a bit daunting. During the course of my representation of him, he had almost always managed to sit through long meetings with social workers and other professionals. The court hearings, although much shorter, were a different matter. Muttering "bullshit" or "fucking bullshit" and storming out of the courtroom had become his stock in trade. The trial would last for at least three days, maybe longer, and he would be expected to sit beside me the whole time *and* stay quiet.

The state attorney in Jacob's termination trial had participated in many of the previous review hearings for the case. I knew he would have developed a good sense of what was likely to set off Jacob, what would get under his skin, and what questions might cause an explosion and angry exit from the room. Mind you, knowing all this was a help in preparing Jacob. He and I met several times, mostly at his college in whatever empty office or classroom we could find, to go over the game plan for trial. We had some great conversations.

I told him based on my interviews of them, Verlander and Carlson and Dahlquist would be great witnesses for us.

Often my trial prep meetings with Jacob drifted away from preparation to more general concerns he had about the girls, about his community college classes, about his own health, and about the past. Once I even tried to diagram on a white board how I anticipated the trial would play out, but before I knew it I was listening to what he was telling me about his mom, about how Mr. Boynton went to prison for molestation, about how he talked to an attorney about suing CPS for the abuse he suffered in the Boynton home but gave up on the idea for fear of how it might make him look, i.e., so damaged he was not capable of parenting. Or for fear CPS would retaliate somehow. We talked about his military experiences, his relationship with the children's mother, about how he felt he had to virtually stalk social workers to get them to talk to him.

In order to terminate parental rights, the state had to prove, under the Revised Code of Washington 13.34.180 and 13.34.190, the following elements:

- the children had been found to be dependent children
- the court has entered a dispositional order
- the children had been removed from the custody of the parent for a

period of at least six months pursuant to a finding of dependency

- the services ordered in the disposition and subsequent orders had been expressly and understandably offered or provided, and all necessary services reasonably available, capable of correcting the parental deficiencies within the foreseeable future have been expressly and understandably offered or provided
- there was little likelihood conditions would be remedied so the children could be returned to the parent in the near future
- continuation of the parent and child relationship clearly diminished the children's prospects for early integration into a stable and permanent home, and
- termination of parental rights was in the children's best interest.

The proof had to be by a standard of clear, cogent, and convincing evidence. That's a standard of proof that falls roughly between "more likely than not" and "beyond a reasonable doubt." It is a high standard, and I didn't think the state could make its case.

Just before the start of the trial, Lois Thorpe left her job at CPS and was replaced by a social worker named Terry Northrup, a thoughtful man who had some real sympathy for Jacob and his predicament. It took Mr. Northrup one trip with Jacob to get him assigned to a therapist at Kane Mental Health.

I knew what type of questions Jacob would be asked, and I encouraged him to think about how he might answer some sample questions, but as time passed, it grew even harder for him to stay focused on preparation. He preferred to talk about our chances of winning and what winning would mean. I said there was a good chance the judge would agree the trial should at least be delayed while the additional service of mental health counseling was offered to him, but I also stressed termination cases were a crapshoot and the outcome uncertain. In my mind, Jacob remained the wild card. Like almost everyone else, I had underestimated the guy.

Termination cases are heard as bench trials, which means no juries, just a judge. That is a good thing, but it also means the judge would make all the difference. We really needed an open-minded judge for Jacob's case, someone who could listen to the department's case impartially. This is not as easy as it sounds, to listen impartially. CPS social workers and the judges work together all the time on committees to improve the flow of the CPS cases through the court system. They attend seminars and conferences together to be educated about the impact of neglect on early child development, on the treatment options commonly used for addicts, on the department's ongoing pursuit of what were called "reasonable efforts" to resolve cases in a timely fashion. These various meetings were also opportunities for CPS social workers to educate the judges on these various issues. All this contact naturally created cordial professional relationships and even friendships. My hope was we would be assigned to a judge who would be able to set aside any previous positive contacts with the agency and be a blank slate for Jacob's case.

We were assigned to Judge Benjamin Wipple, the judge most likely in my opinion to give Jacob a fair shake. I knew he was open-minded enough to weigh impartially the arguments I anticipated would be put to him and strong-minded enough to go against the recommendations of a social worker if he thought the evidence did not support them.

—•—

We were set to start the trial before Judge Wipple on August 12, 2012 at 9:00 A.M. I had done at least a hundred termination trials like this in my career, but, of course for Jacob, this was his first time. For him it could hardly be business as usual. I submitted a lengthy brief on his behalf, summarizing all he had overcome, the very positive testimony the court would hear from his treatment providers, and the legally insufficient assistance the agency had given him.

The state's position was Jacob thwarted the agency's efforts to provide him with mental health services by alternately refusing to sign a release for his VA records and claiming to be working with people at the VA on various issues. Therefore, CPS could not be held responsible for the failure to deliver mental health services. The state also emphasized Jacob had been less-than-honorably discharged. I thought this was a cheap shot since the discharge occurred years before Lexie was born and was not connected to any alleged parental deficiencies. The state concluded the children could not be returned to Jacob due to his untreated mental illnesses.

Throughout the ensuing hours of testimony, Jacob sat beside me, calm if not always cool and collected. He managed to keep his voice down when he reacted to what he considered bullshit and scribbled notes to me when he had questions or wanted to vent about something. I was impressed.

First, we heard from Betsy Wilson. She was fair and honest. She described Jacob as loud and boisterous but never disrespectful. She described Lexie's play therapy as successful and Jacob wrote on his tablet, *but what about us??? Rose was always asking for therapy with Lexie.*

Wilson acknowledged that the Bakers "very much wanted" to be in touch with the children by phone or cards or letters or a personal visit. Even though the Bakers were considered the alternative plan to reunification in the order from the first permanency hearing, and even though the Local Indian Child Welfare Advisory Committee supported placement of the children with the Bakers, they were not allowed to begin having any contact with the children at the time Wilson transferred the case because Elizabeth Grantham was against it. Wilson recalled giving the Baker's contact information to Grantham but did not know if the therapist ever contacted them.

Wilson acknowledged the father's participation in services had been full and enthusiastic and the only things left to do when she transferred the case was to follow through with providing cognitive behavioral therapy and a parenting coach. She agreed Jacob had done his best, and as far as she was concerned, he was conscientious. Regarding visits, she acknowledged if the supervisor ever asked him to stop doing something like asking questions about the foster parents he immediately stopped. At the time she transferred the case, she thought the father needed to address his anxiety, which included what she described as his overreactions. She also said stable housing was an issue.

Wilson acknowledged the children were removed from a foster home in which they lived for many months because of emotional threats and inappropriate discipline. She noted this was hard for Jacob to accept.

And so, the trial chugged along. As anticipated, the testimony of Chad Carlson and Ginny Verlander was credible and constituted ringing endorsements of the dad's ability to process information, change his behavior, and demonstrate his capacity to make the changes permanent. Beth Dahlquist's testimony was equally helpful. She explained Jacob was an inexperienced father, which was not uncommon, and as a result, he had unrealistic expectations regarding his children. Jacob seriously engaged in the work he did with her. He demonstrated by the end of their time together an ability to structure his visits, respond to the children's cues without prompting, and in general make progress in enhancing the parent/child relationship. She also noted the marked change in the children. Lexie went from being the boss to following her dad's lead and spontaneously expressing her love for him. Lucy went from not looking at her dad to paying attention to him and hugging him.

When the state called the visitation supervisor to come forward and testify, I was worried she would undo the good impression made by the witnesses so far, but I was wrong, Jennifer Reisenberg was scrupulously honest. She had been the supervisor of the father's visitation for two years. She explained that it was not her role to coach a parent but rather to focus on child safety. She admitted she never had to stop a visit for fear of safety problem. She agreed once the dad was working with Beth Dahlquist there was a significant improvement in all aspects of the visitation from snacks to activities. She described the father's visits at this time as some of the best she observed.

Ms. Reisenberg described visits over the preceding seven months as a process of four steps forward and two steps back and said there continued to be some improvement from what Dad learned from Ms. Dahlquist. She acknowledged Jacob loved his children and they loved him.

The principal witness for the state, the one who was going to make or break the case for CPS, was Lois Thorpe. Thorpe explained because Rose was in family treatment court, she met with her often and each week the mother stood before the treatment court judge to answer questions about how she was doing and if she needed help with anything. According to Thorpe, the father would not have been invited to address the court even if he had been in the courtroom. This was the mother's time. She did note the court reviewed the case every three months and the father was encouraged to attend the reviews. She described all of her efforts to support the mother's recovery. In fact, just before she realized Rose had relapsed last spring, she had drafted a plan to re-unify the girls with their mother, a plan which started with allowing the mother to have unsupervised visits. Luckily, the mother's relapse was discovered before unsupervised visits were initiated.

Thorpe testified Jacob was never a realistic option for reunification. For one thing, he lived in a men's clean and sober house, no place for children. She never thought the Bakers were a realistic option either. She had been to the foster parent's home enough to see how well bonded those girls were to Christine and George.

Jacob's chair made a loud scraping noise as he pushed it back, but he remained seated, looking down. Thorpe stated she was seeking funding for Jacob's mental health treatment and she had even found a likely provider, but her supervisor told her to put it on hold till they heard from the VA. Thorpe proceeded to describe getting the VA records as critically necessary although in almost the next breath she admitted she, in fact, received a signed release from Jacob last March, allowing her access to his military file, but by then she knew she was switching jobs soon and left the release to be submitted by her successor.

When asked why she had not expanded visits, she explained it was because she saw no progress in visitation. This contradicted the testimony of Beth Dahlquist and Ms. Reisenberg. She could not recall if she observed any visits after Beth Dahlquist's work was completed. She acknowledged Ms. Dahlquist's work gave Jacob some new tools but stated her certainty he could not sustain improvements. She acknowledged she got monthly reports from Chad Carlson and Ginny Verlander. Ms. Thorpe was not certain if she ever spoke to Mr. Carlson, but she was certain she had never bothered to speak with Ms. Verlander.

Ms. Thorpe's testimony was very helpful to Jacob's case. The state had to prove the service of mental health counseling had been provided to him or he rejected it. The blame Ms. Thorpe sought to pin on Jacob for failing to sign a release that would allow her to look at his military file was weakened by her admission she had the release for almost four months but did nothing with it. Jacob's witnesses proved he would likely benefit from individual counseling had he been provided with it. I thought the storyline of the case was breaking our way. I called Jacob to the stand.

Chapter Eighteen

DIRECT EXAMINATION OF JACOB JOHNSON BY MS. PITTS:

Q   Mr. Johnson, could you state your name for the record.

A   Jacob Johnson.

Q   Now, what have been your occupations in life?

A   I was an M1A tank loader/driver in the Army, Army National Guard, then I did nursing.

Q   What kind of nursing did you do?

A   Psych patients. I took care of the dementia, I took care of elderly, I took care of—

Q   Slow down a little bit.

A   —children with ADD. I did a swallowers group in Phoenix, Arizona, where I took care of individuals who had obsessive-compulsive disorder who swallowed spoons, pencils, erasers, paper clips, and they call them the swallowers group.

Q   Let me ask you this. To do the nursing that you are describing, what kind of—what was your title or what was your license?

A   It was nursing certified assistant, then I would go through special groups, because I worked in the Durango Jail, and then like Meadow West.

Q   Are you describing work as a CNA?

A   Yes, ma'am.

Q   That's a certified nurse assistant?

A   Yes, ma'am.

Q   Let me ask you some more questions. Do you have any children?

A   Yes, ma'am.

Q   Who are they?

A   Lexie Johnson and Lucy Johnson.

Q   How old are they?

A   Seven and two.

Q   Do you have any other children?

A   I had one with Rose, but it didn't—it wasn't a live birth. So technically, three, but only two lived.

Q   Do you anticipate having more children?

A   No, ma'am. I have a vasectomy.

Q   And, can you describe to the court why CPS first got involved with you and your kids?

A   First initiation was probably noncompliance. We were drug addicts. I had a legitimate pain that was over controlling, and then there was an incident where CPS stated or the hospital stated that I was with Rose at the time when Lucy had her fingers twisted and broken, and they said I was with Rose at the time and that my stories didn't match. Well, the thing is, I wasn't at the hospital, I was at the house, because I was watching Lexie.

Q   Let me ask you a question about that. Did you subsequently receive from the department a letter saying any allegation against you for abuse was unfounded?

A   Yes, ma'am, I did.

Q   By the time you got that letter, were you less or more involved with CPS?

A   More involved.

Q   So did it keep going from there?

A   Kept going. From there it was a downhill spiral.

Q   When you were first dealing with CPS and the dependency case, were you and the mother together?

A   Yes, ma'am.

Q   You initially visited together?

A   Yes, ma'am.

Q   Do you recall a time when your daughter, Lexie, told you something was wrong in her foster home?

A   Yes, she did.

Q   Now, tell me what you did in reaction to that.

A   Well, I wanted to talk to her to find out what was going on. Since it was at the end of my visitation, Jennifer Reisenberg declined for me to talk to her. I said, "Why? If there's abuse going on, I don't know why," and then I says, since like my nursing license would be in jeopardy of me not calling it in if it was abuse.

Q   Let me stop you there. Do you mean by that that you are a mandated reporter with your license?

A   Yes, at that point in time I was.

Q   At that point in time you still had the license?

A   Yes, ma'am.

Q   Okay. So, your daughter said something to you, you wanted to talk to her further about it, and you were stopped by the visitation supervisor?

A   Yes.

Q   Then what happened?

A   It kind of escalated. Rose was there. I kind of like—I was kind of like shooken up because it brought back traumatic memories from my past, like if this is happening now, I want to talk to the lady about it, and then so she pretty much grabbed the child and put her in the car and said, "We're having a meeting tomorrow."

Q   She who?

A   Jennifer Reisenberg.

Q   So there was a meeting the following day?

A   After the 911 police report was called in, and the police went to the foster parents' house to inspect.

Q   Who called in the 911 report?

A   I did.

Q   Why did you do that?

A   Because, she wouldn't let me talk to my daughter. If there was abuse going on, I needed to report it, and then there is a time frame of mandatory reporting, and I am not going to wait seventy-two hours before I report my daughter being abused. Sorry. I am going to do it ASAP. I did it within fifteen minutes of me being home.

Q   And do you recall if anyone criticized you for calling the police?

A   Raoul Caster told me he was going to—

Q   The court may not know who Raoul Caster is. Who is that?

A   He is the GAL, CASA worker that was assigned to Lexie and Lucy.

Q   And so, how do you know that he didn't think that was a good idea?

A   He threatened me by filing police charges against me. He said I falsified police documentation down in the CPS building.

Q   Let me stop you. Fast forward to a time when you had a meeting when you learn that the children were, in fact, being abused in that home?

A   Yes, ma'am. Ms. Wilson and Mary Ellen Waters told me and Rose on the court house steps right before a hearing that our kids were being abused.

THE COURT: Who did you say did that?
THE WITNESS: Mary Ellen Waters.

Q   (By Ms. Pitts) And who is she?

A   She was Ms. Wilson's supervisor at that point.

Q   So Betsy Wilson, who has already testified, and her supervisor had confirmed there was a problem?

A   Yes, ma'am.

Q   Were your children removed from that foster home?

A   They were removed from that foster home.

Q   Now, did you ever live in foster care?

A   Yes, ma'am, I did.

Q   Why?

A   I had a biological mother who was born breech when she was little so she had a lack of oxygen to the brain, so she was dealing with her own issues. She was erratic, and she was a drug addict, so she made some pretty poor choices in her life.

Q   Did she make some poor choices with regard to you and taking care of you?

A   Yes, ma'am.

Q   Do you recall how old you were when you went into foster care?

A   I think it started off when I was four or six.

Q   Where you in and out of foster care?

A   Roughly.

Q   Now, you have some younger brothers?

A   I do.

Q   How old are they?

A   Twenty-two, twenty-three.

Q   Okay. And how old are they compared to you? Are they ten years younger?

A   Ten, eleven years younger.

THE COURT: How old are you, sir?

THE WITNESS: Thirty-two.

Q   (By Ms. Pitts) What are their names?

A   Jerry and Jack Baker.

Q   Are they twins?

A Yes, ma'am.

Q And, just one more question about foster care. When you were in foster care, did anything negative happen to you? You don't have to tell me what it was.

A Yeah.

Q Did negative things happen more than once?

A Negative things happened, and then they tend to minimize it and say it never happened, then over-justified, kind of downplaying, minimizing how I felt about it.

Q When you became an adult, did you consider some kind of lawsuit against the department?

A Yeah. We had a lawsuit.

Q What happened with that?

A I took it back. I didn't say it didn't happen, I just said I wanted my kids back, and I thought, well, seemed like the snowball effect was going and going and going, and I only thought— well, I called them up and I said, "You know what, my kids are kind of like"—you really can't tell. All I knew is that things just ain't looking right and I said, "I just want my kids back, forget the money." I just wanted my children back.

Q Did the idea of having to go ahead with that lawsuit seem like it was overwhelming since you were trying to get your kids back?

A Yes.

Q Now, do you know whether or not any of your foster parents ended up in prison?

A Mr. Boynton did serve some time in prison for raping the girls and children in the foster home.

Q What was that name again?

A Mr. Boynton, Walter. At Fairfax prison.

Q Now, tell us who Rus and Cathy Baker are.

A Rus and Cathy are a couple that adopted my twin brothers. They always kept me in the family loop since they were placed with them.

Q   When your brothers were in care, they were infants, were they not?

A   Yes, ma'am, they were.

Q   So, Rus and Cathy Baker, B-a-k-e-r, adopted them.

A   Yes, ma'am.

Q   But they included you in the family?

A   Yeah. They would send me money for shoes when I was little or they would send me gifts, and then they would bring Jerry and Jack over every—like every summer weekend, so we can do like a three-day crabbing thing, so they always kept me in the loop, sending me cell phones or pictures of the boys.

Q   And so you were able to maintain contact with your brothers?

A   Yeah.

Q   And do you sometimes or have you sometimes gone to Clarkson where they live and spent holidays with them?

A   Yes, ma'am. I spent last—not this last Christmas, but the Christmas before with them.

Q   Did you actually stay in the Bakers' home?

A   Yes, ma'am.

Q   And do you continue to have pretty regular contact with your brothers?

A   Yes, ma'am. They text me all the time.

Q   And, do you mean every day?

A   Every day.

Q   And would it be accurate or inaccurate to say that you consider the Bakers your family?

A   Yes, ma'am.

Q   Have you considered moving to Clarkson yourself?

A   Yes, ma'am.

Q   And, have you wanted your girls to live with the Bakers?

A   Yes, ma'am.

Q   Why?

A   They were the most stable at the moment. It seems like this case has been dwindling and the fire has just been dwindling and I wanted it to end, you know. I mean like my kids are suffering. We're missing time with them. I would rather them be with my parents.

Q Do you think if they were with the Bakers, it would be harder or easier to spend more time with the girls?

A I think it would be a time and distance issue, but I could see them any time I wanted. I could come over in the middle of the night, come over during the day, come over on weekends and visit. I don't think it would have been an issue.

Q And earlier in this case did you think about moving to Clarkson so you could be close to them if they were with the Bakers?

A Yes.

Q Did you think you would be able to find work over there?

A I was going back to school, so I would have transferred colleges then kept doing what I needed to do.

Q And did you think it would be easier to get your children back if they were living with the Bakers, and then you established a home for them?

A I think it would have been easier for me to get my kids back with my parents.

Q Okay. Now, are the Bakers in a position right now to have the girls?

A No. My dad has got—he worked for KFC for a long time, so he has got foot issues. He needs surgery on the bottom of his feet.

Q That's Rus Baker?

A Yes.

Q Does he have any other illnesses, or does Cathy?

A No, just his feet. He's going to have surgery on the bottom of them.

Q Has their financial situation changed?

A Yeah. They sold the business, KFC.

Q And was that a franchise they had for a long time?

A   Over twenty years.

Q   Okay. Now, how many social workers have you had?

A   Since this has started?

Q   Yes.

A   We had the first investigator, then we had—

Q   Was there someone named Sharon Peabody?

A   I don't think she was then.

Q   Or Jessie Martinez?

A   No.

Q   Okay.

A   She was really tall, a stout lady.

Q   Okay. And, then you had Ms. Wilson?

A   Yeah, Ms. Wilson, and then Lois Thorpe, then Terry, Mr. Northrup.

Q   And have you also had to deal with, I think you said the CASA's name was Caster?

A   Yeah.

Q   And, there's another CASA or GAL in the case?

A   This lady here.

Q   Okay. You are pointing to Ms. Jones?

A   Yes. I am bad with names.

Q   And, have you also dealt with some of the foster parents?

A   No. No. I really haven't dealt with any of them.

Q   Have you met them?

A   I have met them. I don't know them on a personal level. I just know that, you know, like, it's just like, all they do is take care of my children. I don't know any more about anything they do.

Q   You see them sometimes at these meetings at the department?

A   Yeah, and the CPS cases, yes.

Q   Have you ever met with the therapist for Lexie?

A   No, ma'am.

Q   Have you wanted to?

A   Yes, ma'am.

Q   And you have been dealing with Jennifer Reisenberg who su-
     pervises your visits?

A   Yes, ma'am.

Q   Has anyone else done the supervision?

A   Sylvia.

Q   Do you know her last name?

A   No, ma'am.

Q   Is she with Youth for Hope?

A   Yes, ma'am.

Q   Anybody other than Sylvia and Jennifer supervise your visits?

A   (Shakes head.)

Q   Those two?

A   Oh, Jennifer Reisenberg.

Q   Okay. Is she also from that same agency?

A   Yes, ma'am.

Q   So, at least three people have supervised?

A   In the last two and a half years.

Q   And, have you wanted your friends or your sponsor or other
     people to act as supervisors?

A   Yes, ma'am.

Q   What have you done to try to make that happen?

A   We talked to Lois at the last LICWAC meeting. Since I
     wasn't—I wasn't enrollable, so that's where we had to go to
     do all of our talking about stuff, so....

Q   Let me stop you for a minute. What's your tribal affiliation?

A   Seminole and Cree.

Q   And Cree? Is it on your mother's side?

A   Yes, ma'am.

Q   And is she 100 percent?

A   I think she is half. That makes me a quarter.

Q   And the girls are not eligible as far as you know?

A   It's still—I mean, I guess from what they say, but it's in my record
     that like there's a certain trace of like Native American history.

Q In them.

A Right.

Q From you.

A Right, and that's likely why we went to the place over in Bayview, like they helped us out, the meetings with LICWAC and stuff.

Q Say that last sentence again.

A Like they helped us with LICWAC meetings, so that's why they likely took us in, from the last time.

Q And, so you were going to tell me about friends that you hoped to get to be supervisors. What did you have to do for that?

A Um, I was supposed to give them the name, the number, and then they had to come in and do a background, see if they were eligible. They had to be, you know, licensed, insured, registration.

Q If they transported?

A If they transported, and then they had to have the car seat. I could probably like borrow one from the department.

Q Did you get paperwork for them to complete from Ms. Thorpe?

A No.

Q Did she explain the process to you and that they might have to come in themselves?

A Um, that was kind of vague. It was kind of vague how it was done. I have been there several times waiting before visits. I usually come an hour or two before visits just to sit there and do my homework and wait for the girls to come. There were a couple times I waited for Mrs. Lois, she never arose from her office.

Q Do you come early like that to make sure you are on time?

A Yeah, so there's no questions asked. I always come an hour and a half early.

Q And was it your understanding that you could not have more than two hours once a week unless you found somebody to do the supervising yourself?

A   Yes, ma'am.

Q   Now for treatment. You had an inpatient counselor, didn't you?

A   Yes, ma'am.

Q   Do you remember who that was?

A   Samantha.

Q   Samantha?

A   Uh-hum.

Q   Then you worked with Mr. Carlson?

A   Yes.

Q   And you continued to see him occasionally?

A   Yeah.

Q   And you worked with Ginny Verlander? Do you remember working with Ginny?

A   Yes, ma'am.

Q   What did she do?

A   She helped me—she helped me deal with like the anger issues and helped me to understand that you never understand somebody on drugs, you are never going to understand it. I don't understand like the dysfunction, so she helped me process some of the information. And I was so, like, not really understanding, and then, like modeling behavior, then the timeouts, and then the anger, and then, I guess like they are broken down, like acronyms about pride and so forth, so it comes down to like breathing machines, and then taking timeouts in sessions.

Q   When you say breathing machines, do you mean like nebulizers if the girls have respiratory problems?

A   No. They have like a system, like you do breathing treatments like for yourself, like you do—

Q   To calm yourself down?

A   Calming down. You do four in, three out, two in, two out, one in, one out, so forth.

Q   Now, in addition, Chad did drug/alcohol treatment with you, but he was also an instructor for some of your parenting classes?

A   Yes, ma'am.

Q   And was the same true for Ginny, that she worked with you
     on domestic violence and anger issues, but she also taught a
     parenting class for children who had seen domestic violence?

A   That was through 1600 Lake Ave.

Q   Are you saying 1600?

A   Yes.

Q   Thank you. You have had in addition to Mr. Carlson and Ms.
     Verlander some parenting instructors?

A   Yes.

Q   For classes. And did you work with a CCO?

A   Yes, three of them.

Q   Three of them. Okay. Now, is it true or not true that you had a
     charge in, or a conviction in Ashland County and one in Kane?

A   Yes, ma'am.

Q   So, did you work with two different CCOs in those counties?

A   I worked with—Yeah.

Q   So, are you on DOC now?

A   No, ma'am.

Q   How long have you been off DOC?

A   December 2011.

Q   Okay.

A   The 21st.

Q   December 21st?

A   Yes, ma'am.

Q   Let me ask you another question. Have there been times that
     you have been angry in court?

A   Yes.

Q   Why have you been angry?

A   Why have I been angry? Because I have done this rodeo for
     twenty-five months plus, and no matter what you do right, it
     doesn't matter. You can do everything right for these people,
     and they say they are going to hold you accountable. These

people have a master's degree, a bachelor's degree, and their level of performance is less than ours, and we are trying to fight for my children back. Their whole perception of this case is to try to make me look like I'm a moron, I'm incompetent, and I can't take care of myself. I am thirty-two years old and I have been doing this for a moment, and I have two kids, I have been in the service and I have walked through things people have never seen, and you know what, I mean, I was a National Guard soldier, so for these people to sit here and take my personal inventory and tell me I am incompetent and I don't know what time of day it is, that I hear voices from the veterans, because I have hearing loss, and, it's rough.

Q   Let me stop you there and ask another question. Let's go through all the services that you have done to get your children back. How many parenting classes do you think you have taken?

A   I did about two hundred hours. That was for teaching children in recovery like certain aspects, and they have packets, and the packets are like sixteen to twenty-four weeks long. So I have been doing this since 2010. I did all of the classes that they have requested to me, and then the DV treatment, the parenting in recovery, parenting beyond, parenting kids that witness domestic violence, the DV treatment for a year, then all the additional services that weren't put on my social worker's report that I have done.

Q   And you have done both—You did a drug alcohol evaluatio

A   Yes.

Q   And then you did inpatient?

A   Inpatient, outpatient, and intensive 2.1.

Q   And you have actually completed your outpatient program. You are just seeing Mr. Carlson for support.

A   Yes, ma'am.

Q   You have a sponsor?

A   Yes, ma'am.

Q   Who is that?

A   Skipper.

Q   Skipper? Okay. Is this someone you can turn to?

A   Yes, ma'am.

Q   And do you have other people that you rely on maybe through your church?

A   Yes. Bob Markievich from Celebrate Recovery.

Q   Is he someone else that you can get support from?

A   Yes, ma'am.

Q   Do you know if he's a father?

A   Father?

Q   Yes. Does he have experience as a father?

A   Yes, he does.

Q   We have heard some testimony about you living in what's described as clean and sober housing.

A   Yes, ma'am.

Q   When you live in housing provided by the treatment program, are there rules you have to follow?

A   Curfew, no using drugs or alcohol, no phone calls after ten o'clock, no stealing, lying, or cheating.   At any point in time they can ask you for a UA. No washing laundry after ten o'clock.

Q   Have you been using the twelve-step program?

A   Yes, ma'am.

Q   Do you know how many times you have been through those steps?

A   Several. It's a daily recurrence.

Q   Now, one of the things that Dr. Chan had recommended was that you get some parenting coaching. Do you recall that?

A   Yes, ma'am.

Q   And, there are a couple other things—and he also thought that mental health counseling would be helpful. Remember that?

A   Yes, ma'am.

Q   Now, there's a couple other things that you have done to improve your situation, are there not? For example, have you changed your housing?

A   I have changed my housing.

Q   Describe your home.

A   I live in an apartment, the third floor. I have a two-bedroom apartment. It's very clean, very tidy. I pay rent in three-month increments, so all my bills are paid up for ninety days.

Q   Now, are you also back in school?

A   Yeah, I am back in school.

Q   Where do you go to school?

A   BC College.

Q   That's Bayview Community College?

A   Yes, ma'am.

Q   And let's step back for a minute and look at your income history. When this case started in 2010, you were working as a CNA?

A   Uh-hum.

Q   And, do you still have that license?

A   No, ma'am.

Q   How did you lose it, if you did?

A   I went home. I got a domestic violence charge. Somebody else was in my house, and I had an issue with it.

Q   Although you have completed domestic violence treatment, do you believe that was a trumped-up charge?

A   I do.

Q   Now, so as a result of that conviction, you lost your license?

A   I did.

Q   Okay. So, what did you turn to for income when you lost that?

A   VA. The VA gave me money to go back to school.

Q   Right, but I want to go back in time a little bit. Was there ever a time when you were able to get some assistance from the state

A   Yes, ma'am. GAU.

Q   And, how much money did you get a month from GAU?

A   339.

Q   And that's what you lived on?

A   Yes, ma'am.

Q   For how many months or years did you live on 329—389?

A   339.

Q   —339 a month?

A   Well, the economy took a blow a couple times, then it went from 339 to 266 to 187.

Q   Wow.

A   So when the price fluctuates, then our rent fluctuates with the pricing.

Q   Your rent?

A   Yes.

Q   Is the current place you have a Section 8 housing?

A   No.

Q   So you are paying full rent there?

A   Full rent.

Q   How much is that?

A $575.

Q   Now, recently have you qualified for an educational loan from the Veterans Administration?

A   Yes.

Q   Is that what you are paying Bayview Community College with?

A   Yes.

Q   Does that give you a stipend to live on?

A   Yes, ma'am, it does.

Q   Is that more money than you have been able to get in the past

A   Yes, ma'am.

Q   When did you start at Bayview?

A   June.

Q   You have had one complete quarter?

A   Yes.

Q   How did you do?

A   I passed all my classes.

Q   Tell the court what classes you took.

A   I took Zumba.

Q   What is Zumba?

A   Dancing.

Q   Dancing.

A   It's spicy dancing with a bunch of women.

Q   How did you do in that class?

A   I got a 4.0.

Q   Did you take any other classes?

A   Yeah. That was prime of my classes. It was awesome. It was a very humbling experience. I did Zumba and I took MS Visio and I took —

Q   What was that second?

A   Visio. MS Visio is an application that you do platform software. I took a computer course to learn more about how the processing of a computer works, input and output and processing.

Q   How did you do in that class?

A   I got like a 3.0.

Q   Good.

A   So the VA gave me a lady to use once or twice a week and then I don't know if they paid her independently, but she took me on as a tutor.

Q   As a tutor, so she was an educational advocate for you?

A   Yeah.

Q   How many credits did you take?

A   I took twelve credits.

Q   Are you currently enrolled at BCC?

A   Yes, ma'am.

Q   What classes are you taking this time?

A   I take English 91 because my English is not up to date, and then I take Study Skills to help me, maybe because it's all about learning, so I am trying to figure out how to study better and process information better.

Q Did you find that it was hard work taking those tests last quarter?

A Yeah. Zumba wasn't easy, but everything else was a piece of cake.

Q Now, why have you done so many services?

A Because they think of me as a weak link or damaged goods. Nobody goes to the store to buy, you know, damaged goods, so I want them to know that this guy has done everything we asked even when we don't expect him to. They don't expect me to complete or they don't expect me to get my kids back.

Q They don't expect you to benefit from services?

A They don't expect me to benefit.

Q Let me ask you another question. Do you think you have benefited from the services you have done?

A Yes, ma'am, I do.

Q And is that across the board?

A Across the board.

Q And, do you think that Beth Dahlquist helped you?

A Yes, ma'am, I do.

Q How did she help you?

A I think she helps me to really relate to my daughters in a way that I never had, had that experience. Lucy is a very strong resemblance of me, of Lexie when she was little, but Lucy has this persona that like, the way she acts and the way she is, the way she talks is so my style, it's like me, like a junior me, a mini me. And then she had like three bananas, and so now she is in this era where she can—she knows how it feels, it feels different when she goes to the bathroom after three bananas. That sounds bizarre, but when you are sober and you are clean and your daughter is telling you this, man, that's awesome that you can relate that when you have more than two bananas it comes out different.

Q It might be a little bit too much.

A   Too much.

Q   Is that the kind of thing that Ms. Dahlquist helped you with?

A   Yeah.

Q   Knowing about nutrition?

A   Nutrition, about—I mean, CPS has got this issue about over-doing it with food, but Beth Dahlquist told me it's not a food issue. If that's the only thing they are going on, then that's just beans. I mean, I bring a multitude of food so they can have a choice. It's all about choices in life, so you bring them an opportunity to pick what they want.

Q   In the past, before you started at BCC, did you devote a large part of your income to making sure they had the right foods at your visits?

A   Yes, ma'am.

Q   And what kind of places did you go to get that food? Did you have to be creative?

A   I got chocolate rocks that were not chocolate, they are just rocks that are formed in chocolate, but I went to the mall to buy rocks that were edible, and then I have to explain to them, "Okay, now, do we normally eat rocks? No, but these are magic rocks."

Q   Let me ask you more questions about this. Did you notice a change in your children as you applied the skills you got from Beth Dahlquist?

A   Yes, ma'am.

Q   What change did you see?

A   They were eager to obey, eager to obey, eager to listen, want-ing to know what was next, what daddy had in the bag, and they were eager to comply with whatever demands I made.

Q   So do you think that the skills she gave you actually improved not just your parenting, but your relationship with the children?

A   Yes, ma'am.

Q   Let me ask you another question. What kind of feedback did you get from Ms. Dahlquist?

A She wasn't playing games. She is not here to play games. She told me, you do the hard work and if you reap, you will reap what you sow, so she was pretty—I mean, she says I did everything I possibly can, I worked hard, I put the time in, did the activities, I brought the timer with.

Q Did you get the result you wanted?

A I got the result I wanted. I wanted to try to strive, I want to succeed.

Q Would you describe her as strong-minded?

A Yeah, very much so.

Q Was that a style that worked for you?

A Yes.

Q Do you know if she had ever been in the military?

A She was.

Q Now, what is your understanding of why you are not allowed more visitation?

A Their perception of progress. Their perception. It's all about how they look at it. If they don't like what they see, or they don't like what they like, or if they don't like you. I mean, people say they don't pass judgment, but people pass judgment. I mean, they don't have to like me to give my kids back to me.

Q That's right.

A That's not like a prerequisite for my children coming back, but it seemed like that does take a big part in this case.

Q Whether they like you or not?

A Sure. You don't have to like me.

Q Do you think that you have been treated fairly?

A No. I think I have been treated—When you do everything right and you are staying clean and in a house longer than what you would normally do, and do meetings like you are supposed to do, you are meeting the children regularly, old faithful, and you bring them healthy snacks, then they want to pick apart things you do, what you say, I mean, when it's not an issue, but they want to turn it around and make it sound like it's an issue.

Q Now, have you wanted visitation to happen in your new home?

A Yes.

Q What's the response been?

A Nothing. I have called everybody I possibly can do. What more are you supposed to do?

Q So you have asked to have more time with your girls and it's been declined?

A If I could have somebody supervise me with them in my house approved by CPS then I might get more time

Q Yes.

A I have got to find somebody that's willing to go down there and deal with the CPS issue.

Q Have you been allowed to attend your daughters' medical appointments?

A No, I have not.

Q Have you wanted to?

A Yes, I wanted to.

Q Have you been allowed to go to their school events?

A No, I haven't.

Q Have you wanted to?

A Yes, I have.

Q Has it been your goal for the whole case to get your kids back?

A Yes, ma'am.

Q Now, Dr. Chan also talked about mental health counseling. Other than the VA, where have you tried to get that service?

A I went to Beacon Hill.

Q No, I don't mean VA, I mean agencies here.

A Sullivan Community Health.

Q What happened there?

A Well, it's a medical issue or it's an insurance issue. I went to

Uniform Family Clinic, I went to—Stevenson Hospital won't see me due because of an insurance issue.

Q When you go to these agencies, they look at your card and say what? You are in the wrong place?

A First they tell you over the phone, "Yeah, we'll take your insurance." By the time you get there and they see your card, "Oh, you are one of those kinds. We don't take this insurance."

Q Have you ever tried to go to KMH?

A Several times.

Q And, before Mr. Northrup got this case, what happened when you went to KMH?

A I was not eligible for services.

Q And did they explain to you why you were not eligible?

A Financial. Financial, because they don't pay enough on their co-pays. I mean, that's like the logistics of the case.

Q When you went to these agencies to try to get services, particularly counseling, did you think that it was hard or easy to explain to them what you needed?

A It's hard to explain to them.

Q And, have you found that when you have somebody go with you that knows what you need, that helps?

A Didn't help. It took—it took a couple times. I mean, Lois said she called and she couldn't get anywhere, and she is a higher person, like, you know.

Q Did she ever go personally with you to any appointments?

A Never. She never picked me up, never took me out, never did anything.

Q Now, let's turn to the awesome subject of the Veterans Administration. So were you ever in the army?

A Yes, ma'am.

Q And was this through the National Guard or some other?

A It was active army, then I was put into another unit through the Army National Guard unit.

Q So it started with active army and you went to the Guard?

A Uh-hum.

Q Do you recall when you joined up?

A January 2001.

Q How long were you in the service?

A Two years, seven months, one day.

Q Where were you stationed?

A Fort Knox, Kentucky.

Q Anyplace else?

A South Fork, Washington....

Q What were you trained to do?

A Kill people.

Q I need you to be more specific. There's lots of different ways to kill people.

A I was a tank armor crewman. I drove M1A1 tanks. I was with a group of four complete soldiers, a tank commander and a gunner and a loader and a driver, and I was on the front half of the tank.

Q So in terms of the four people on the tank, what was your job?

A Either driver or loader.

Q Okay. And when you say loader, are you loading weapons?

A You are loading the main machine gun, or like the main weapon. It's an MM 120, firing bullets, about 60 pounds, 80 pounds, and it goes into the big machine gun. It's like a bore. It goes in the bore and that's how you load it.

Q How did you like being in the service?

A I liked it.

Q Do you remember why you left?

A I had some training accidents.

Q Where did the training accident occur?

A Montana Training Center outside of Livingston.

Q Were you injured in the accident?

A Yes.

Q Okay. Now, already in evidence is your letter of discharge. I will ask you a couple of questions about that.

THE COURT: I have a question if I might. Were the training accidents during your period of active service in the army or while you were with the National Guard?
THE WITNESS: National Guard.
THE COURT: Okay. Thank you. When approximately did the accident occur?

Q (By Ms. Pitts) How close to when you were discharged? If you were discharged in 2002 —
A It happened in 2001.
Q Now, exhibit four indicates that your discharge is described as under other than honorable conditions. Do you understand that?
A Yes, ma'am.
Q And has the fact of that status made it difficult to access services from the VA?
A Yes, ma'am.
Q Now, you have to bear with me because I know you know more about this than I do. Does the Veterans Administration operate on different levels?
A Yes, ma'am, they do.
Q What are those levels?
A State, local and federal.
Q So do those agencies talk to each other or are they separate?
A Not well.
Q Not well.
A Not well at all.
Q Okay. Now, exhibit twenty-five is a letter from the Veterans Administration from the Jackson Federal Building. This would be the federal Veterans Administration?

A   Yes, ma'am.

Q   And it is a denial of disability benefits.

A   Yes, ma'am.

Q   Is it your understanding that you did an evaluation with Christy Anderson as part of this process?

A   Yes, ma'am.

Q   And then you got denied.

A   Yes, ma'am.

Q   And then exhibit twenty-six is a letter from the Department of Veterans Affairs, which I assume is different.

A   Yes.

Q   Pacific Health Systems, Lake Randall Division, Littleton, Washington.

A   Yes, ma'am.

Q   Have you gone to Littleton and talked to these people?

A   We had an audio conference with them before.

Q   When you say we, who do you mean?

A   You and I.

Q   We did? You mean Mr. Stephenson, or Mr. Smith?

A   Stephenson and Smith.

Q   Let me ask you some specific questions. This would indicate this is the state veterans' group.

A   Yes.

Q   The folks down in Littleton at Lake Randall and they thank you for applying, and then they say, "Because of the quality of your discharge, you are going to be denied services."

A   Yes, ma'am.

Q   Okay. So who's Joe Stephenson?

A   Joe Stephenson works for the Disabled Veterans Administration Association.

Q   Did he help you to try to get disability benefits?

A   Yes, he has.

Q   Is he still trying, as far as you know?

A   Yes, ma'am.

Q   And you and I have met with Mr. Stephenson?

A   Several times.

Q   Okay. And who is Peter Smith?

A   Peter Smith is — he's a service representative that helps families that are being deployed.

Q   Is he employed by the National Guard of Washington?

A   Yes.

Q   And at some point, did you or did you not come to the conclusion that you needed to get that discharge changed in order to get some services?

A   Yes, ma'am.

Q   Okay. So, have you applied and would this be to the Pentagon?

A   The Pentagon.

Q   To change your discharge status?

A   Yes, ma'am.

Q   What has happened with that?

A   They have a certain time frame to, within the guidelines to return it back.

Q   Right. So is it accurate or inaccurate to say that you are waiting to hear from the Pentagon?

A   Right, yeah.

Q   And Mr. Smith helped you with those forms.

A   Yes, ma'am.

Q   So, you have been trying to get services from the Veterans Administration.

A   Yes, ma'am, at three different levels.

Q   Sometimes you have gone to North Cape?

A   North Cape.

Q   You have talked to people over there?

A   Uh-hum.

Q   Sometimes you have gone to Franklin Army base?

A   Yes, ma'am.

Q Or had conferences with them? Sometimes you have talked to people over in South Fork?

A Yes, ma'am.

Q How would you describe your struggle against the Veterans Administration to try to get some services?

A Because of the denial letter, because it's—because of the RE code.

Q RE code?

A There's a code at the end of your service time. If it's stamped with a good code, then people talk to you. If you have a code on it, it's like you are blackballed. Because I didn't finish the four years in the National Guard— I mean, I have an honorable discharge from active Army, but I have a less-than-honorable because I didn't serve my time out with the Guard, and I couldn't perform my military duties.

Q Because of the accident?

A Because of the accident.

Q So, it was catch-22.

A Catch-22. Then they said I had to find soldiers from my unit, so I found soldiers from my unit to file paperwork on my behalf.

Q Let me stop you there. So was one of the requirements when you were trying to get disability benefits, getting declarations from other soldiers who were injured or at the accident so that they could say what really happened?

A Yes, ma'am.

Q Did you go out and do that?

A I did.

Q And it didn't make any difference, did it?

A It didn't make a bit of difference.

Q Thank you. Now, Ms. Thorpe I believe testified that she was often confused about your status with the Veterans, is that right?

A She was.

Q And, is it accurate or inaccurate to say you found it confusing, too?

A Yes, ma'am.

Q   Now, when Ms. Thorpe testified, she talked about some sort of program you were going to in California.

A   Palo Alto.

Q   Would you tell us what that was about.

A   Palo Alto is an extensive thirty-day post-traumatic stress disorder counseling for anybody that's been in a hostile environment.

Q   Let me stop you for a minute. The diagnosis of PTSD came from the military, or from before the military?

A   Well—

Q   I don't mean your experiences. I mean, who told you you had that?

A   Well—

Q   Do you recall? Let me put it a different way. Do you think that one of the things you suffer from is post-traumatic stress disorder?

A   I don't really know. I mean, I have been diagnosed with so many different categories and numbers that they all kind of blend together.

Q   Okay. So who did you talk to about this program in California?

A   Peter Smith, and a lady at Franklin.

Q   And, what would make it possible for you to go to California?

A   Somebody has got to pay $150,000 for me to go to it, and the Pentagon has got to sign off on my letter.

Q   Your letter changing your discharge?

A   Changing my discharge.

Q   So you really couldn't go to California without becoming eligible for services.

A   Amen.

Q   Kind of a catch-22 again.

A   It is.

Q   And that conversation I believe was just last summer, in 2011.

A   Yes, ma'am.

Q   Do you currently have an intake assessment scheduled at KMH?

A   I did my intake.

Q   When did you do that?

A   Last week or the week before.

Q   Okay. Who set that intake up for you?

A   I did it with Terry.

Q   Mr. Northrup, who is in here?

A   Yes.

Q   How did that work? Did you do it by phone? Did you go over there?

A   He took me in person. He drove me over there. We drove to three or four different places over there on the east side.

Q   Looking for someone who would take you?

A   With my insurance.

Q   So he physically took you to each place.

A   Physically took me.

Q   And, KMH said, okay, we'll do the intake?

A   That was the last place we stopped in, and I brought him with me. I let him do the footwork so he could experience my issues and struggles. I say, "They tell you over the phone, but when you get there, oh, we don't take this insurance." Well, he told me over the phone one thing.

Q   When you went to KMH, did Terry do some of the talking?

A   I let him do most of the talking so he could get a feel of what I go through on a daily basis.

Q   Is it fair to say that as a result of his intervention, you got in?

A   Yeah.

Q   You are scheduling regular counseling appointments now?

A   Well, with the summer vacations and then he couldn't be there one day, then he was sick, and then the trial. I missed appointments due to him not coming in, and me coming in to trial today.

Q   So you haven't actually had a counseling appointment, but you are set to start that.

A   Yes, ma'am.

Q   Okay. Do you think that if you had a chance to learn some new skills in terms of ways of thinking, that you would be able to benefit from those skills and learn them?

A   Yes, ma'am.

MS. PITTS: Those are all the questions I have. Now the other attorneys may have some questions for you.

THE COURT: Thank you. Ms. Turpin-Smith? (She was attorney for Rose)

MS. TURPIN-SMITH: No questions, Your Honor.

THE COURT: Very well. Mr. Uchida?

MR. UCHIDA: Thank you.

CROSS-EXAMINATION BY STATE ATTORNEY MR. UCHIDA:

Q   Mr. Johnson, early on in your testimony you talked about an individual that went to prison?

A   Yes.

Q   Who was that individual?

A   Mr. Boynton, Walter Boynton?

Q   Yes, I believe that's the name you used.

A   He was a foster family that CPS put me in.

Q   As part of your testimony, you said something about the girls. Are you referring to Lexie and Lucy?

A   No. There were children in the foster home that were being abused. We were all being abused. Some got abused certain ways, some got abused a certain other way.

Q   But he had nothing to do with Lexie and Lucy. They weren't even born yet.

A   No. I was fourteen, fifteen.

Q   So when you mentioned the girls, you are not referring to your children.

A   No.

Q   Okay. Ms. Pitts asked you some questions about tribes and native heritage. Did you testify that you are not enrollable?

A   Um, we have had issues with enrolling me and my family because I have certain paperwork that was burned up in a church or—It's been difficult. We have done this before where we tried to enroll. Since I was in foster care, I don't know, my biological parents, like my mother, I don't know her side of the family very well, so it's very hard to trace people down and when they are crazy to begin with, you are not going to get a fresh answer out of them.

Q   Did you say that you are enrolled or not?

A   I am not enrollable at this point in time, but it could change in the near future, you know. Things could change.

Q   But at this point you are not enrollable.

A   At this time I am not enrollable.

Q   Okay. Ms. Pitts asked you some questions about involvement with a CCO, community corrections officer. Why did you have a CCO involved with you?

A   I made poor decisions back in my using days and I got a DUI back in '09, so I have made some human errors, and then I fixed them by taking carefully of my financial responsibility and going through the program and paying off all the wreckage.

Q   As part of your convictions, did you serve any time in jail?

A   For which charge?

Q   Just in general.

A   Oh, yeah, I have served time.

Q   In Kane and Ashland?

A   Ashland County. I served forty-five days. I served twenty-three days for the DV charge in Kane County. I didn't serve any time for my probation violation.

Q   Approximately when were you in the Ashland County Jail?

A   I think it was in the fall 2010.

Q Was that around the time the dependency case began?

A Yeah, I believe it was.

Q Now, as part of the domestic violence conviction, I believe you testified that someone was in the home? What were you referring to there?

A Jason Lewis.

Q And approximately when did this happen?

A I came home after treatment. Treatment would be—I got in November, December, January. I got out in January.

THE COURT: What year, sir?
THE WITNESS: '11.
THE COURT: Thank you.

Q (By Mr. Uchida) You said you got out. Are you referring to some type of inpatient program?

A Thirty days of inpatient.

Q And upon completing the inpatient program, you returned home to find Mr. Lewis there?

A Yeah.

Q Now, both yourself and Ms. Faraday have been involved in drug treatment, right?

A Yes.

Q How did your family's substance abuse begin, when you and Ms. Faraday were together?

A Well, we both have legitimate pain concerns. I don't think I need to go into the detail in that department, but if you need to know, I can tell you. We both have pain management issues, and we both got pain meds. That's pretty given. Our relationship started out, I get mine on the 5th, you get yours on the 12th. That's a great relationship because when I run out, you have got some, when you run out, I have got some.

Q So it was sort of mutual?

A Yeah.

Q As opposed to one person starting, then the other person being brought into it?

A Yeah. It was pretty much, we would just kind of like help each other out until we got our next prescription.

Q Now, did you testify that you wanted the children to go to the Bakers—the children I am referring to, your two children—to the Bakers in Clarkson?

A Yes.

Q Why?

A Well, I was on a lot of financial obligations. I lost my nursing license; I can't work as a CNA. I lost my right to bear arms. My employment has been kind of rocky. I am fighting with the VA for my disability. You kind of see where this is kind of going. I wanted my family to take them. We owned a KFC in Clarkson. Not me, my parents owned it, so they have a substantial amount of money to raise my children until I get back on my feet, you know. Like my parents are not suffering. My kids would never suffer. I mean, they would have all of their—they wouldn't have any needs, wants, or all their needs, wants and desires would be met by them.

Q It sounds like right now that the Bakers are not an option for the girls.

A Uh-hum.

Q So, what is your current plan for the girls?

A Well, I have housing. I wasn't expecting to come into any of this money, I wasn't expecting to get housing, I wasn't expecting any of this stuff to come, and so—

Q By you weren't expecting to come into all this money, what are you referring to?

A For college, college money to go back to school.

Q And you are getting this college money from the VA?

A I think, from how I was directed, how it was told, it comes out as a loan. You get your grades above C and that loan turns into a grant. I don't know how it works. I just go with the flow.

Q   How did you get this loan?

A   You apply for it with your FAFSA. It's underneath your FAFSA pay, your Pell grants and FAFSA alike. I don't know how much it is, but it comes out to be like you get so much money every three months, and then you get this much money to start out with, then every three months you get more money.

Q   Where did you apply for this? Through VA?

A   No. A VA representative was the one that talked to me about it. He said, I will tell you a secret. This is how you get some money to live, this is how you get money to pay off your housing and get nice clothes and take care of yourself.

Q   So, it was somebody from the VA informed you of this program, and you have taken advantage of it.

A   His name was Steve. I don't remember his last name. Steve something. He wasn't with the Disabled Vets he was another gentleman that works at the post in South Fork.

Q   He works at Post for what organization?

A   It's Veterans —

Q   Just say it slowly.

A   It's Post Veterans of War. It's like —

Q   VFW?

A   Yeah, VFW. They have barbecues and —

Q   Okay. Thank you. You were just talking really fast and it was hard to understand.

A   I apologize. I do that from time to time.

Q   Why do you think you do that?

A   Well, I am in the hot seat right now.

Q   When did you move into your current apartment, Mr. Johnson?

A   Thirty days ago.

Q   Up until I guess the end of the year, you were living elsewhere?

A   Living…in that men's housing.

Q   Could the girls have lived with you at that men's house?

A   No way would I want that to happen.

Q   Besides whether you want it to happen —

A   No, they could not. It was only a men's house.

Q   So, thirty days ago your living situation changed so that you have a place in which they could live with you.

A   Could live.

Q   Now Ms. Pitts asked you some questions about this California PTSD program.

A   Uh-hum.

Q   Did you tell the girls that you were going down to California for this program?

A   Matter of fact, I talked to Lois Thorpe prior to so it didn't come out wrong. I asked her if she wanted to be part of it to make sure it didn't—It seems like anything you say gets kind of turned around, so I wanted to make sure I had somebody there as a witness, and I brought Lois Thorpe in there and I said, this is what's going on. I might have to be gone thirty days, but this will start the process of all my VA benefits and then the retro pay, and then like the medical and the treatment

Q   Were you expecting to start that program any time soon?

A   No. No. It was kind of like on the back burner. They didn't know exactly what paperwork was going to come back. They didn't really know a whole lot. All I know is that the seating there is hard to get into because it's a high volume of people that go through there and the cost is like people's salaries for a year just for thirty days, so it's very intense. So the price of it would cost a lot and I needed to have the Pentagon sign for it.

Q   Now, Ms. Pitts talked about exhibit number twenty-four, which is your discharge.

A   Uh-hum.

Q   How did you come about being discharged under other than honorable conditions, given you said your army discharge was favorable?

A   Lack of time in service. When you sign up, you sign up for a commitment. My commitment was a four-year commitment, or it was a six-year commitment, and then I did the time in service, then I still owed them like a couple more years, it was like a year and a half or something like that, and then they put you on inactive reserve. I didn't finish the time because when I got injured it was two years, seven months, one day, so there was still time ticking on the back of my—when I got injured, and they wanted me to stay in the unit. I couldn't perform my military duties.

Q   So did you essentially quit or go AWOL?

A   They got me out on a AWOL. I told the sergeant I was having issues, but they didn't know what to do. Firstly, I asked if I could go active duty so then I don't have to worry, you know what I mean, I didn't have to worry about it, but if I could be transitioned to another job. They said they couldn't do nothing for me. I says, these are the opportunities I have. I don't really know what to do. I was having nightmares, I was having insomnia, I was having—I mean, because it was so intense, it was so intense, the accidents were so intense.

Q   By the accidents, you are referring to what happened in the Montana training ground.

A   Yes.

Q   So, it sounds like you then didn't return to your unit?

A   No.

Q   Was your discharge status ever absent without leave?

A   No. They kind of got me off easier than what I should have. I could have had it worse off than what I do now, but....

Q   So, would it be accurate to say that the circumstances may have been an absent without leave discharge, but it was just reported as under other than honorable conditions?

A   Yes.

Q   They kind of said, well, we'll massage it a little and make it less than honorable?

A   No. They felt bad because they knew what happened. So there was a group, there was like about fifty guys, and it was a traumatic event.

Q   So as a result of this, you just said I can't do this anymore and that was the end of that.

A   No. Well, I mean, I talked to two officers beforehand, before this transition was set in stone. So, you know, it wasn't like I am not going to show up and I am not going to take care of my responsibilities. I told them this is what's going on and these are the actions I need help with.

Q   So you made some decisions, and—

A   They made some decisions and they said we'll help you out the best way we know how, and this is what I got out of it.

MR. UCHIDA: Thank you very much.

THE COURT: Okay. Any redirect, Ms. Pitts?

MS. PITTS: Thank you.

THE COURT: All right. Just a minute. I may have a few questions. Let me look back through my notes.

EXAMINATION BY THE COURT

Q   With respect to the altercation with Mr. Lewis—Is that his name?

A   Yeah.

Q   What was the charge in connection with that?

A   Domestic violence stalking.

Q   Pardon me?

A   Stalking charge.

Q   Do you remember if it was a felony or a misdemeanor?

A   It started off as two felonies, trespassing, voyeurism, because I walked in onto them having sex, so I got—they got me for voyeurism, which I don't know how the hell that's a possibility.

Q Do you remember what you ultimately pled guilty to?

A Domestic violence, telephone harassment.

Q You don't remember whether that was a felony or a misdemeanor?

A I don't know. I think it started off as domestic violence felony.

Q How long do you think your benefits at BCC will run, or at least what's the maximum period of time you can receive benefits, do you know?

A They told me four years.

Q Okay. And what are you hoping to accomplish?

A Business management degree.

Q How old were you when you went into foster care?

A Roughly six. I don't know. I mean, I would assume six. That's the youngest I can remember.

Q Were you in foster care until you became an adult?

A Yes.

Q Approximately how many places did you stay over the years?

A In foster care?

Q Yes.

A Seven or eight.

Q Here in Washington, or someplace else?

A I went to California as well. I went to my grandmother in California, and then I went to a boys' ranch in Sacramento.

Q Do you have any criminal history as a juvenile?

A No, nothing.

Q Just a minute here while I look through my notes. If you are able to engage in counseling at Kane Mental Health going forward from now, what would you want to accomplish with that?

A Just continue progressing, moving forward, doing what I need to do to do well. I am not trying to use it as a crutch. I am using it as a stepping-stone to the next place.

Q   What do you think counseling can help you with? Maybe that's a better way to ask the question.

A   I don't know—I mean, is it childhood issues? I don't know what they are looking for. I don't know what—I mean it's such a broad spectrum. I don't know what color they are looking for. I don't know what I need. I don't know, unresolved childhood issues? I don't know if it's my kids being in foster care? Some guy threatened me because I made a falsified police report? It could be a range of issues. My kids being abused, and they are telling me one thing and I find out another, then they send me a paper in the mail saying that it's not. I mean, I don't know. They are all stressful that could require counseling. I mean —

Q   You say, "I am not sure what they are looking for," and I am assuming you are making a reference here to the —

A   Department.

Q   —the department, is that right?

A   Yeah.

Q   What would you be looking for?

A   To heal, to heal from all of this trauma that my kids had to deal with and the fact that I put myself in a position in my life to have to deal with these people. That's what I want. I want some kind of closure. I want something to—I mean, you have got to think, dealing with these people for two and a half years, you are going to need counseling just to deal with them or to deal with the aftereffects. There are a lot of aftereffects. I have got to deal with these people. I have got to see them every day after this case is closed, if and when. I would probably say I need some severe counseling to deal with the aftereffects of the trauma and abuse I have been put through by the department.

Q   If the girls were going to live with you in this apartment, what, if any, additional assistance do you think that you would need in order to parent successfully at this point?

A Well, I do attend school, so the mother doesn't—she doesn't work, so I would assume that mother could watch the children. I don't know, like, I don't know how this all pans out. Parenting is a two-person deal, so she needs to take responsibility and watch them and take care of them. I mean, it would cost me $435 a month to put Lucy into day care at school with me, which I have the funds for that, but I mean if I don't have to pay that, I don't want to. I would rather put that maybe in a college fund for her or some kind of clothing voucher or clothing.

Q Well, would you be able to get some additional funds from what you are receiving presently to cover day care?

A Yeah, I would get extra funds.

THE COURT: Are there any additional questions for Mr. Johnson based on the court's examination, Ms. Pitts?

MS. PITTS: Yes. Thank you.

REDIRECT EXAMINATION BY MS. PITTS:

Q Mr. Johnson, do you ever feel like your thinking gets stuck?

A Sure.

Q And have you ever had the experience that it's hard to think about something else when you keep thinking about the thought that is right here in your face?

A Yes, ma'am.

Q Okay. Do you think you would benefit from skills that would help you unstick yourself?

A Yes, ma'am.

Q Okay. And, I think there was some testimony in this case about a book about post-traumatic stress disorder that you looked at?

A That I got from the VA from Peter Smith that I gave to my children to understand me so we could both understand each other.

Q Did it help you understand you?

A It gives me a reason and rhyme to the way I come off or do the things I do.

Q Now, you have described some of the techniques that you already can use. I think you described breathing exercises.

A Yes, ma'am.

Q Does that help get you a little bit unstuck, if you take the time to do some breathing?

A If you acknowledge it and utilize it before it becomes an issue. It's all about, you know, doing it before it becomes an issue.

Q And do you have the experience now that sometimes you're well into the issue before you think about, I should take some breathing exercises?

A Yeah.

Q Okay. Now, we don't know what this court is going to decide, but if the court said, I don't think the children should be with Ms. Faraday, but maybe they can be with you, would you be willing to be separate completely from the mother?

A Yes, ma'am. I would do whatever it took.

Q So, your testimony when the judge asked you a question was parenting is a two-person affair.

A Uh-hum.

Q Do you think you could find other suitable people to help you?

A Yes, ma'am.

Q And, one of those people or one of those things would be day care at BCC?

A Yeah.

Q Have you seen the facilities there for the day care?

A Beautiful.

Q Can the children be there all day?

A Lucy can be there for eight hours. I mean, my classes are not eight hours a day, but that's the maximum.

Q   It's really only Lucy that would need day care because Lexie is in school?

A   Lexie would be in school, and I already have the funds to cover Lucy's expenses. I already did an application and I have already put her on a waiting list.

Q   For the day care?

A   For the day care.

Q   Now, are there other people, like through your church or through friends that you have that you think would also be able to help you have the kids, babysit if you need to go someplace or do something?

A   There is a church next door to where I am living at—they have a—the Four-Square Church, they have like a little playground set up and they have day care.

Q   Do you anticipate you might change your allegiance or affiliations to that church?

A   It could. If it's more cost effective, and put my daughter in school, put my daughter in school and I go to school. I mean, it could be cheaper in the long run, but it wouldn't bother me either way.

Q   Do you live close to an elementary school?

A   I live like dead center between two of them.

MS. PITTS: Those are all the questions I have. Thank you.
THE COURT: Mr. Uchida, anything else?
MR. UCHIDA: Yes. Thank you.

RECROSS EXAMINATION BY MR. UCHIDA:

Q   What is the current status of your relationship with the mother?

A   She is just the mother of my children.

Q   In answer to the judge's questions, you were talking about, you said it's a two-person deal, the mother caring for the children, so it sounds like —

A I mean, eventually. I mean, I believe parenting should be a two-person, but there's a lot of children that don't have a mother or a father, but I mean, I will raise them on my own if need be. If that's the way it's supposed to be or has to happen, I will do that. So there's no question about us reflaming our relationship or getting back together. Just because we talk and hang out doesn't mean that we are trying to rekindle old flames, because I know that gets kind of speculated a lot. Observations kind of demonstrate people's behaviors, so just because we talk and just because we hang out or have a cup of coffee together doesn't mean we are trying to hook up.

Q Are you separated from the mother then?

A I have—She lives life on her life's terms and I live life on my life's terms.

Q And you have kids in common?

A We have kids together, so I mean, I will always love her. She gave me two beautiful children and she is the mother of my children. I will always have a love for her. For me to say that I don't love her is crazy because it's a continuing relationship, you know what I mean? I mean, you could love somebody and not be in love with them. You love the person and hate the behavior.

MR. UCHIDA: Thank you very much, Mr. Johnson.

THE COURT: Anything else?

MS. PITTS: No.

THE COURT: All right. Thank you, Mr. Johnson. You may have a seat.

Jacob stepped down from the witness stand and I could hardly contain myself. High fives would not have been appropriate, of course. I grinned at him and patted him on the back. Then I scribbled across the tablet we used for communication. *This was picture perfect. I'm proud of you!*

More than just maintaining his cool and showing respect to the court, Jacob had demonstrated he was a dad working hard to get his kids back, and the one thing he still needed after more than two years was the one thing CPS never provided.

The day after Jacob testified, the state attorney filed a motion for voluntary nonsuit without prejudice with regard to Lexie and Lucy Johnson. This was a request, more like an announcement, CPS wanted to have its petitions for the termination of parental rights dismissed. The case against Rose was dismissed too because her attorney was able to prove her treatment services had never included the dual diagnosis approach she clearly needed. When such a motion for voluntary nonsuit is made, the moving party, in this case CPS, has a right to have its petitions dismissed. Judge Wipple seemed pleased with this turn of events and signed the order granting the dismissal.

Wow. We had won! The petitions were dismissed by CPS and now CPS needed to provide mental health counseling. I had every confidence this was the last piece that was needed to turn Jacob into an adequate single parent.

There was even more good news. Judge Wipple agreed to hear the next review on the case. We would be in front of a judge who knew the whole sad story of the case and who would hold the agency's feet to the fire. The review hearing was set for August 24, 2012. This hearing would get us back on track for reunification. As we left the court room, Jacob started calling me Johnny Cochran.

Chapter 19

Judge Wipple's order from the August 24 review hearing required a new round of parent coaching for Jacob with Beth Dahlquist. Jacob was already set up with individual counseling at Kane Mental Health. The parties were ordered to meet on a monthly basis with Mr. Northrup to make sure any issues were dealt with as soon as possible. The judge also wanted the parents to participate in Lexie's counseling. Unfortunately, he conditioned the participation on the recommendation of her therapist. This limitation was problematic (more than I knew) but with the recognition the plan was now reunification, I hoped some type of family counseling would soon be provided, if not with Grantham then with someone else. Visitation remained supervised, but language was added to the order that it could be expanded for each parent by agreement of parties. It was anticipated any expansion would quickly move to monitored and then un-supervised visits. Judge Wipple had a positive attitude about reunification and thought in the next six months or less the girls could be home with either mom or dad. He thought we should have another hearing in just a few months, but there was some bad news too. Judge Wipple was retiring in a matter of weeks. Judge Bennett-Carey would take his place for all future hearings on the case.

We had our first group meeting on September 27, 2012. We discussed some problems Jacob was having with KMH. The therapist assigned to Jacob was being flaky. One-time Jacob said they spent the entire session talking about the therapist's experience in the army. Another time Jacob waited in the lobby for *two-hours* before someone told him his therapist was out sick. Then, instead of rescheduling him, Jacob was sent into a fifty-five-minute session with a woman he had never met before. It was a waste of time. Mr. Northrup gave KMH the benefit of the doubt and suggested they were only trying to help.

I wanted to scream, "He needs cognitive behavioral therapy for managing PTSD and for excessive rumination. He doesn't need to chat about the army or start fresh with a new person," but I bit my tongue and Terry Northrup agreed he would contact the therapist to straighten this out.

The children's mother was making progress in her recovery. As she approached the four-month mark in her most recent sobriety, she was hanging in there and stayed clean and sober. Like Jacob, she too, was in mental health counseling. Each parent asked about family therapy with Lexie, and the social worker promised to look into it.

Although Jacob's visits were still supervised, they were expanded from two hours to two-and-a-half hours and could now be out in the community. We discussed his plan to take the girls on a ferry ride to North Cape. Everyone approved. We discussed the new contract with Beth Dahlquist and the possibility of further expansion of visits assuming the current visits went well. Jacob was fixing up the children's bedroom in his apartment so they could visit him there for extended times.

The ferry visit went well. Jacob met the children with Ms. Reisenberg at the ferry terminal in South Fork. The ferry ride to North Cape and back took about two hours. These Washington state ferries are massive car carriers with plenty of room inside and out for families to explore the multiple decks, each with spectacular views of sound and shore and mountains. Jacob came armed and dangerous—he had stopped at a bakery for day-old bread and brought with him no fewer than ten loaves. Before and after sharing a meal of fish and chips, Jacob and his daughters spent the time on an upper deck feeding the gulls. Between the incessant calls of the always-hungry seagulls and the happy squeals of the children as they threw whole slices of bread into the air, this was a community visit at its finest. Jacob was happy.

He began to think he might get to be a real father again. He talked to the girls about getting a pet and asked them what they would like. There was a discussion of a pig. At his visit on October 5 he showed Lexie a fat wad of cash which he had her count—$650. But when she asked if she could have some of it, he said no, he needed all the money to buy stuff for her room. She said nothing.

———•———

Among the nuggets I did not discover for some time, the extent to which the foster parents were involved in Lexie's therapy was perhaps the biggest one, but there was another one buried in a pile of paper I would not receive for several months that was also significant.

At his monthly visit to the foster home, about six weeks after the trial, Terry Northrup met as usual with the Johnson girls' and their foster parents. He had previously let the foster parents know what happened to the termination petitions. On this visit, he was sitting in the living room, chatting with the foster mother, and Lexie was on the floor with her sister. Pipping up into a lull in the conversation, Lexie asked,

"When is my adoption?"

"We are still meeting with a judge." Mr. Northrup replied

"I want to see him to explain. I want to see Rose and Jacob, but I really want Mommy and Daddy to adopt me." She was talking about Christine and George.

Terry promised her he would let the judge know she wanted to see him, but he didn't let the judge know. He simply wrote a note in his file about the home visit and included what Lexie said. He may not have realized how this exchange might be understood by Lexie. In the ensuing weeks of regular meetings on this case, Mr. Northrup never mentioned to me or the mother's attorney what Lexie said. We all knew adoption was off the table and reunification was the plan, but Lexie didn't know it.

Months later, when I was piecing this altogether I saw a visitation note from the week following Mr. Northrup's chat with Lexie. She had barely been in the room more than a minute when she said to no one in particular, "Adoptions are good."

Jacob immediately replied, "I wonder if you know what it really means? They are not good—it's when kids are taken away. Parents never get to see their kids again."

This ended any discussion, but what it makes clear is these two people, Lexie and Jacob, needed to talk to each other about the recent trial, about the current plan, about Jacob's progress, and about what Lexie thought might be or should be happening. This was what family therapy could provide, a safe place to talk.

Two weeks later, Jacob was able to take the girls to his new apartment for the first time. The children's advocate, Martha Jones, joined them. Among the other activities Jacob had planned was a bubble bath. He used to give Lexie bubble baths and she loved them. Lucy was very happy with the idea and immediately stripped off all her clothes and jumped into the tub Jacob was filling up. There were bubbles everywhere, but Lexie hung back, and to his credit, Jacob quickly became aware of her hesitation.

He turned to her and said, "Maybe you got too big for me?" She nodded her head and he suggested she check out the books in the living room.

Martha Jones gave Jacob credit for picking up on Lexie's cue and said, "Girls get too old to play in the bath with their daddy."

He agreed. Jacob was anxious to show Martha Jones how well he had furnished the apartment. He was sorry to say he did not have beds yet for the girls, but he thought a buddy of his from school would lend him some. This exchange occurred at the end of the visit when they were all in the living room getting ready to leave.

Martha said, brightly, "Girls look out the window and tell me if Jennifer is here yet." Then she asked Jacob to let her stay and talk more with him. He agreed.

Once the girls were gone, Jones explained to Jacob she was concerned the chatter about the beds would upset Lexie.

"Why?"

"Well, it makes her think she'll be staying here."

"That's the point isn't it? Once I get unsupervised visits, we have overnights, right?"

"I understand, but we are still not there. You just have to be careful not to jump the gun with her. Let her get used to the place before we talk about overnights, okay?"

---·---

On October 19, 2012, when the supervisor arrived at the school to take Lexie to the Friday afternoon visitation, the principal intercepted her. "Lexie has been crying all afternoon. She says she doesn't want to go to her visit today. We can't force the issue. We called her mom."

"You called Rose Faraday?"

"No, no. I called Christine. She came right over. They are in the office."

Lexie was sitting close to her foster mom.

"I don't want to go," she whimpered.

The supervisor and Christine each asked her why not, but Lexie just shook her head. Jennifer Reisenberg needed to know more. Finally, Lexie said she didn't like the visits with Jacob or Rose because all they did was play with Lucy, and if she ever told Jacob she didn't want to do something he just keep asking her why, and it was uncomfortable. Rose was the same way, asking her too many questions.

Jennifer made a deal with Lexie. They would go to the visit, but if she felt uncomfortable for any reason, she should tell her father she was sick and then they could leave. Lexie agreed. She called ahead to let the CPS receptionist know they were running late and Lexie was little under the weather.

When they got to the visit, Jacob immediately told Lexie to let him know if she needed to leave early because she was sick. She was standoffish at this visit, but she did enjoy making a list of the foods she wanted him to bring next time. Then Jacob asked her what hurt, was it her tummy? He went through various other parts of the body that might be hurting, head, throat, and each time she said no. He asked her if she was just not feeling talkative, and she did not reply. A few minutes later, she walked over to the supervisor and asked if they could leave because she was not feeling well. Jacob, thinking she was really ill, agreed to end the visit early and told Lexie he hoped she felt better soon.

The following Monday October 22, there was the regularly scheduled visit between the girls and their mother. The visit was shortened by about forty-five minutes because Lexie was not feeling well.

Behind the scenes there was a flurry of emails, discussing the situation. Martha Jones wanted to know what could be done. Jennifer Reisenberg worried they were encouraging Lexie to manipulate the situation. Terry Northrup said he would try and get a contract started soon for Beth Dahlquist. He also thought they needed some advice from Elizabeth Grantham.

This exchange was dutifully memorialized in the social worker's email folder which I would not receive for another four months. No one contacted either parent.

On October 26, Lexie wanted to leave early from her visit with her dad. She told Jacob she still wasn't feeling great. It was okay with him to end the visit about thirty minutes early. Northrup, meanwhile, asked Christine to address Lexie's resistance to parental visits with Grantham.

Martha Jones thought maybe Lexie would feel more confident about the visits and other things too if she felt her voice was being heard. She could write a letter to the judge, of course, but Jones thought the best idea would be to get Lexie her own lawyer. Lexie liked the idea. A motion was to be heard on November 6, 2012 at 10:00 A.M.

Meanwhile, Rose was organizing a special Halloween celebration. Instead of sitting in the CPS room on Monday, she had permission to move her visit to the 31st. Jacob agreed to have his visit at that time too. They would go to HotRod Alley, a pizza place where the booths were shaped like cars and there were lots of video games to play. Everyone would be in costume. Rose asked her new boyfriend Charlie Gilbert and his mother to come too. Northrup limited the guest list to the parents and Grandma Dee.

But on the day of the event, Rose got a ride from her boyfriend and then he came into the restaurant and sat with his mother at a nearby booth without being introduced. Jacob recognized him as Rose's new boyfriend. His presence steamed Jacob, but there wasn't much he could do about it. The guy was sitting three tables away.

The girls arrived with Jennifer Reisenberg. Lucy was dressed in a bunny costume. Lexie was a fairy princess, complete with crown and wand. Jacob had arrived dressed, he said, as a student but with a pocket full of change for Lexie to play video games. The burgers were good, but the chocolate cake from Grandma Dee was better—it had a ghost and a witch and a pumpkin on it and the girls' names too. Jacob maintained his cool, but later in the day, he called Martha Jones. She agreed with him Rose showed poor judgment in trying to bring her boyfriend and his mother around the children. Jacob wasn't certain if Lexie knew who the guy was, but Lexie noticed him too and told her foster parents she liked the restaurant, but she did not really want to meet new people.

On November 6, the parties gathered for a hearing to ask the court to appoint an attorney for Lexie. At that time in Kane county, children did not get attorneys appointed to represent them unless they were at least twelve and expressed a desire to be represented. Even then, there was nothing automatic about it. There were only two attorneys in the pool who regularly represented children in dependency cases. At the time of this hearing, Lexie was two months shy of her eighth birthday. Her reluctance to participate in visitation was seen by all as something that needed to be addressed.

At this time, neither I nor counsel for the mother had seen the social worker's notes or the visitation notes, so we were not aware of the dynamics of her resistance, much less how she had been encouraged to think the adoption was still being considered by the court. We knew visits were ending early but had no idea Lexie had been coached to pretend she was sick.

I didn't like the idea of appointing an attorney for Lexie because she was so young, but Jacob thought anything that might help Lexie express herself or feel better was a good thing, so we agreed an attorney should be appointed for her. The court accepted the representations that Lexie was a very mature child who knew her own mind and was old enough to work with an attorney to make sure her positions were adequately represented.

The morning of the hearing, Terry Northrup brought us all copies of a fax from Elizabeth Grantham. She recommended, due to recent changes in the case (unspecified), a child psychiatrist should be brought in to evaluate Lexie's emotional development. I didn't know what to make of this bombshell, but if Grantham was stepping aside or even just moving over, that had to be good for Jacob. Everyone agreed to the evaluation.

On Friday November 9, 2012 the girls were at the CPS office waiting and waiting for their dad. He had been running late at school, and in his haste to catch the bus to get to the CPS office on time, he jumped on the wrong bus. When he realized what he had done, the bus had gone a few miles in the wrong direction. He called the office to say he could not make it. Then the following Monday November 12, Mom called to cancel her visit because she was ill and did not want the girls to catch anything.

On November 16, 2012 Lexie attended the visit with her dad without any objection. She was a bit standoffish at first and argumentative. She complained about the food he brought. When Reisenberg allowed them to step outside, she thought Lexie was a little too aggressive with her father, throwing pebbles at him. She refused to give him a hug. She didn't want her picture taken, but she never mentioned being ill and the visit did not end early.

Then, the following Monday November 19, 2012, Lexie was scheduled to have her visit with her mom on her own without Lucy. This was done to let Lexie be the center of attention. Reisenberg picked her up at school, but before they got to the car Lexie told her she was scared and didn't want to go to the visit. She was afraid to visit without her sibling because then her mom would spend the whole visit asking her questions. She would not go. The visit was cancelled. From this point on, Lexie refused all contact with either parent.

On December 5, 2012, Northrup let me know he found a better therapist for Jacob, one who worked in the same agency as Elizabeth Grantham. We both hoped this proximity might lead to contact between Grantham and Jacob's therapist. Maybe there might be an opening for some therapeutic contact between Jacob and Lexie.

On December 21, 2012, the social worker talked to Lexie during his monthly health and safety visit to the foster home. She had little to say about her father. She told Northrup she did not want to visit either parent. She offered no explanation. When he asked her how she felt about Lucy continuing to have visits with their parents, Lexie shrugged her shoulders but said nothing.

Chapter Twenty

Knocking out the agency's termination petition was a big deal. By showing the flaws in the state's case we managed to get the state to back down. Even if there was still a clock ticking, the case was moving, or so I thought, in one direction toward reunification. I believed time was on my client's side. It was better than a fresh start because Jacob had already accomplished so much. There was an excellent chance Jacob would benefit from the individual counseling now being provided. I really thought we might be home free and CPS had been chastised enough to really help this father. Between his individual therapy and the family therapy I anticipated would soon be offered, Jacob and Lexie would finally be able to look at and fill in the gaps that had developed between them. In family therapy, they would have a chance to reassess each other realistically.

But behind the scenes, wheels were turning that would crush Jacob's chances to resume parenting his daughter Lexie. There was still much that was buried in paperwork I had not yet received. I was not sure why, but the monthly meetings were becoming exercises in futility. We were finally told about the extent of Lexie's opposition to visits. Jacob rightly demanded to know what the agency was going to go about it. We discussed the selection of that child psychiatrist and hoped he or she could do more than complete an evaluation of Lexie's emotional development. At each of the meetings the parents requested family therapy. They wanted to be included in a session with

Ms. Grantham, but if not with her then some other therapist and maybe the child psychiatrist could provide family therapy. Now that Lexie was refusing all contact, the need for family therapy was more pressing than ever. Mr. Northrup agreed to explore the idea.

Mr. Northrup instructed the parents to give him the questions they wanted Elizabeth Grantham to answer. Each parent took this request seriously. Here is what Jacob asked:

> *When did the whole subject of adoption first come up? What do you say if Lexie brings it up?*

> *I know there is another child in the foster home that has been adopted and I wonder if you think this might confuse Lexie...like maybe Lexie feels he is loved more or better because of that?*

> *I wanted to be adopted when I was in foster care, can you let me talk to Lexie about that?*

> *When can I talk to you directly?*

Terry Northrup promised us he sent Jacob's questions and the questions Rose gave him to Ms. Grantham as soon as he received them, but she never replied. The parents never got any response, much less answers, to their questions. Meanwhile, the agency was obligated to bring the issue to the court's attention because Lexie's refusal to go to visits was a de facto suspension of the parents' visitation, without just cause. Nothing in Jacob or Rose's conduct made it legally necessary to suspension visitation. Visits were suspended at the insistence of a very young girl.

Jacob's visitation with Lucy had finally progressed to monitored visitation in the community. This meant he was no longer under a microscope. He needed to let the social worker know where he was going and what he planned to do on the visit, and he had to stay within his time allotment. Since he had no car, much of the visit was spent traveling by bus to the mall or park or restaurant. Often, however, his social worker would give him extra time to travel back to the CPS office or give him a lift, which was very helpful. Visits occurred at his apartment, which was a few blocks from the CPS office. This allowed the social worker, Martha Jones, and Beth Dahlquist a chance to drop by and see how he was getting along with Lucy. There were never any health or safety problems. Lucy enjoyed being with her father. Maybe she enjoyed being the only princess in the room.

Northrup simply recited the facts of Lexie's resistance at the hearing to suspend the parents' visitation on January 4, 2013. He did not mention her knowledge of adoption or her easy separation from her sister for purposes of not visiting. He had not yet determined if the child psychiatrist could provide any family therapy. He was at a loss.

I blithered on too long about all Jacob had accomplished, including the significant expansion of his now virtually unsupervised visitation. I raised Jacob's main concern someone had prematurely discussed adoption with his daughter even though Judge Wipple ordered a sole plan of reunification last August. I asked the court to not tolerate the suspension unless there was a concrete plan to address Lexie's rejection of her father. Although there may be no visitation at this time, there must be contact of some kind.

Judge Bennett-Carey couldn't force the child's therapist to do anything. Nor could he force the child to go to visits. He directed the newly identified child psychiatrist, Dr. Paulette Steiner to review the situation and tell us how to get back to regular visitation. He was hopeful her work would include family therapy. The permanent plan remained reunification.

———•———

By April 2013, Rose had established seven months of sobriety. Northrup was promoted to supervisor of a newly created unit and a new social worker took over the case, Rachel Banks. She was enthusiastic about moving forward with the plan for reunification of Lucy with her mother. Rachel talked with Jacob about how much Lucy loved her visits with him. She wanted to know how he felt about Lucy living with Rose. He conceded it was a good plan, even though

Rose was by this time living with her new boyfriend. Rachel was aware of him, and he had already submitted to a background check, and there were no issues. Jacob wanted his children out of foster care more than anything. If CPS would let Lucy go to her mother's home that was acceptable to him.

Jacob admitted to Rachel he was using his apartment just for visitation with Lucy and was living with his girlfriend Melinda the rest of the time. If Lucy was going to live with Rose, he saw no reason to keep paying for the apartment. Jacob was also trying to think of something he could do for Lexie even though he could not see her or talk to her anymore. He wanted to give Rachel three hundred dollars to pass on to Lexie, but she declined to take it. It was too much money.

Dr. Steiner, called Rachel on May 22, 2013.

"I don't think I am the right person for this job."

"You are perfect."

"This is not a time to flatter. I had a meeting with the foster parents yesterday and then privately with Lexie. There is no movement there."

"What do you mean?

"She's made up her mind, and she politely told me to quit thinking anything would change her mind. When I said I thought I had read somewhere in the file she wanted to be adopted but still wanted to see her parents, she was quiet for a full minute. Then she said, 'Yes, I used to think that.' She was like a politician changing her mind after due and full consideration. I'm not sure I have ever met a child quite like Lexie. I am afraid you have to grant her request. I think her identify is wrapped up in having the adoption go through. I mean it would damage her to be denied. She's been in care for three years!

"Okay, but can't you give us a report? I need you to stay on this since you have already met her. Don't make her start over with someone else. Just tell me if there is any way we can set up contact between this child and her parents, and if we can't, we can't, but my own opinion is not going to carry much weight. You're the expert."

Dr. Steiner groaned. " Let me meet the parents and see what I can come up with. I should be charging double!"

Lucy explained to Rachel on their first meeting she had a visitation-daddy, Jacob, and a home-daddy, George. She seemed happy with this arrangement. She also liked visiting her mom at her new apartment. She was too young to be told she was about to begin a slow transition home to her mother with a targeted return sometime in July after several overnight visits.

These transitions were often a special sort of crapshoot. Children often react badly when they have to go back to foster care after a weekend with their parent(s), for example, and this hardly indicates there was something bad happening in the birth parents' home. More typically, it is the result of being forced out of the birth home again and again, likely triggering recollections of the initial traumatic removal. Or, it can simply be the result of the confusion any child would experience if they did not know for sure where they were really living.

In this case, Lucy went back and forth fairly easily, but because of her mother's spotty track record maintaining a drug-free lifestyle, the transition was strung out over about ten weeks. Charlie, the boyfriend, had no concerning history and was now a live-in boyfriend. Melinda Graves also had passed CPS muster and was approved as the visitation monitor for Jacob. Intensive in-home services had to be set up for Rose. The biggest hurdle once Lucy was back home was likely to be the parents' difficulty with each other. Jacob and Rose had to learn to work together to manage his visitation schedule without the social worker acting as a go-between.

Lucy was officially returned to her mother on July 19, 2013. It was a Friday. Every thing went well but when Sunday afternoon came around, when she was usually returned to George and Christine, she stayed with Rose and Charlie. Monday morning, she started asking about it.

"Home-Daddy," she said, meaning George.

Rose told her home was now with her and Charlie, but she would still see Daddy Jacob. No doubt she was puzzled, but at age three and with the offer of ice cream, it was too soon to worry much.

But by Wednesday night, she was having trouble sleeping.

"Is Lexie coming?" she asked, and when she was told Rachel was setting up visits for her with Lexie, Lucy could not have known what that meant.

Lucy had been through a lot. She was just three months old when she was abruptly taken from her parents and put with the Samsons. Her placement with relatives lasted only a few days, and she was moved again, this time to foster care with her sister Lexie. Being with Lexie helped, but she missed her mommy and daddy and cried herself to sleep each night. We know there was physical abuse in this home, although it seemed to be primarily directed toward Lexie, but it was at this time Lucy developed significant respiratory issues and needed daily albuterol treatments. When she was just eight months old, she and her sister were placed in their second foster home. Within a few months, she seemed to be getting back to normal. By her second birthday, she no longer had respiratory issues. She adapted to the routine of visits, enjoyed going anywhere with Lexie, and clearly adored her sister.

What were the girls saying to each other about their parents as the months rolled by? When Lucy had her second birthday, Lexie expressed concern to Rose that Lucy called Christine and George Mommy and Daddy. Rose didn't know what to say. Meanwhile, Lucy's health was good. She loved princess toys. At visits with her dad, she was growing less and less interested in him, imitating Lexie's disinterest.

Lucy responded enthusiastically to the structure Jacob learned from Dahlquist. The quality of the visits improved for everyone. When the termination trial was going on in August 2012, what was Lucy hearing? This time, her routines were well established, she was in daycare, saw her parents weekly, and lived in the foster home with the people who wanted to adopt her—people she now knew as Mommy and Daddy.

Then Lexie quit visiting. This may have made visits easier for Lucy because she did not have to share her mom's or her dad's attention with anyone. Jacob started another round of instruction from Beth Dahlquist, and Lucy thrived in the expansion of her contact with him. Beth Dahlquist noted Jacob had retained much of what she had previously taught him, and she observed his relationship with Lucy was now blossoming without much help. She was mystified at the turn the case had taken with regard to Lexie.

Although Jacob hated being called the visitation-dad, he recognized being a weekend dad was probably all he would ever be. He accepted the plan to move Lucy into her mother's home because she would finally be out of foster care, but Lucy had no way of knowing what it meant when her visits with her parents were expanding, especially when her visits with her mom included spending so many nights at her mom's house. Once she got a sense she was going to stay with Rose and Charlie, she freaked out.

By July 25, 2013 Lucy was unwilling to finish her meals, and no amount of ice cream made a difference. She had lost her mommy and daddy again. This time it was Christine and George. She had lived with them for two-and-a-half years. It was likely all she remembered of her early life. She missed Lexie terribly. She missed her daycare friends and teachers too; everyone was just gone. To make matters worse, she never saw George or Christine again, and worse than that, the visits she was supposed to have with Lexie were delayed.

She cried and cried for the people who were gone, and her mother, try as she might, could not console her. Lucy resisted everything from her mother's schedule and structure and discipline to the meals put before her and the clothes she had to wear. She didn't like Charlie. Nothing was right. CPS set up individual therapy for Lucy, but the first available appointment was not until November. She still liked seeing her visitation-dad and often did not want to go back to her mom's house after her visits with him and Melinda.

At the review hearing on September 13, 2013, Judge Bennett-Carey found both parents in full compliance and making progress. It was reported to the court Dr. Steiner had seen each parent once and Lexie at least twice. She wanted to see Lexie one more time and then would be able to write her report. The mother's attorney and I renewed our plea for the provision of family therapy, but the judge refused to order this until he was able to see the Steiner report. The next hearing was scheduled for mid-December. In a note in the social worker's file, Rachel's supervisor wrote Lexie was seeing Dr. Steiner with the intent of starting family counseling with both parents. I did not see this note for several months. It was, of course, entirely wrong.

Jacob was continuing in school, seeing a counselor, and trying to get his driver's license back. This was no small task, as it meant endless calls to different county and municipal courts and even personal trips to these jurisdictions courtesy of Melinda's mom and grandmother. Melinda did not drive, but she helped Jacob pay enough to get payment plans established for all the fines and costs he had accumulated for various traffic infractions. Once the plans were accepted and in place, his license was reinstated. He then purchased a truck and was able to show Rachel his valid license and proof of insurance. He was then allowed to transport Lucy. This made his unsupervised visits much easier.

Chapter Twenty-One

Dr. Steiner submitted her five-page report in the middle of October, 2013. It was her opinion Lexie should stay where she was and be adopted by her foster parents, Christine and George. The mother was described as sympathetic, even willing to discuss giving up her parental rights, but the father was impatient and unwilling to accept reunification was not possible.

Not surprisingly, this report infuriated Jacob. He was aware he may have made a bad impression on Steiner, but he was frankly past caring. He just wanted to see his daughter, and all he was getting was the same information over and over—Lexie says no, Lexie wants to be adopted. What was the point of all the work he had done, of Judge Wipple's plan for reunification, if this doctor was just going to go along with what Lexie wanted? What was the point?

My assessment of the situation was bleak. The Steiner report stated the obvious, and it was not going to get us anywhere. Apparently, family therapy was a service the agency had abandoned. The status quo would be maintained indefinitely. Lexie might not be going home, but how could she be adopted? What court would terminate the parental rights of Jacob or Rose when they were both doing so well, when Lucy had already been returned to Rose?

There was a small ray of hope, at least in terms of contact. Of course, Steiner supported sibling visitation, but she also thought it was possible for the parents to have some contact with Lexie once she knew what she was recommending. The mother's attorney and I suggested even a single session of family therapy would be helpful to let the parents and child simply see each other in a therapeutic environment, a safe place for Lexie. Steiner rejected this plan and recommended instead a "chance encounter." Let Rose and Jacob on separate occasions seem to run into Lexie when she was out and about with her foster parents. A few weeks after the report, Rose, as instructed, pretended to catch a glimpse of Lexie at the Safeway checkout line. She had Lucy with her, who had received no warning. When Lucy saw first Christine and George then Lexie, she ran like a bullet into her foster father's arms. Tears started to roll down his cheeks.

Lexie pulled on Christine's arm. "I want to go to the car," she pleaded.

"Lexie, how are you?" Rose asked, trying to make it casual.

Christine apologized and took Lexie out to the car. In spite of George's cooperation, it took Rose another ten minutes to extricate Lucy from his arms.

The following Sunday, as the foster family walked down the sidewalk after church, Jacob walked toward them. Lexie was dancing around her foster parents, telling them what she had learned and done in Sunday school. Other parishioners, aware of what was happening, crowded behind the family. On a spin, Lexie saw Jacob. She froze and then she ran back inside the church, and several people with Jacob and the foster father in the lead, took off after her. The foster father stopped in the vestibule, as did the men with him, and let Jacob go into the church alone.

Jacob was in a panic. Why was she running? He called her name and started down the main aisle.

"Are you okay? What's wrong? Lexie, what's wrong?"

He went down the side aisles and then headed up to the choir loft. George headed up after him. Jacob found her trying to hide between the organ bench and the pedals. She was whimpering.

Jacob reached down. "It's okay, honey, I won't hurt you. Come on out of there. Tell me what's wrong."

George was in full rescue mode at this point.

"Don't touch her! Can't you see she's frightened?"

"Why is she afraid?"

"What does it matter? I have to ask you to leave."

Jacob flushed with anger. "You don't get to tell me what to do." Then Jacob saw several men coming up into the loft. Now he feared for his own safety. He started to back away from Lexie.

"All right, all right, but don't think you're going to get away with stealing her. CPS and you are brainwashing her against us. We got Lucy out of foster care!"

He pounded down the stairs and out into the sunshine. He was nearly blind with rage, but he started counting, and then he did his breathing exercises. Ten blocks later his heart slowed down. Then he called me. My office was in my home, and when I saw who was calling I answered.

Jacob was still angry and gave me a jumbled version of what happened—Lexie hiding, running after her, trying to help out of her hiding place, George making him back off from his own child.

"And this posse showed up. I was just trying to help her, my own daughter. Why is she afraid of me? What are they telling her?"

I couldn't believe my ears. This looked bad.

"What the fuck is *wrong* with you?" I yelled into the phone. "Couldn't you just back off for a moment? Couldn't you see how freaked out she was? My God—it doesn't matter if CPS made her that way or if some long gone advocate poisoned her brain about adoption—you have got to get yourself into the here and now. Don't you see how this will be used against you?"

Jacob was silent.

I was shocked by my outburst. I got a grip, "I am so sorry, Jacob. I should never speak to you like that. I know you are doing the best you can."

He replied, "Yeah, yeah. I'll call you tomorrow," and he hung up.

"I thought we were done," he later told me. "You just unloaded."

It would be months before Jacob trusted me again, and many more months before I had the time to organize all the documentation in Jacob's file and saw how he had been set up to lose Lexie from the beginning of the case.

Working directly with each other to organize Lucy's visitation with her dad had not gone very well between Rose and Jacob. These arrangements inevitably involved Rose's boyfriend, Charlie, from time to time. He might be the only one home when Lucy was picked up or dropped off. He might be the one who answered the phone in the evening when Jacob called to tell Lucy goodnight. Rose wanted Jacob to follow a specific schedule and to call a few evenings a week, not every evening or whenever he felt like it.

Jacob thought now that he was arranging visits directly with Rose she would give him more time than CPS allowed. Instead, she wanted to impose a fixed schedule consistent with what Banks wanted. Jacob resented all the time Charlie was getting to spend with Lucy. He thought this was especially unfair since Charlie had done nothing to get unlimited access to Lucy except screw Rose. As so often happened with him, the issue of Charlie was one he could not easily let go of, and his perseveration kicked in big time.

This gave him an opportunity in his therapy to examine how he became obsessed with an issue like Charlie, but Jacob was a work in progress, so to speak, on such issues. When Rose complained to the social worker she felt pressured by Jacob, the social worker created a formal schedule and told Jacob to follow it. She gave a copy of the schedule to Rose and to Melinda too. CPS officially approved Melinda as the visitation monitor for Jacob and the social worker appreciated the calming influence she had on Jacob and how Lucy was bonding with her doing girlie things together.

Jacob occasionally lapsed into his interrogation style with Lucy. He wanted to know more about Charlie. What did they do together? Why didn't she like him? One day, Lucy told Jacob that Charlie had touched her private parts and she didn't like it. Jacob went up like a roman candle. He immediately called Rose who was in the middle of a session with some services providers in her living room. They would report to the social worker they could hear Jacob screaming on the phone, chastising Rose for letting Charlie abuse his daughter. An investigation of the allegation of sexual abuse against Charlie would show Charlie sometimes gave Lucy her bath, and in the course of bathing her, he wiped her genitals clean with a washcloth. Rachel Banks told Rose to do the bathing herself.

On another occasion, Jacob told Lucy if she didn't like what Charlie was saying to her to tell him, " I don't have to listen to you, you are not Dad." The first time Lucy tried this out on Charlie, Rose overheard her. It was hard enough to get Lucy to obey without having her head filled with contrary crap from Jacob.

Lucy was still having a rocky time with Rose. As soon as Rose took her eyes off her, Lucy was off doing some mischief. One day, Rose thought Lucy was playing quietly by herself in her bedroom. She found her later "painting" the wall with her feces. On another occasion, Lucy left the house on her own to play on the swing set in a nearby park. She only came home because she fell and badly scraped her knee. Rose had fallen asleep on the couch. Jacob, for all his issues with Rose, was reluctant to complain too loudly about any lack of supervision because, above all else, he did not want his daughter sent back to foster care.

Lucy started full-day Head Start in the September 2013. She was a disruptive influence in her classroom, noisy, belligerent, and demanding. The school often called Rose to come and either settle her down or take her home. After just five weeks, the school announced they were moving Lucy to the half-day room. Banks and Rose and Jacob thought Lucy needed more, not less time in the structure of school, but the teacher refused to budge.

Chapter Twenty-Two

It was not long before Rachel Banks took us back to court for a hearing to inform the judge Lexie was traumatized by her "chance encounters" with her parents. She also wanted to restrict Jacob's visitation to make it supervised again. The hearing was on November 15, 2013.

The court hearing did not go well. Rachel Banks recited Jacob's shortcomings and attributed at least some of Lucy's adjustment issues to his disruptive manipulations of Lucy. Fair enough. I explained to the court Jacob had a very strong fight-or-flight response. Jacob understood it was not good for Lucy to be caught in the middle of conflict, but it was awfully galling for Jacob to have a stranger—Charlie—allowed to spend each and every day with his daughter Lucy when he was allowed only a night or two a week. I asked if the court wanted to reimpose supervision Melinda Graves be made the sole supervisor of Jacob's visits. There should be no reduction in his visit time. We asked that his visits be merely monitored rather than supervised.

I did not know what to say about the "chance encounter." I asked that we try cards and letters rather than end all contact. I then argued strenuously the agency allowed the child to become alienated from her parents which sabotaged reunification even as Jacob worked so hard to become a successful parent.

On the issue of Lexie, Judge Bennett-Carey was willing to agree it was a valid complaint to say the agency may well have failed to intervene years ago to promote certain relationships, but that was not meaningful now when Lexis was so upset by contact. Therefore, all contact between the parents and Lexie was now prohibited, and the sibling visitation that had not yet started was limited to every six weeks. No one mentioned family therapy. The court returned Jacob's visitation to strictly supervised status but accepted Ms. Graves as Jacob's supervisor and did not reduce the time. He still had his overnights.

As we walked out of the courtroom, we met Sharon Peabody in the hallway. I assumed she was there on another case, but she came up to Rose and then Jacob and handed them each some paperwork. To my surprise, it was a petition for termination of parental rights for Lexie only. Jacob immediately recognized what it was and stepped in front of Rachel Banks as he threw the documents in my direction.

"I'll sign on the dotted line," he exclaimed, "if she wants to be adopted, but I want her to tell me to my face!"

Was Jacob letting us all know his conditions for resolving the case?

—•—

In 1990, Washington state law was amended (Revised code of Washington CW 26.33.295) to create the authority for implementing communication agreements between birth parents and adoptive parents for post-adoption contact. The statutes does not limit the nature of these agreements, but it does require a finding by a court such an agreement is in the child's best interest. Further, the parent's consent must be given freely and voluntarily, with full knowledge of the consequences, and not the result of fraud or duress or undue influence, and not in exchange for something. However, that is exactly how these agreements were and probably still are used in dependency cases in Washington state. In exchange for giving up his or her rights as a parent, a parent gets the promise of some type of continuing contact, even visitation, with the child. From the outset, these agreements were used by the state to settle termination cases.

In order to take advantage of a communication agreement, the birth parent was required to "voluntarily" give up his parental rights. The agency saved considerable time and money when a parent relinquished his or her rights. The cost of trial was saved, there could be no appeal, and the absence of appeal saved more money and time. An adoption could be established within thirty days of a relinquishment. The parent gained something precious, the chance to have some type of relationship with the child through written communication or visits. Even where the parent was not allowed to communicate with the child, agreements might still bind the adoptive parents to a promise to update the birth parent at least annually about the child and provide photos of the child.

In almost all dependency cases where a termination petition is pending, some version of these agreements is offered to the birth parent. Any parent confronted with the prospect of facing a termination trial is under layers and layers of stress. Advice comes at them from all sides, the agency social worker, their attorneys, their own parents and extended family, parents they sit next to in AA meetings, and friends. Add to this barrage of opinion, in some cases, the parent facing termination is impaired by continuing drug abuse, unmanaged (or unmanageable) mental health disorders or both.

As a rule, social workers do not like to go to trial. Social workers do like to get their cases moved to the adoption unit. (Remember the financial incentive—four thousand dollars for a "normal" child and six thousand dollars for a special needs child.) The parent's attorney, meanwhile, is weighing the likelihood of prevailing at the termination trial, usually near zero, against what seems to be the certainty of some type of ongoing contact.

Jacob had already endured a termination trial. The fact he prevailed would hardly mean much as he stared down at a new termination petition, again summoning him to trial. I wondered if he might be able to relinquish his parental rights to Lexie if only he could sit down with her and hear her tell him adoption was really what she wanted. I had a full-blown fantasy: Lexie and her parents in a comfortable therapy office, Steiner in the background. Each parent tells Lexie all they have accomplished. They tell her how sorry they are it has taken them so long to get ready to have her back. Then Lexie, calmly and sweetly explains why she wants to stay with Christine and George. No offense. Jacob tells her about his own hopes of being adopted. Lexie puts her arm around his neck and says,

"They will adopt me, Jacob. Let them do it." Tears all round. *Curtain*.

When I stopped daydreaming, I called Rachel Banks and asked her to check with Christine and George to find out what they might be willing to offer under a settlement. It wasn't much.

Jacob was offered an agreement for one-way contact. Once a year, the foster parents would let Jacob know via an email address how Lexie was doing. No response would be allowed. Some parents cling to the idea if they just agree to give up and sign on that dotted line, no matter what the document says, they will still get to see their child post-adoption. An attorney representing a parent who is contemplating giving up his parental rights and consenting to adoption may never feel confident the client really understands what all this means. I was lucky. Jacob understood perfectly well what it meant. I was not surprised he found the proposed deal easy to reject.

Chapter Twenty-Three

Rose missed some UAs. Then she had a UA that was positive for marijuana. Banks was fed up and set another hearing requesting Lucy be placed back with Christine and George immediately. On December 27, 2013 we were standing in front of Judge Bennett-Carey again. Luckily, Rose had already secured a room at an inpatient facility that would allow her to keep Lucy with her. Her attorney argued strongly in favor of this plan. Jacob also was in favor of letting Rose keep Lucy: relapse is part of recovery, Lucy could be hard to handle, what could be safer that an inpatient treatment program?

I also argued if the court decided to remove the child she should not return to the foster home where Lexie lived. This was a treacherous argument. If Lucy were ordered back into foster care, the transition would be made infinitely easier for her if she returned to a familiar place, a familiar family where her sister still lived, but understandably, Jacob was totally against the idea of Lucy being returned to Christine and George. If she went back there, she would be exposed to the same influences that led Lexie to reject, even fear him.

We were all surprised when Judge Bennett-Carey agreed Lucy should stay with her mother. Removal was not in the child's best interest. He tightened the rope he expected Rose would hang herself with, however, by requiring her to comply with all orders and rules, 100 percent of the time. If she failed to do so, CPS could remove Lucy without any further court hearing. As for Jacob,

Rachel was quite positive about him. She quoted extensively from his therapist whose remarks showed Jacob was fully engaged in therapy. Judge Bennett-Carey ordered Jacob's visit become unsupervised again with Melinda present to monitor all overnights. He also set the termination trial for April 28, 2014.

Two weeks later, Rachel Banks left the agency for a new job. Sharon Peabody was again assigned to the case. Rose was already a star at the treatment center. Lucy was in therapy there too. The facility was in the North Cape area, fifty miles from where Jacob and Melinda lived. Jacob drove with Melinda to North Cape each week on Melinda's day off to pick up Lucy for a visit. They did fun things, shopped, and ate together. Like her dad, Lucy loved the All-You-Can-Eat restaurant. These visits could be as long as six hours, but Melinda had to stay with Jacob and Lucy the whole time. Jacob was fine with this and felt it protected him from false accusations and misunderstandings.

Sharon brought Lexie to the treatment facility to see Lucy. Rose agreed to make herself scarce. Lucy was overjoyed to see her sister. For the first ten minutes, she could not stop hugging her. Sharon took them out to a nearby play area and the girls played together. Then, toward the end of their two-hour visit Lucy said,

"Wanna see Mommy? She's right inside."

Lexie froze, then she moved away to a bench and proceeded to crawl under it.

Lucy followed her, "I can see you!" she hollered.

Lexie said nothing.

"Come on out," Lucy encouraged her, "let's swing."

But Lexie stayed where she was.

Sharon intervened. "I think Lexie got really tired, Lucy, we had to drive a long way to get here."

She slowly drew Lexie out and they all walked to Sharon's car. Sharon strapped her into her seat and then walked with Lucy back to the facility. Lucy was already planning the next visit.

"I have this glitter I wanted to show Lexie, like pens only they print glitter. I'll save them for her."

But when the next time came, six weeks later, Lexie would not go. She didn't like the facility. She didn't like how Lucy was always talking about Rose or Jacob or Melinda. She did not blame Lucy for wanting to be with their mom; it just wasn't the same for her.

"What if you never see Lucy again?"

Lexie was clear. "I want to be adopted. Lucy doesn't."

Sharon went to the facility at the scheduled time for the visit without Lexie. When she told Lucy that Lexie would not be coming for any more visits, Lucy cried and then sobbed.

On January 4, 2014, Jacob received a letter from the Department of Veterans Affairs. His discharge was changed, and he was now listed as Discharged Under Honorable Conditions. It was a bloody miracle! Jacob's persistence and the help he got from Peter Smith had—unbelievably—paid off. Jacob got a big army decal and stuck it proudly on the back of his truck. He renewed his efforts to get benefits from the VA. This started Jacob off on another round of what I call "VA Hunting": going to a variety of offices to see what services and benefits might now be provided to him by the VA. The answer was still none, but nothing could diminish the pleasure he took in being an honorably discharged soldier.

I asked CPS again and again for consideration of some kind of contact between Jacob and Lexie—letters, pictures, gifts. Unfortunately, when Lexie was consulted about it, she promised to put anything sent to her from either parent in the garbage, unopened.

Jacob continued with school and managed to satisfy all the requirements that turned his tuition from a loan into a grant each quarter. He was enjoying his studies, was happy with his life with Melinda, and saw Lucy every week. By Valentine's day 2014, he started to have Lucy for an entire weekend. His visits were no longer supervised. As for Lexie, Jacob and I were now getting ready to fight to the bitter end to preserve all he had left of her, his legal relationship with her.

I thought the law was, at least technically, on our side. We had succeeded last time because important services had not been provided, and it was clear

Jacob would benefit from them based on his track record. This time, he was a successful parent as far as the elements were concerned. How could the agency prove his deficiencies were not corrected? He was co-parenting Lucy as a successful weekend dad.

Rose had returned home with Lucy on April 1, 2014. Charlie was waiting for her. Lucy was much easier to handle. Making arrangements with Jacob and Melinda, mostly Melinda, was going smoothly. She felt strong in her recovery, but she could not face another trial. She was offered the same open adoption agreement that had been offered to Jacob—one-way contact, once a year. She held out hope there might be more down the line, but in any case, she accepted Lexie wanted to be adopted. So be it.

I told Jacob we had a chance of succeeding as we had previously, but it would not get him what I thought he wanted, a real relationship with Lexie. He explained to me he wanted to stop the agency from terminating his parental rights because if he had no relationship with Lexie, it was the agency's fault. After my review of the record, I knew he was right.

I pulled out the mountains of paper I had received in discovery and all the CDs and flash drives and began to review every piece of information about the case start to finish. Much of what I saw was familiar to me: agency court reports, evaluations, and the narratives maintained by each social worker detailing their activities on the case. There were guidelines, even rules they were supposed to follow in maintaining these records. For example, they were to make their entries as contemporaneously as possible to the activity recorded. Each entry had a date and time for the activity and a date and time for the entry of the note. Sometimes pages of these narratives would have many different activity dates but only one entry date. We never knew if there was another set of notes the social worker made, their scratch paper notes made to help them remember details.

When I prepared for the first trial, I scanned the record for any evidence the agency had provided the crucial services recommended by Dr. Chan. There was no such evidence, and that was as far as my review needed to go, or so I thought, but now I discovered and absorbed for the first time the extent to which Elizabeth Grantham had involved Lexie's foster parents in her therapy from the moment the child was placed in that home. Jacob and I knew Lexie was in therapy, but none of us on the defense side knew the family therapy Jacob had asked for at the parents' very first visit with the children at the CPS office was being done, and effectively done, too, with the foster parents. This put me back on my heels, literally. I had no idea family therapy with the foster parents started in December 2010. No one could begrudge Lexie or her foster parents the advantages they gained from this family therapy, but there was no reason to think Jacob would not have similarly gained a deepening relationship with his daughter had such therapy been provided to him too. The seed of the alienation between father and daughter was planted years before. CPS never once intervened to include the parents in the therapeutic process. I hoped the court would not let the agency now claim the alienation it promoted was a legal basis for terminating parental rights.

I also learned Raoul Caster had done real damage to the parent/child relationship by introducing Lexie to the possibility of having to leave Christine and George behind to live with people she did not know, the Bakers. Someone made Lexie aware her parents had lots of problems and people she didn't even know would make decisions about where she and Lucy would live. Now Lexie added to her list of worries whether or not her parents could get fixed soon. This was a subject that could not be discussed in visits, so Lexie's information on the subject of her parents' progress was never corrected in a parent-friendly place like therapy.

I had a chance to thoroughly consider the experience Lexie had in her first foster home and its likely impact on her relationship with her parents. Before she was removed from her parents' care, Lexie was able to rely on her parents completely. Suddenly they were no longer able to be the people she turned to for sustenance, nurture, safety, knowledge, and 24/7 love, and when bad things happened in that first foster home, Daddy could not save her; Mommy could not deliver her from harm. The family therapy that could have mitigated the consequences of this trauma between Lexie and her parents was never, ever provided. They were never allowed to rebuild their close relationship. Instead, Lexie's growing attachment to and reliance on Christine and George, which was a healing process, excluded her parents. The record showed the agency social workers deferred to Elizabeth Grantham's therapeutic approach and un-accountably sanctioned her total rejection of Lexie's parents. Lexie's capacity to form healthy relationships with others was salvaged. Her relationship with her parents was not.

As I prepared exhibits for trial, I was newly overwhelmed by the evidence of all that Jacob had done.

- Certificate of Achievement, Intensive Inpatient Treatment
- Certificate of Completion, Parenting Class for Children Who Have Witnessed DV
- Certificate of Accomplishment, Intensive Outpatient Treatment
- Certificate of Completion of Parenting Class for Toddlers and Beyond
- Certificate of Completion, "Developing Capable Young People,"
- Certificate of Completion of DV perpetrator/anger management treatment
- Certificate of Completion of Parenting the Positive Discipline Way
- Certificate of Completion (Dahlquist) parenting coaching program
- Certificate of Completion of parenting as prevention
- Certificate of Completion 2-year Sisyphus program
- Certificate of Completion (2nd round with Dahlquist) parenting coaching program
- Letter altering discharge status to honorable

Chapter Twenty-Four

The judge we drew for the second termination case was another lucky draw for us. Like Judge Wipple, Judge Maureen O'Grady was fair-minded and unlikely to be swayed by a social worker's opinion if it was not substantiated by significant evidence. I was happy to have a judge who brought to the case not only impartiality, but a wealth of practical experience from the real world of trial practice.

The trial began on April 8, 2014. The state took the same position it had in the earlier trial: Jacob was an unfit parent because of his mental health issues. As a result, he did not have an adequate insight into his own mental health issues and was unable to understand and empathize with his daughter. A parade of witnesses came before the court to prove the state's case—five social workers, Elizabeth Grantham, Martha Jones, Paulette Steiner. Beth Dahlquist testified on Jacob's behalf again, as did Melinda Graves. I submitted the trial transcripts of the testimony of Chad Carlson and Ginny Verlander. The state agreed to let me submit a glowing letter from Jacob's therapist in lieu of testimony.

Sharon Peabody testified Jacob had made progress in his relationship with his daughter Lucy, but so long as Lexie was not willing to be with him, there was no chance Jacob could parent her. She really couldn't say if it would have made a difference if Jacob had received the same guidance the foster parents received.

Even when confronted by the judge with an order signed by Judge Bennett-Carey, which stated "father will participate in family therapy with Paulette Steiner," Ms. Banks insisted family therapy was never the intent of Dr. Steiner's work on the case.

The judge also had questions for Martha Jones, Lexie's advocate.

"When Lexie first showed reluctance to visit, was there any reason, right then, family therapy could not have been put into place for the child and father?"

Jones testified, "I don't know. Elizabeth Grantham never recommended it."

Lexie's foster parents each testified. They confirmed the extensive work they had done with Lexie and Elizabeth Grantham over the years she had lived with them. The foster father also confirmed Raoul Caster was the first person to talk to Lexie about the option of adoption. More surprisingly, he confirmed Caster had remained an important figure in her life. "Uncle Raoul" saw Lexie often. The foster mother confirmed they had always wanted to adopt Lexie and Lucy.

Elizabeth Grantham testified it was her policy not to have anything to do with biological parents unless others, the court or the social workers, told her reunification was the plan. She claimed she was not a decision-maker in the case. It was not her job to share anything with the child about her biological parents.

Dr. Steiner testified Lexie wanted to be adopted. Under questioning by the judge, she provided the really damaging evidence. First, she thought the history of the mother's improvements and relapses led Lexie to conclude both her parents were unreliable and she simply declared she was done. Meanwhile, her foster parents were reliable. Second, it was important to respect Lexie's decision not to see her parents because disrespecting her decision by ignoring it would make her feel she didn't matter. Third, Dr. Steiner concluded, in spite of the work the father had done to turn his life around, she could plainly see the window of opportunity for reunification was closed.

Lexie testified too. By this time she was a mature nine-year-old. There is a special procedure for presenting the testimony of the child—she got to have a dog with her, Jacob had to watch her on closed-circuit TV so she would be comfortable, everyone was quite gentle in their questioning of her.

She didn't remember too much about the years she lived with Jacob. She acknowledged she did not want to see Lucy. She talked about her life with Christine and George and how great they were.

When the judge asked her if Jacob had ever hurt her, she replied, "No, I'm just done with him."

Jacob was the last person to testify. He was so perfectly himself, so true to what he knew and believed. Jacob's testimony was similar to his testimony in the first trial. He was unflappable, sincere, and funny. He was still in college, and he had been on the dean's list twice. He discussed his heavy use of prescribed pain medication at the start of the case, his experiences in the army, and his attempts to get benefits or services from the VA. He explained nothing was possible until he got his discharge changed, and even then, he was unable to access VA services. He described some of his experiences in foster care. He explained how he had wanted the Bakers to have the girls, so he would have some possibility of being a real dad for his children. He described how long it took CPS to acknowledge the mother in the girls' first foster home was abusive, how she had an alcohol issue of some sort, and how the girls were suddenly moved from the home. He recalled a time at one of the visits when Lexie wanted him to hold her and rock her, but the visitation supervisor intervened and said it was inappropriate; she was too old for that. This was, of course, exactly the instruction being given to the child's foster parents, to hold her like a much younger child.

Jacob described his success in his recovery and how much he admired Chad Carlson his chemical dependency counselor.

"I changed from the inside out working with Chad Carlson," he said. But that advocate Raoul wanted him to give up, he started talking to Jacob about how he should do the right thing because Lexie was happy with her foster parents.

Jacob thought he was doing the right thing getting treatment, working with his DV treatment provider, consistently providing clean UAs, and routinely attending visitation.

He admitted he had trust issues with most of the social workers assigned to his case, but Beth Dahlquist was someone he was able to work with, and he saw real changes in the children's attitude toward him as he implemented her instructions. Visits started to be fun. One day, long after he was required to do UAs, he had provided the girls with cupcakes they could frost themselves with wildly colored frosting he also provided.

He wryly noted, "They asked me to do a UA the next day. It was clean"

Throughout his case, Jacob asked for family therapy. This was the service never provided.

"All this money is spent on foster care and on therapy, and still no one can figure out how to put this family back together again," he said.

He made it clear he wanted Lexie taken out of her current foster home because the foster parents were clearly hindering return. He also thought Elizabeth Grantham should be replaced. In that first year, Lexie was begging to come home. CPS did not care about the attachment she had to him and to her mother when CPS removed her. The parents had Lexie for five-and-a-half years, but reunification services were never given. When Lexie was afraid of losing her parents, CPS didn't care.

The judge had several questions for Jacob. After listening to Lexie's testimony, what did he think was in her best interest?

Jacob stood his ground. "She needs another place to live. That seems awkward, but when people are standing in the way for you to reunite with your kids, what else will work?" Jacob went on, "I can't talk to her. I can't see her. It is unheard of to tell her all I have done or let her know about the things that never happened, like Lucy's fingers were never broken."

He wanted Lexie to know the truth.

"I have been on both sides in foster care and what this has done to me is it led me to contact my bio mom, just to get her side of the story. I didn't like hanging out with her, but I do want to find out what really happened. I wanted to know what pain they put her through, and how she tried to get me back. I think kids should be reunified with their family...."

In terms of social workers he added, "We never had one good fair shot... one person doesn't know what the next person does. Put her in a different foster home, give her a different therapist, start from scratch."

The judge then asked, "What do you think the consequences to Lexie would be?"

Jacob replied, "What do you think the consequences have already been? The damage they have done to my child right now is high. Proper services were given to the foster parents and not to us. I mean, they haven't even given me a person I can actually talk to about my child."

The judge asked, "Do you think Raoul Caster the CASA is behind the statements Lexie is making today?"

Jacob answered by way of describing a psychology course he was taking that indicated kids just tried to make people happy. They didn't want to hurt anyone. The judge then asked if Jacob could use his own experience of being eleven and wanting to be adopted to understand where she was in her head right now.

Jacob acknowledged, "…it is hard to put yourself in someone else's shoes," but where she was living was not therapeutic. How could she change so completely? "It just seems to me there is a lot more to the story."

Chapter Twenty-Five

On May 30, 2014 we gathered to hear the judge's decision. When Judge O'Grady came into the courtroom and walked up the stairs to her imposing desk five feet above us, she was carrying an armload of files and notes and exhibits. She settled in and greeted us, and then she began to speak.

She said Jacob was a credible witness, and in addition, she found him to be earnest, cooperative, and guileless. She specifically found he was willing to engage in and make progress in and complete all the services ever offered to him. He had no parental deficits. She made it clear the dependency for Lexie was not based on any physical abuse and referred to Lexie's own testimony in which she readily acknowledged her dad never hurt her. The judge said her dad never posed a risk of abuse, and the judge found he was an appropriate parent for Lucy.

Several times during her oral ruling, the judge returned to the period of time she described as the critical juncture when family therapy, or as she characterized it, reunification therapy should have been provided to Lexie and her father. This was the missed chance to preserve Lexie's relationship with her dad. She emphasized the fact Lexie's refusal to see her father was not connected to any parental deficiency. This made the case unusual, if not unique. Three factors accounted for the current dilemma facing the court: (1) the lapse of time, (2) the failure to provide reunification therapy in 2012, and (3) Lexie's strong attachment to her foster parents.

Judge O'Grady said the most credible witness she heard from was Paulette Steiner. This witness assured her it was too late to repair the parent/child bond. The Judge concluded the current circumstances were not the father's fault, but the chance to reunify this family no longer existed. She had no choice but to terminate Jacob's parental rights.

She looked at Jacob and said, "I am sorry," to which Jacob succinctly replied.

"Because they didn't do their damn job."

The judge then expressed the hope Lexie would eventually come around and one day would want to see her father again. Nothing in the trial record supported this hope.

As we shuffled out of the courtroom, I was already nattering away at Jacob about the next steps he could take if he wanted to challenge the decision. I thought the case was factually unique enough to be reversed on appeal. This may have given me some solace, but Jacob had just been punched in the gut. He promised to call me later and was still shaking his head over the ruling as he got into his truck. He had done everything that was ever asked of him, he had demonstrated his ability to learn and apply what he was taught, and they could still terminate his parental rights. It was a body blow.

—·—

Jacob directed me to pursue an appeal of Judge O'Grady's decision. I filed the notice of appeal and supporting documentation on August 12, 2014. It was at this point I handed Jacob's case, as far as Lexie was concerned, to a gifted appellate public defender, Rainy McKenzie. Jacob was in good hands.

The appellate process is a long one. Briefs on Jacob's behalf were first read by an appellate court commissioner. She also heard oral arguments from the litigants. She basically agreed Judge O'Grady was right. This decision was made in April, 2015. Jacob's attorney appealed the commissioner's decision to a full panel of judges in the same court. They also heard oral arguments but eventually agreed with the commissioner, and the order upholding the termination of Jacob's rights was issued on August 3, 2015

The case was then appealed to the state Supreme Court. This court wanted to hear from other people than just the parties to the case and put out a call to the legal community for additional briefs. Five organizations, mostly opposed to Judge O'Grady's decision, submitted briefing. Then the Supreme Court, nine justices in all, heard oral arguments. Some of the justices were clearly upset by the conduct of the agency and clearly believed CPS had failed in its duty to provide reunification services such as family therapy. Some of the Justices complimented Jacob on the correction of his parental deficiencies. We both felt, walking out of that courtroom in the Temple of Justice, the decision against him might be reversed.

Then, on December 6, 2016, the Supreme Court issued its decision. All of the justices, some happily, some regretfully, agreed Judge O'Grady had no alternative but to terminate the father's parental rights. Jacob was shocked. Me too.

Chapter Twenty-Six

Shortly after we filed the notice of appeal, Lucy's CPS case heated up. Rose took Lucy to their primary care doctor to discuss the possibility some of Lucy's impulsiveness was due to attention deficit disorder. The physician agreed and was ready to prescribe Adderall. Jacob strenuously objected. He did not want his daughter medicated, and he wondered if Rose wanted the medication for herself. In any case, the agency had to get the court's permission to authorize the use of the drug on any child under CPS supervision.

The court directed CPS to facilitate a second opinion from a physician Jacob trusted, a woman who had treated Lucy when she was a newborn. This physician agreed with the diagnosis of ADHD but thought a much less radical medication, Intuniv, should be provided, at least to begin.

Another hearing on this issue was set by CPS for July 2, 2014. Although the central issue was the question of medication, everyone recognized another even more fundamental issue was the continuation of the case itself. The law required a dependency case be supervised by CPS for at least the first six months following the return of a child to a parent's care. Lucy had been back with her mother for nearly twelve months. On behalf of the parents, the mother's attorney and I asked for dismissal. The parents had corrected their parenting deficits and were ready to submit a parenting plan to family court.

The plan they agreed to left Lucy living with Rose and Jacob with weekend overnights. The plan was approved by CPS.

The judge noted the parents were able to work together now as evidenced by the respectful conversation they had been having about the medication issue. It was time for CPS to get out of this family's life. Four years after she was removed from her parents on a bogus allegation her dad had intentionally injured her, Lucy was finally out from under CPS control. The dismissal ended my representation of Jacob, but we continued to stay in touch regarding both Lucy and Lexie. As we left the courthouse, I told Jacob when I retired I would like to write a book about his case. His stamina and steadfastness were amazing to me.

"Does this mean we can go on Ellen together?"

———•———

Jacob ended up agreeing to try Adderall, but only for a few months. The shared custody plan was accepted by family court. Melinda had taken over the pick-up and drop-off duties for Lucy while Jacob waited in the car. Charlie seemed to be around less and less. One day about three months after the dismissal, October 20, 2014, Melinda brought Lucy home from her weekend with her and Jacob only to find Rose passed out on the couch. Melinda signaled Jacob to come in from the car and she then left with Lucy.

"Your mommy needed a nap, and she is still asleep. Let's go to the park until she wakes up."

Jacob found empty beer cans in the kitchen and a few full ones in the refrigerator. He could not find much food. He brought a cold cloth into the living room and, spreading it over Rose's face, he managed to get her up.

"What's happening?" he asked.

"What do you mean?"

"It's three-thirty in the afternoon. Have you been drinking?"

"Jacob! I just fell asleep—it's hot in here."

"There are empty beer cans in the garbage."

"Those are Charlie's!"

"Okay, but there shouldn't be anything like that around you."

"Don't make a big deal out of this."

"What if CPS came by?"

"Stop it! They won't come by anymore unless you call them."

—·—

Jacob went back to the family court to get the parenting plan changed so he was the primary/residential parent of Lucy and the mom had the weekend visits. This process was complicated and frustrating. He could not afford an attorney. After several false starts, a sympathetic court facilitator in the clerk's office helped Jacob get a real hearing set on January 28, 2015. He had properly notified Rose, and she appeared. Jacob had also submitted a statement regarding his issues with Rose, especially her alcohol abuse. Jacob was awarded temporary custody of Lucy and a special advocate was appointed to investigate the situation and report to the court regarding what was best for Lucy. The advocate was an attorney from another county, an experienced litigator in family law matters as well as an experienced child advocate.

Meanwhile, Lucy was often defiant and totally unable to master the principle of cause and effect. The consequences of her actions seemed to shock her, almost as if another child—her evil twin—had performed the action, and she had to deal with the consequences. Once she was with her father full time, she attended therapy regularly. The whole family, Jacob and Lucy and Melinda, engaged in family therapy to allow them to hear each other and to make sure responses to Lucy were consistent at school and at home. Lucy's defiance lessened, and her mastery of herself increased, but she was still pretty mad.

Sometimes out of the blue Lucy would ask her dad, "Why doesn't Lexie want to see me?"

He didn't know what to say; it was a mystery to him too. Lucy was mad at her mom. In therapy she was given permission to swear as a way to help her express the anger she felt. She could swear a blue streak. She demanded her therapist show her the paperwork her mom signed to give Lexie away—how could she do that? Jacob got the documents to the therapist.

The advocate for Lucy reviewed records and met with Jacob and Melinda, tracked down and talked with Martha Jones and Jennifer Reisenberg, consulted with Lucy's therapist, and she talked with Lucy, but she was unable to get any response from Rose. After the initial hearing, Rose dropped out of sight. She did not contact Jacob or Lucy. No one knew where she was, although Jacob saw on Facebook she had a new boyfriend and was living somewhere in North Cape. He never knew what happened to Charlie.

The advocate left messages for Rose that were never returned. Phone numbers no longer worked. The months dragged on and still no sign of Rose. The court order now required her to set up supervised visitation if she wanted to see Lucy. She never called Lucy or sent any cards. Then on Christmas Eve 2015, she called Jacob demanding a visit with Lucy right then. She wanted to come by and pick her up for a few hours. He said she had to follow the order. She berated him for keeping her daughter from her. He held firm. There was no contact after that.

On June 3, 2015, the advocate submitted a report to court, which described Jacob's care for Lucy as attentive, stable, and consistent. He was doing everything he could to provide her with all she needed most, especially the educational help and mental health therapy she needed to thrive. It was a wonderful report. The parenting plan was officially modified placing Lucy permanently with her father. The advocate had no concerns with Jacob. She asked the court to limit the mother's access to the child, should she appear, to supervised visits. The father could be relied upon to see Lucy's best interests were consistently protected. He was deemed to be a good dad. Two weeks later, the court awarded him full custody of Lucy and modified the visitation order to prohibit any contact between Lucy and her mom unless her mother could show proof of clean UAs and participation in treatment.

Not long after that final hearing, Jacob woke up in the middle of the night with tears streaming down his face. He missed Lexie. It felt like death.

"I know it's not the same because I know she is alive somewhere. I just can't see her or hear from her."

Periodically Rose surfaces, demands a visit, and then disappears again. On two occasions, her mother, Grandma Dee, called begging Jacob to let Rose see her daughter. He explained he cannot violate the court order but was happy to bring Lucy by to see Grandma Dee so long as Rose was not there. One time recently, a police officer came to his home. He said he had a report Jacob violently struck Rose Faraday during a fight they had two nights ago. The officer showed Jacob photos he had taken of the injury, a nasty bruise showing clearly across the left side of her face.

Jacob gave the officer some of the backstory, the custody issues, showed him the current order, and told him he had not seen Rose in almost three years. At the officer's request, Jacob held out his hands, knuckles up, to prove he had not hit anyone or anything recently. The officer apologized and departed.

After years of struggles at school, changes in medications and therapists, Lucy, aided by Melinda and her dad, suddenly figured out how this cause and effect thing worked. She now has friends in and out of school, is getting solid B's and A's, ran for class president, and when she didn't win, accepted with real grace the consolation prize of being a student rep on one of the school's committees. She loves to read and bead bracelets, play video games with her dad, and do those things Jacob describes as "girlie things" with Melinda. She no longer asks about her sister or her mother. She is an amazingly resilient and beautiful child, living, you could almost say, happily ever after, with her equally resilient father and his loving partner.

EPILOGUE

Some social workers really liked Jacob, but those who liked him did no better by him than those who treated him like an irritation. Few were able to keep their eyes on the big picture, none could acknowledge the trauma their own actions caused, and none promoted Jacob's relationship with his daughter Lexie as a priority in their case management. Overworked and underpaid, social workers often miss opportunities to do good.

As for the legal process in these cases, it does not work very well. Judges and commissioners have no time to know the whole story of any case, and the lawyers often don't know it either. They are in a rush to learn only what they need to know for the next hearing or the next meeting. In this case, I did not appreciate the role family therapy, offered exclusively to Lexie's foster parents, played in alienating her from her birth parents. If the parents and Lexie and Lucy, too, had been provided with regular family therapy to sort out all the brutal changes and happy accomplishments that occurred between 2010 and 2014, their relationships would have been securely sustained. I think it is also true this case would have moved more quickly to resolution had this simple service of family therapy been provided.

Of course, I want you to care about what happened to Jacob Johnson and his daughters. Lexie was allowed—indeed, programmed—to give up on her parents and pick new ones, and she became willing even to renounce her sister to get what she wanted. She was well-bonded to her parents when she was removed from them, and she suffered the trauma of removal as so many children have suffered from removal in Washington state and across the United States, but unlike most of them, Lexie was turned away from her parents by a therapeutic process, which systemically encouraged her to pick new parents. This was beyond what most foster children are subjected to, and the result was probably inevitable. The total exclusion of her father from her existential life lead to her total alienation from him.

Lucy suffered through multiple transitions. She, too, was traumatized by the loss of her mommy and daddy. She lost the foster parents who became her new mommy and daddy, too. She felt her sister's rejection keenly. Then her mother disappeared from her life as completely as Lexie had. She was badly hurt, and she was furious too. Nonetheless, her father stood by her side, always, enduring the reduction to visitation-dad and then rising to the occasion of being her single, reliable, loving parent.

Jacob had good and truly lost his daughter Lexie, but Lucy was another story, and in a different courtroom without the awful weight of the CPS thumb on the scales of justice, Jacob was seen not only as a viable parent but as his child's saving grace.

Where did Jacob get the strength to be a dad when the entire child welfare system had failed him twice? When he was very small, he was not rescued from his mother as he should have been, and when he was a parent, his children were rescued from him when they should not have been. He lost his grasp of the child who rejected him, but he did not give up on the child who needed him most. I hope this book fills in some of the blanks for Lexie so she can someday, after learning the whole story, admire her first daddy and maybe even give Lucy a call.

Acknowledgements

I would never have been able to complete this book without the help of many people. Jacob and Melinda made themselves available to me every step of the way and I am grateful for all their help. It was not always easy for Jacob to revisit scenes from his past, especially from his childhood but he did it to answer questions I had and I am so grateful for his willingness to do so. Esme Evans did a major editing job for me and gave me a variety of invaluable comments and observations. Her hard work on this manuscript made a huge difference. Amelia Watson read through the entire manuscript at least twice with great attention to detail and made this a better book than it would otherwise have been. I started this project by taking the Great Courses class Writing Creative Fiction taught by Tilar J. Mazzeo. Her guidance was clear and very helpful. I have to thank Jonathan Milstein for always doing his best to save me from myself. My sister Peg generously shared her time and expertise and has always been an enthusiastic supporter of my projects. Claudia Johnson gave me early encouragement and help. Katharine Cahn gave me a perspective from the field that was very helpful. Sharon Slebodnick shared her enthusiasm in the subject matter of this book, topics so often well away from public view.